Amends

Eve Tushnet

AMENDS

Printed in the United States of America

First Edition: July, 2015

ISBN-13: 978-1514603062

ISBN-10: 1514603063

For my parents

Contents

Acknowledgments

Like all of us, I owe more than I can repay. I'm deeply grateful to everyone who read this manuscript and coaxed it through its long larval stage. My deepest thanks to Catherine Addington, Meron Begashaw, Jeremy Biltz, Rachel Manija Brown, Jim Henley, Matt Jones, Gebre Menfes Kidus, Will McDavid (who also did the book's design), Dori Ostermiller, Ivan Plis, Anne Tiffen Taylor, and Will and Nicola Wilson. The infelicities and tackiness which remain are mine, not theirs.

Medea would point out that my parents gave me my DNA, many of my habits (though not the ones this novel is mostly about), and the gift of life, just for starters. They also generously gave me a place to stay while I worked on the first draft of this book.

Amends

Chapter 1: The Manure Element

J. Malachi MacCool was born in Berkeley, California, in the last decade of the Cold War, to parents who deserved better. He had a dilapidated body and a face like the last days of the Raj: jowly, discredited, eager for the final defeat. He was thirty-two, he lived in a cockroach-infested studio apartment in Washington, DC, and fans of his writing—for magazines like *Intimations*, *Hound and Gentry*, *The Anglican Militant* and *Tempus*—considered him one of the great unwanted geniuses of a degenerate age. His favorite term of praise was "civilizational," and he lived by the creed, "Alcoholism is what raises man above the utilitarians." The J stood for Jaymi.

At the time he received the email from the reality show "Amends," J. Malachi was on his seventh Stalin of the night (port and vodka, the drink that won the Great Patriotic War), and he had reached the point of drunkenness where he watched Thatcher-era Conservative Party political broadcasts on YouTube and ranted to his pet shrimps about the defense of the realm.

He refreshed his drink and his inbox. They were equally

lurid and depressing. He had several right-wing spam emails:

"Be Your Own Banker" Webinar.

ECONOMY IN MELTDOWN: How Long Do You Have Before It All Goes Dark?

Seven Things to Hoard Today.

You're White, You're Guilty, You're Dead!

"Come on, I'm not dead," he muttered.

He deleted that, but the next one was no better: Now Obama Wants Your Conscience, Too!

"He'll have to find it first," J. Malachi said, and defiantly gulped his Stalin.

There was one email which looked different. "Referred to you by Ferdinand Attanasio," the subject header said. Inside, the sender claimed to be casting a new month-long MTV reality show "featuring a diverse cast pursuing experience-based explorations into contemporary cultural questions. What does it mean to make amends? Do we have too much of a 'culture of confession'? What do we owe one another? Can people really change? That's what our show will try to figure out. Ferdinand said you'd be great at representing an articulate conservative viewpoint which gets beyond the stereotypes."

And then there was this tricky little paragraph: "The show uses alcohol rehabilitation as a space to explore contemporary issues. We want to see how 'real world'-type participants experience and interact with an alcohol treatment program—regardless of their own level of substance use. This treatment will be provided at no cost."

There was something greasy about that paragraph.

"'We're not saying you have a *problem*,'" he paraphrased it, sucking down another gulp of Stalin. "'We're just saying we'll pay for the solution.'"

He did not feel good about the fact that they'd gotten his name from Attanasio. That meant Attanasio had seen the words "alcohol treatment program" and thought of him.

Virtue ethics, hypocrisy, decline; cravats, ascots, college scarves, neckwear generally: These were things J. Malachi hoped people associated with his name. *Alcohol treatment program* did not sit comfortably in that list.

The email ended, "Please take a look at the contract attached, fill it out, and get back to me. Thanks so much!" It was signed by "Jeremy," no last name, identified only as an MTV editorial assistant.

A childhood spent reading British children's books from the 1970s had made J. Malachi suspicious of anyone named Jeremy. A month was also a fuck of a long time. Would he have cameras on him, hidden microphones, no access to the outside world? Would he get to go home at night? J. Malachi was a great believer in home.

He was about to close the email, continue his war of attrition against the Smirnoff bottle, and put off thinking about this offer until the deadline had already passed, when an email from Attanasio himself appeared.

Just seeing the name made his gut twist guiltily. Ferdinand Attanasio was a gentle, fatherly arts editor at *Inside the Whale.* He was used to what J. Malachi called "my style": the hamstrung punchlines and swollen insights. He Frankensteined them into something like a book review or a shambling, twitching "occasional" piece. Attanasio made sure J. Malachi got paid even when he turned in misspelled ballet reviews two months after the ballet closed.

"Hey J. You probably just got an email from some friends of mine. They're trying to do good work and I hope you'll say yes. Think of it as a favor to me."

No fair using guilt, J. Malachi thought. But he was ideologically aligned with guilt. He was, in general, on guilt's side, and never more than when it was directed at himself.

A month without drinking.

Fine. I used to give it up for Lent. (For the past three years he had given up mixers instead.)

He opened the attachment, briefly considered spelling his name wrong just in case he wanted out of the contract later, then decided that probably wouldn't stand up in court. He tried, or pretended to try, to read the details of the contract but they bored and scared him, so he signed it and sent it back. "Thanks; see attahced." He was never drunk enough to use a comma splice.

*   *   *

Emebet Gebremichael slowly silvered into consciousness to the gentle sounds of rain. She was lying on some kind of hard tile, and she stretched, feeling emptied of self. She was happy. The rain dropped and trickled by her cheek, on her hair, tracing a thin teardrop line along her skin. The gentle rain reminded her of the word of God, for which she thirsted. Her eyelids fluttered. She stretched out a hand—and touched the base of a urinal.

Suddenly she was completely awake. The consoling haze resolved itself into a hangover as her self was jammed back into her skin. Emebet sat up and groped around for her sunglasses. She had fallen asleep next to a urinal filled with ice, and what had trickled onto her face and hair was not entirely water.

She scrambled onto her knees and then her feet, and scuttled to the sink. Vaguely she noticed that her wrists and legs were bruised. She felt jolty and shivery. Her teeth ached, and her hands were bruised and cut. She wondered why. She washed up, glancing fearfully at the door of the men's room. She pulled her sunglasses on and stumbled out the door on spider-legs: cringing, hunching, shuddering. She saw that she had been in a bar and it was almost dawn, so probably someone had seen her. *You're lucky you weren't locked in.*

Outside, in a back alley, she buttoned up her jeans, tried to buckle the straps on her broken shoes, and checked her possessions. Wet wipes, bug spray, prayer beads, gauzy white headscarf, two changes of clothes and a church dress, an empty bag of corn chips, purse with two dollars somehow still in it. Two dollars and thirty-six cents, actually, which was two dollars more than she felt she had in her moral accounts.

Emebet was just shy of forty, but there was something younger about her face, something lost. She looked fresh off the boat, even though she'd actually come to the States when she was sixteen. She had thin lines below her eyes and a deeper furrow between her brows, and an expression like someone trying to explain that she was just a few dollars short.

She looked like a beggar, she thought; but she looked like an honest one, which was lucky for her. It would be very easy to get liquor by noon. She'd ask someone at the CVS to buy her Tide detergent—the fact that she smelled a bit might even help her—and Tide had become a kind of prison-currency of the homeless. Tide could be bartered for vodka, with a quick pit stop in the middle at American legal tender.

The harder part would be finding a liquor store staffed by Salvadorans, not Ethiopians. Emebet wasn't willing to burden her countrymen with the guilt of selling to her.

She heard about "Amends" because she made a mistake that day. She tried to buy vodka from the Lay Back Liquor owner because he looked American. But he said, "Don't you go to my brother's church?"

He remembered the television intern who had stopped by earlier that week for a handle of Jack and a quick chat about casting: Did anyone unusual ever come to the Lay Back Liquor? Anyone who might represent an underprivileged group, give the show some diversity?

And that was how Emebet Gebremichael became the second-most-famous Oriental Orthodox reality star, after Kim Kardashian.

*   *   *

Posted at the Den of Acceptance, July 16, 2012:

Hey packmates! Many of you know my story: For several years I was an active heroin addict and alcoholic, but I realized, with your support, that what I was looking for didn't come in a needle or a bottle. As I recovered my memories of pack life and began to accept my true identity as a gray wolf, I got my life in order and today I'm *almost* two years clean and sober! Yeah, I can't believe it either. But the wolf doesn't like whiskey.

Now I have an amazing opportunity to share my story with the world—and help non-kin understand our lives and struggles. I'm going to be on TV! Can't share details until the show starts airing but filming is secluded, so I'm letting all my packmates know that I won't be around much until it's over. From a monkey on my back to a wolf in my pack... it's been a great journey and it's just getting started! Howls to all you guys and I will let you know when the show airs!

--sharpercanine12 aka wolfjulie aka barfightexpress

UPDATE: I apologize to all those who were offended by my characterizing addiction as a "monkey." I did not mean to suggest that monkeys or monkeykin are unpleasant or harmful in any way, but I take responsibility for the hurt my words caused.

SECOND UPDATE: I also apologize for my use of the word "harmful" in a negative sense. Some members of our community have informed me that self-harm can be a valid coping strategy, and I don't want to disrespect other otherkin's choices or beliefs. Thank you for educating me! And don't forget to watch me on TV!

*   *   *

Medea Chu-Childe signed up for the show in the hospital. Medea was the twenty-six-year-old authoress (her preferred term) of *Cockatrice*, a play about a gay male couple so desperate to acquire a child that they procure the services of an oppressed Indian witch. She casts a spell which allows one of them to magically impregnate the other. But their daughter is a caricature of testosterone run amok: She slaps the doctor when she's born, and becomes a pirate so she can fuck and kill without consequences. "She's like *Pippi Longstocking* meets *Rosemary's Baby*!" one of her fathers wails.

Medea was herself the child of two gay men, an egg donor, and a surrogate. She responded to all questions about whether the couple in the play were her own parents with a laugh: "Memoir is tacky. I write fables." *Cockatrice* was only the most recent of her fairy-tale attacks on the constructed family; her early plays had titles like *The Wicked Sperm Donor* and *The Twink's Child*. But *Cockatrice* was her big hit.

Her bitterest critics accused her of being a lesbian because it was the only way she could get away with writing what she did.

Some women would have responded to this accusation by talking about all the girls they'd loved before, but Medea had a different strategy. She didn't talk about her exes—the recent ones had already been strip-mined for her plays, and her first love was a tender secret. Even Medea Chu-Childe could respect certain conventional emotions, such as puppy love, especially when they belonged to her.

Instead she toyed with the top clasp of her bustier or twined a finger in the glossy black ringlets piled on her head like loops of film, and in a voice filled with covert pleasures, she said, "People say I chose to be a lesbian. Did you choose to think stealing is wrong? Could you drown a kitten just for fun, if you really tried? This is how I feel about *coitus*."

(She had in fact performed what she called research with men, but she was skilled at misdirection, so this subject didn't come up in interviews.)

She got exasperated reviews with lines like, "I can't believe I have to say this, but feminism is not coterminous with man-hating"—and fan letters with lines like, "Every girl is a gun." Women sent her letters by postal mail just so they could sign in menstrual blood.

At the cast party for *Cockatrice* she had grappled her way up an actress, declaimed, "The age of chivalry is dead!", and collapsed. When she couldn't be revived the partygoers called for an ambulance.

She'd done a blurry intake interview ("What day is it?" "Yesterday! No, wait, these days it's always tomorrow") and the doctors had made her lie down on a bed they wheeled out into the waiting room. She didn't like being among all the people so she pretended she could only hear the television.

In a commercial a man stood on a box, hooded and shrouded, his arms held out to the sides. The ragged cloth he wore had grass and dirt stains on it. A smiling soldier sprayed him with a fire hose marked LEADING BRAND, and he choked and fell off his box. Then the scene switched to a housewife dunking a man's hooded head into a bucket of LEADING BRAND bleach, over and over, as he struggled.

"Don't torture your fabrics! Use Tide Gentle Touch! Because these colors don't run—" over a shot of the American flag—"when they're treated gently, with Tide."

*　　　*　　　*

Gair Cupek was just washing his face after shaving when his teammate barged into the bathroom.

"Hey, Cupcake," Dylan Hall caroled, leaning back against the door frame to block Gair's way out.

"Morning," Gair said mildly. Dylan grinned, and the dimple on his cheek sprang into place like an asterisk noting the manufacturer's disclaimer. Gair hoped the stinging in his cheeks was just from the aftershave. "Wow, you smell unusually terrible."

"Natty Light," Dylan apologized. "Keggers can't be choosers."

"Did you get *any* sleep?"

"I got slept with, if that counts."

Dylan looked like a sock hung on a doorknob, and he had a streak of what seemed to be glitter over one eye. Gair was reluctantly impressed by his ability to get glittered in a hotel full of male high-school hockey players. Dylan could find a train-wrecky girl at the bottom of the ocean, or in outer space. His number was saved in a hundred girls' phones—as things like "You Deserve Better," "Dumpster Diving," "Actual Werewolf?", and "JUST NO."

Gair tried to make his face look concerned, but not scolding. "The night before the title game—was that really a good idea?"

"It was definitely a blonde idea. Come on, I've already got a coach, what I need is an alibi."

"What you need is a therapist."

Dylan laughed and shucked his liquor-soaked shirt over his head. "What I need is an exorcist."

He prowled around, getting ready in his own way: stealing Gair's toothbrush and mouthwash, trying to make Gair smell his armpits. When they were both more or less ready he grabbed a little silver cross necklace, which had spent the night curled up peacefully on the side of the bathtub, and slipped it over his head. It winked teasingly between his collarbones.

Gair couldn't help asking: "Why do you wear that thing?"

Dylan looked at him, uncertain for once. "Does it bother you? I can take it off if it's, like, offensive."

"No, just—can I ask if you believe in God? I mean have you accepted Jesus?"

"I tolerate Jesus," Dylan said.

Gair rolled his eyes.

Dylan looked uncomfortable—he looked like he'd been caught doing something, which was bizarre, because usually he liked getting caught—and then he said, sunnily, "I believe God sees everything we do."

He ducked out of the bathroom then and headed out of their hotel room, past the ragged sign Gair had put up reading, DYLAN IS NOT ALLOWED. (The long list which followed had been lost to the ravages of Dylan.) He grabbed a protein bar and a handful of condoms on his way out.

Gair looked after him in several different kinds of frustration.

*   *   *

Colton Rodman was at the "sucking vodka through a Jujube" stage of in-cubicle drunkenness. Over the years he had worked many jobs he lied about at parties: porn star, exterminator, pet mortician, children's birthday-party clown. The collection agency was definitely the worst. Even the cubicles here were coming apart. His supervisor would wander by and greet him affectionately ("Hi there, spooky freak!"), then stand around picking at the top of the cubicle. Big white crumbling chunks of it would come away in his hands like cake. This did not create an impression of job security.

Colton had many strategies to hide his drinking. He mixed his vodka with obscure sodas whose scents nobody recognized, Moxie and Mr. Pibb; he waited to go to the john until his coworkers were all safely entombed in their cubicles, evading them like Pac-Man dodging ghosts. He affected a different fake accent with each cold-called client, so any slurring in his speech would seem deliberate.

In other workplaces this might have been seen as offensive. At the collection agency, employees played the "best" customer calls over the loudspeaker and competed to craft the most obscene insults for each one. "I wasn't even a racist until I worked here," one of his coworkers had told him once. "No offense."

"None taken," he said easily, smiling with lots of straight white teeth. Smooth tan skin, eyes blanked out by sunglasses, and two rows of perfect teeth.

I'm a social media ghostwriter for Joel Osteen. I rehome neglected exotic pets. I'm in a seasonal job right now, as a children's detention center Santa. I'm a disgruntled postal worker. I'm in between jobs currently, but I have a lot of experience as a cactus.

For this client he was Jamaican. "It's okay. It's okay, mon, don't worry. We're actually calling to let you know that you've been pre-approved for our special debt reduction package!" He brought a little ersatz island breeze, a little good feeling, into the life of this woman whose child had just been hospitalized, and by the end of the call she was crying and thanking him profusely.

Later that week the collection agency would send someone out to install a device in her car which kept the key from turning if she didn't make her payments. She had also signed over all her child-support payments and agreed to direct debiting, even though their records showed that she had already been overdrawn twice that year.

Colton hung up, and took a moment between calls to grab a drink. In his natural, snakeskin voice, he said, "No, thank *you.*"

A light on his phone which had until that moment always been black suddenly flashed red. He jumped as if he'd seen a spider. The light stayed red, steady, shivering a little at the edges. Someone in the main office wanted to talk to him.

Colton, his heart pinballing, picked up the phone.

*   *   *

A door whooshed open and Ana Ruiz stepped into a giant mouth. This was the lobby of Fainting Goat Studios: a white reception desk curving across the red-carpeted floor like teeth, with plush red hangings on the ceiling to represent cupid's-bow lips. The carpet was broad and pebbly, darker in the tongue section and paler on the sides. The lobby was two-story and wide open, with slender, curving silver staircases on each side. Ana had to stare at them for a moment before she recognized them: The Fainting Goat lobby wore a retainer.

"Make yourself at home away from home!" the receptionist chirped. She had a Splenda voice and wiry, muscular arms.

The receptionist didn't step out from behind her teeth-desk, but she waved her arms to indicate all the things Ana could do in the lobby. "This is what we call our *quirkspace.* It's no ordinary workplace! We believe that play is just another word for work. So feel free to provoke your creativity with foosball, Skee-Ball, or mini golf! If you punch the clown's nose," indicating a trollish, painted plastic thing, which came up to Ana's shoulder and leered at her from her nightmares, "fair-trade gorp with M&Ms will pour from its mouth!"

"...Fair-trade M&Ms?"

The receptionist went from Splenda to Sanka. "No, real ones," she said sharply. "Bentley will be out in a minute."

Ana wandered past the gap in the teeth and into the dental quirkspace. She gazed up at the second floor, where she could see the closed door which hid her new boss, as well as an open door in the very center of the roof of the mouth, which revealed the empty office of Fainting Goat's founder, Whelkin Jeames.

There were large soft blocks in the quirkspace, big enough to sit on or arrange into towers. A glass tank was built into one wall, but instead of fish it contained hamsters, shredding *Variety* and running on a little wheel. A human-sized wheel was outside the glass, and Ana stepped into it and began to run.

Bentley Woad came up behind her. "A little on-the-nose, don't you think?"

Ana jumped, and the wheel kept moving, so she stumbled getting out of the thing. *Should've picked Skee-Ball,* she thought. She introduced herself and held out her hand.

"I know who you are. Well, let's go upstairs and talk about the show. The wheel stops for no hamster!"

The producer of "Amends" was a bottle-blonde with lacquered, bitten fingernails. Her black t-shirt, with ripped-off sleeves, said I KNOW, I'M WORKING ON IT. At the end of her stone-washed jeans her veiny feet were in red open-toed stilettos, and her painted toenails didn't match her fingernails.

Once they had climbed the retainer to her office, she turned to Ana and said, "You know that I don't want to do a standard junkie exploitation show. The point is to show a new side of addiction to the viewing public. We're looking for smart, articulate people who are fucked-up in stupid, articulate ways. We're breaking stereotypes here, okay? We're not going for the bottom of the barrel—we want to show that the barrel is pretty much all bottom. These are people who think they're high-functioning," Bentley said, with a rueful smile. "They are wrong. Do you have any experience with addiction?"

Ana had prepared for this question. "I'm codependent!"

Bentley boggled at her. "Yeah but—that's not a *thing*, that's not an addiction. That's a job-interview answer! 'Oh, my biggest weakness is that sometimes I just *care too much!*' No, okay, I'm putting you down as no experience with."

Bentley seemed to be trying to lean intimidatingly back against her (white, enameled, plaque-free) desk, but she kept fidgeting.

"So you have a lot of catching up to do. Here are the rules." She grabbed a green smoothie off her desk and gulped it for punctuation, nearly falling off her heels in the process. She glowered at Ana.

"Addicts, when we're using, are basically rat terriers with the personal judgment of peanut butter. Talking to them or trying to reason with them is like getting stuck in an endless time loop. They can't see a way out so they just repeat the same thing, we get stuck like a record, which you probably don't even know what that means because you're an infant, *God*. They already know everything you're going to tell them and they are already bored."

Her voice was raspy and authoritative. She sucked her smoothie through its plastic straw until it gurgled. When she opened her mouth again her tongue was stained green.

"There's a saying that addicts get stuck, mentally, at the age we were when we first started using. And we don't start getting older until we get clean. So hey, you know, congratulations to me! I'm a producer at age seventeen! *I am that good.*"

Ana nodded compliantly, and Bentley scowled at her. "Addicts have a weird relationship to time in general. We don't like it. The past and future are the enemies and the present sucks, so we cling to the idea of the One Last. One last big good time. A using addict lives in a perpetual subjunctive tense. Woulda coulda shoulda. If I hadn't, if other people would just. If I could start again I would be better."

Her voice sounded sad, then, for a moment: childlike and humbled. It was the first moment Ana felt leadership from her, not just attempted intimidation. She noticed that "better" was a low bar.

Bentley got back into her groove. "Most of our talent is gonna have the mental age of negative six. They're basically evil fetuses. Their hearts are mosquitoes, they only land on someone they want to bite.

"Addicts are... gooey. Our morals are very stretchy. We don't have a clearly-defined self because we've crossed so many of the lines which used to define us. 'I'll never drink on the job,' 'I'll never have sex with a guy just because he has drugs,' those are things you use to draw a line between you and the world, that's your skin. And when you cross those lines it's like you don't have skin anymore and you're just oozing all over the place... you do whatever you can get away with."

Ana suddenly remembered high-school physics. *Addicts*

are gassy, she thought, and suppressed a giggle. *Expanding to fill the space they're given. But then*, she wondered, *who doesn't?*

She was pretty sure she still didn't understand the addict mentality. But she understood what Bentley said next: "Our job with 'Amends' is to help people figure out that humbling themselves, admitting wrongdoing, and trying to make amends to the specific people they hurt will actually make them happy."

"That sounds like a tough sell," Ana said.

"Nobody *wants* to chew off his own foot. But if you're stuck in a trap, you'll be happier if you chew off your foot than if you just sit there until the hunter comes."

"Won't you just be less unhappy, not happier?"

"Not done talking."

"...Okay."

"I view this show as a form of service. It makes me *happy*. It's not exploitive so get that out of your head." Bentley picked up a pen and chewed on it, just for a moment, then put it down and picked up a novelty pair of walking teeth.

"Most of the people they need to make amends to wouldn't take an apology from them if it came with a million-dollar check, but the camera can open those doors. It is, you might say, one of the many Higher Powers with which we work."

She had wound up the teeth and now set them on her desk, where they chattered their way to the edge of her laptop and then toppled over onto the keyboard. The little pink feet paddled helplessly in the air. Bentley picked up the pen again.

"We're providing an experience for the talent—a recovery experience. Please think of them that way, also: as talent.

Talented people, even if their only talent is for turning their personal lives into melodrama. We can help them monetize that drama. And when we're rough with the talent or cynical about them that is because we know them, better than they know themselves."

She gnawed on the pen as she figured out how she wanted to close this set-piece speech. Ana waited.

"We are going to be putting their lowest moments on national television and if we do our jobs right, they will thank us for it later. Do you see the size of your task here?"

Ana was trying to figure out what to answer when Bentley started up again. "As production assistant you will be herding all of us, the fuck-ups in management and the *abject* fuck-ups in talent, you will be the one person whose internal clock actually works like a clock and not like a Mobius strip, you will be the oldest child. Are you, by the way?"

"I'm the middle child."

"Hmm, it shows. I'm an only though, I shouldn't talk. Anyway, on set you're the oldest. Old movie productions used to have what they called a continuity girl. Addicts' lives lack continuity even out here in flesh reality; in television reality it can get even crazier. You're going to keep us all in one piece, pull together a person out of a bunch of pixels. You won't have to do the *grodiest* work. Gross is good television, so if there's anything funky—and there will be—the talent will have to shovel that mess themselves. Like if somebody swallows his microphone, he gets to be the one who hunts through poop for it. But if you have a keen sense of smell this might not be the easiest show for you."

"I can wear nose plugs."

"Ooh, that's good. That gives the audience a sense of the difficulty here, the *visceral* side of things. The manure element. And hey, as long as we're talking wardrobe, what is with your dress?"

Ana beamed nervously. She had been hoping someone would ask.

"I have a friend who's a designer. She made this—the sleeves represent pills," white and puffy, on either side of a corset bodice, "and the skirt represents a pill bottle. One of those orange ones." The skirt was sheer, so you could see Ana's black bike shorts through the neon orange bubble.

Bentley laughed out loud. "Fuck me all over. Turn around?"

She made a turning motion with her hand. Ana complied.

"Nice. Yeah, wear that on camera. That's beyond stupid, I love it. Have you looked at the casting videos?"

"Oh yes, I've familiarized myself with all the material I was sent."

Bentley gave her a deeply seventeen-year-old look, all hooded eyes and instant boredom. Ana was beginning to understand that her Rough Guide to Addicts lecture was more than just a self-aggrandizing stunt.

"Okay, my mind gets really drifty when you talk like that. Which ones did you *like*? We have to have the one who thinks she's a wolf, by the way. I know it's a little bit Freak of the Week but she's a bat mitzvah buddy of Jeames's niece. What did you think of the others?"

"I liked Emebet, the Ethiopian Christian. All reality shows need a Christian. Also I liked the playwright, Medea; she'll make a good villain. We need one of the gay men, unless the writer in the bow tie is gay. My favorite of the ones who are already out was Colton, the debt-collection guy, since he also brings racial diversity."

"Oh my God, it speaks," Bentley said. Ana smiled primly. "Yeah, yeah, we need the debt guy, he's a supervillain in this economy and he's *personally* racially diverse, and he did porn so there's eye candy. Right now most of our talent looks like the wreck of the *Marie Celeste*; even the bow tie looks like he was dragged backwards through a hedge fund. Whereas Debt Be Not Proud still has his cheekbones."

She favored Ana with a sharky smile.

"I approve of all your choices and I agree. You and I are so compatible, we are practically the same species. Now please go away, do all of the tasks I assigned you in the fifteen emails I have already forgotten, and when filming starts, wear gloves."

Chapter 2: One Last Good Time

Most of the cast of "Amends" decided that they would use their last night of pre-reality TV freedom to have a great time, one last time. Shayna Miller (who preferred to be called Sharptooth) was the sober exception. She spent the night online with a Canadian who was trying to figure out if his true inner nature was a snowy owl or a great horned owl. Being of service to others helped her fight her drug cravings, and she was completely reliable in any Internet-based crisis.

J. Malachi sat down at his hulking, sticky desktop computer and tried to write. He owed his editor at *The New Flâneur* an art review, but all of the art shows he'd seen lately were the same old thing. Contemporary Russian-Americans posed to imitate famous Soviet propaganda posters; piles of dime bags on the street corners of gentrified neighborhoods. Portraits of theocratic dictators made with lipstick. They were captions, not pictures. They reviewed themselves.

He felt weak and scared, gulping at a vodka and orange soda (his own invention, the Clockwork Orange: the name was because it removed your free will), picking at bits of fluff and food stuck in his keyboard, and wondering how anyone could expect him to work sober. He'd been frightened ever since he realized what he'd signed up for. He felt a low, stomach-based panic, but it didn't call up his flight-or-fight reaction; he thought maybe he had disabled that mechanism. All he could do was sit there, drinking, waiting for the alcohol to eat up the present and excrete it as the past.

Shaggy gray cobwebs hung from the corners of the ceiling. There were cockroaches trapped in the scotch tape holding up the vintage Tory poster (LABOUR ISN'T WORKING) that he'd put across from the computer to prick his conscience. Car headlights swinging by on 16th Street lit up the mosquito netting by the door; he'd taken it down from around his bed when he realized it had become a roach habitat, but he kept forgetting to throw it away. When the white lights hit it, it seemed to foam and surge like possessed yogurt.

He thought he'd heard that you were supposed to toast when you drank vodka. He wanted to do what you were supposed to, especially when it required drinking.

"Here's to the era of personal responsibility," he said to his shrimps, and lifted the traditional red solo cup. Then he realized he had to think of another one right away, since he wanted another drink. "Uh... here's to waiting! Here's to the waiting room of life."

That seemed a little *too* accurate—a little too reminiscent of the night he'd spent, about six months ago, in the Georgetown University Hospital emergency room. He had set off the fire alarm in his apartment while trying to make steak Diane from a recipe he'd found at his favorite reactionary food blog, The Counter-Revolution. He vaguely remembered lying on the kitchen floor, then lying on the bathroom floor, then lying on a gurney, and then trying to walk a straight line next to a hospital bed to prove that he was sobering up.

"Oh come on, I was always picked last for gym, I can't walk a straight line even when I'm... ah, what's the word for when you're not drunk? Hungover."

This hadn't impressed the nurses.

He had then, out of some half-remembered impulse he'd probably gotten from a book—one of those books he talked about but hadn't read, like Kant or de Tocqueville—asked if Georgetown was still a Catholic hospital.

"I don't want birth control, don't worry," he said, very sincerely, convinced that he was now quite well and could be allowed to go home. "I was wondering if you could fetch a priest? I'd like to talk to a priest about the state of my soul."

When the bewildered nurse had told him this wasn't possible, he had nodded solemnly. "Oh, of course. I'm sure you only call them when it's time for Last Rites."

Several hours later he had walked home barefoot, carrying his penny loafers with two fingers hooked into the penny slots. Cherry blossoms were fluttering down around him. He was filled with a great lightness and relief, which he later identified as giving up.

He didn't especially like thinking about that night, or about any of the nights he remembered better when he was drinking.

"Hospital," he mumbled. "Everything's a hospital these days. I feel like I could be sitting by the stage to go up and get my Pulitzer and it would feel just like a hospital waiting room."

*   *   *

Emebet spent her grand last night in style: with a pint of Gordon's vodka on a bus shelter bench. It was one of the benches she thought of as un-Christian, the ones with the metal dividers to keep homeless people from sleeping on them, but it was positioned so that she could keep an eye on the broken newspaper box where she had stashed her extra clothes. She would later learn that this bench was only three blocks from J. Malachi's desperate studio apartment; she knew his building because you could sneak into it through the convenience store.

As the bottle emptied and the few passersby filtered off the streets and out of the stiffening darkness, Emebet felt like she was swallowing the world. *The True Cross was found in a garbage heap*, she thought, trying to comfort herself. *I wonder what I'm hiding.*

She fell asleep sitting up, and had bad dreams.

*   *   *

Colton didn't even know why he was in this situation to begin with. He was restlessly drinking—at a bar, for once—with, or at least near, a few people he had hated in high school. He was dressed business casual, in a bar whose mostly-white clientele was more familiar with business illegal.

"This is so weird," he complained to the bartender, a short and paunchy man with the face of a nightmare leprechaun. "Unexplainable."

"It's inexplicable that your employers would want you to stop drinking at work?"

Colton hadn't mentioned the reality-TV angle; they were supposed to keep it a secret. "No, I know why they want me to stop drinking—not just at work, by the way, everywhere. It's because they're sick people with a dominance fetish, they get off on controlling other people's behavior. But why now? I've been a lot more of a fuck-up before. I'm maintaining here, okay? I'm not coming in to work three hours late with rotisserie chicken in my hair. I'm not trading blow jobs for Adderall with my manager. This, where I am right now, this is not that big a deal."

The bartender gave a long, low, hollow gutter-ball laugh. "This is not the worst you can do. That's your argument?"

"Why is this place so expensive anyway?"

"That drink in your hand is two fifty. Only place you'll get cheaper is if you drink at home."

"Yeah, and the company's better there too."

"Have you talked to your sister about this?"

Colton narrowed his eyes and leaned aggressively over the bar. "Why, how do you know my sister?"

The bartender lifted his hands in frustration. "What do you mean, how do I know her? How the fuck do I know you? I grew up here, jackass. I live literally four blocks from your childhood fucking home. In *my* childhood home."

Colton had no idea which "childhood home" the guy meant—they'd been evicted from a series of increasingly seedy apartments—but he was willing to give the benefit of the doubt. "Really? You look surprisingly toothy for somebody from the old neighborhood. Surprisingly be-toothed. Anyway Rian isn't gonna help. The last time I saw her she threw me out."

"Why, what did you do?"

"I called her boyfriend her dealer by mistake. He does

in fact supply her with pot so you can see how I would get confused. But Rian thinks it's trashy to sleep with your dealer, so, you know, I'm glad she has standards."

"If I were a better person," the bartender said, "I'd 86 you."

Colton, deeply offended, knocked back the last of his drink and said, "For fucking *what*? Anyway it doesn't matter. 'If I were a better person.' What bullshit. Nobody's a better person. Everybody's an asshole."

"I agree, that is a very handy excuse."

Colton was in denial about his better nature, though. He had meant to leave "Is AA for You? Twelve Questions Only You Can Answer" as his tip, but in the end he couldn't go through with it. He had worked too many terrible jobs. He tipped fifteen percent with a barely-legible note saying, "This would have been 20% if you weren't such a." He got distracted before finishing the sentence, and sloshed out into the night.

*   *   *

Medea had meant to go out and insult friends, but she got into a ferociously domestic mood and decided to improve her habitat. She was a spry little drunk, hurtling after her cats on all fours so she could adorn them with ruffles she'd ripped off her lampshades. She washed a lot of dishes and utensils badly, and tried to clean the lipstick off the carpet. She was playing the same song over and over at top volume for inspiration. She had lost her short-term memory, so each repetition was equally great. Occasionally she would jig until she fell down.

She got a dirty lampshade ruffle around the fattest cat, whose girth had prevented him from wriggling under her bookshelf. He meowed mournfully and writhed in her arms.

"You look fantastic, my friend," she cooed. "You are the

best. Who's gonna love you like I love you?"

The cat tried to bite her, and kicked with his hind feet but got his claws stuck in her sweater.

"Oh, poor thing," she crooned. "Poor kittycat. You look great, though. I made you a tutu! I've fixed the lamps now and also decorated the cats, this night is awesome. I'm filled with efficacy." She had a hard time getting her mouth around the corners of the word. "Homemakers and life-takers, man. Homemakers... and life-*takers*."

✳   ✳   ✳

For Dylan the last night before "Amends" was marked by periodic trips to the men's room of the only sports bar in Duluth that didn't card. He would stagger around, fall against the bathroom mirror and stare at himself, and try to remember what he had just done or said. Over the course of the night he repeated this performance about ten times, his hair becoming progressively more tired and emotional, until it was standing almost entirely on end. Still, he managed to keep a smile on the front of his face.

He kept finding himself in the middle of conversations for no reason. "I just got back from the john," he announced, "so I have no idea what you guys are talking about, but I completely support your business model. I think teeth are the next big thing. Like after they fix health insurance, next thing is teeth."

A little while later, but possibly part of the same discussion, "No, I can hook you up! I met a guy the other night, my friend knows a guy who trains those little birds to come and peck tartar and stuff off your teeth. Just like with hippos." And then, musingly: "Tartar. Tar-tar-tar."

Somebody—a former teammate, and also one of Dylan's

many ex-stepsiblings, elite junior hockey being a fairly small world and both of his parents being the remarrying kind—asked him whether it was true that he was going to rehab.

"Uh, kind of? I'm not allowed to talk about it, I signed a thing."

"Jesus, what do they think they can do with you in rehab? You were never habilitated, how the fuck do you plan to get *re*-habilitated?"

"That is an excellent question."

"What do they do there?"

"God, your guess is better than mine. I mean I think I'm going to get crucified, I think it'll be good for me. I think I'm really going to get it this time." He put his head down on the bar, and wondered what his tartar was like. "They're really going to nail me down this time," he said.

"Might be what you need."

"Oh, no," he said, lifting his head, "I totally agree. Couldn't agree more. I'm a total banana boat at this point. I'm a basket case with no basket. I think it'll be good, I'll learn to have shame and shit."

His ex-stepbrother laughed. "I don't think that's how it works."

"No, I read about this," Dylan insisted. "They teach you to have shame, like, respect for yourself, to not put yourself in... situations."

"Shame and self-respect are opposite things."

"What? No, shame is the thing that helps you make good choices. This is basic kindergarten stuff. Anyway if you say that I shouldn't feel shame, aren't you, like, shaming me for my feelings? You're shame-shaming. Don't shame-shame."

Tar-tar-tar.

In the bathroom, after dropping his phone in the sink and on the floor, he managed to type out a text to Gair that looked like a hockey player's teeth: wht foes it feel likr to b sfa gofod prdson?

*   *   *

J. Malachi came to with his face against the flocked linoleum of his bathroom. A large cockroach was crawling toward the bottom of his shower curtain.

"Bleh," he said. "Pleh." He coughed. "...Why do I have two copies of *The Last Gentleman*?" (The answer was that he'd vomited into one of them. He probably should have thrown that one out instead of just dropping it over the side of the bath.)

There was something sticky-looking by his face, and also his foot hurt. Slowly, like a mountain forming on the earth's crust, he rose up on all fours. The sticky patch was orange. There was also something not-orange and smeary which turned out to be blood.

"Good day to you, I'm Sherlock Holmes," he muttered, as he examined the clues laid out before him. The blood was from his foot and the broken Corona bottle—when had he bought beer? There was blood in the bathtub, and another broken bottle, and a large pewter eagle he'd bought at a yard sale; his khakis were also soaking wet. He added these facts together and deduced that he had taken a bath with his eagle.

"Sherlock Holmes. Now there was a great Victorian. In this decadent age they'd run an intervention on him."

The sticky thing was vodka and orange soda! He felt intrigued. He wanted to lie down again so he did, face down, closer to the sticky patch. He put out his tongue and lapped at it experimentally: hair of the floor that bit you. Couldn't hurt.

Not bad at all. Definitely vodka and orange soda. A heavy, freighted, nostalgic taste, slightly furry, with a strong bouquet of aspirin or maybe Liquid Plumr. That might be the floor though. He licked for a while, until he felt strong enough to get up and figure out what to do about his foot. He pulled the glass out, washed the foot in the bath, and poured the very last of the vodka over it to keep it clean. It stung a little, which he was pretty sure meant it was working.

* * *

Colton awoke naked and covered in chicken korma. He looked around and, seeing that he was alone in the bed, muttered, "Oh thank fuck. ...Why is it always chicken?"

"Morning," a sepulchral voice said from the darkest corner of the apartment.

Colton shot upright in bed. There was a giant white man in his underpants standing propped against the windowsill, implacable, with an albino python winding around his shoulders.

"Oh my God, I fucked the Ghost of Christmas Past."

The white man laughed. The python tasted the air. Colton, feeling that his number had come up at last, leaned over the bed and retched into the fat ghost's Stetson.

* * *

Medea staggered to the door and let in her least-alienated friend, a woman named Salome (they had bonded over their names), who was coming to pick up her cats. "Sheeit," Salome said. "You look like lesbian bed death. I hope the publicity is worth it."

Medea made a rumbling noise which was intended to be threatening. Then she yawned. "They're hiding," she said. Her voice sounded unused; the rest of her seemed definitely used too much. Her thick black hair was a mass of snarls and split ends, and she had a fake eyelash stuck to her cheek. For a vertiginous moment Salome expected an eye to blink open underneath it. "Here kitties."

"Do you have any food you can put in the carriers to lure them?"

"It won't work, they're too smart for that," Medea said proudly—and then corrected herself. "Not that intelligence is everything. I would love them even if they were retarded. No, we'll just have to wait until they decide they *want* to get in the cages. Don't worry. Everybody chooses the cage in the end."

But Medea's cats were fed up with her. They had been hiding under the bed—a horrifying waste ground where they never went unless they were truly desperate—but as soon as the carriers were opened they bolted out and buried their ruffle-bedecked forms inside. Medea raised her eyebrows, but she got the cage doors shut and the animals began to calm down. "It's okay, kitties, I'm here," she sang, and tried to poke her fingers through the wire doors to pet them. They hissed and snapped at her.

Salome had known Medea back when she was new-sprung from Barnard, coltish and even shy. She'd been a poet then, not yet a playwright, with a terrified, fluttering laugh. She'd hold forth tipsily ("Walt Whitman never wrote a poem in his life—he *oozed* them") and sit in your girlfriend's lap, and just when you were about to haul her up and throw her out she'd give that high, shaky laugh, like the flag of some tiny defiant country. She'd turn her round face up to you and smile, daring but not disingenuous: She just wanted to know how much she could get away with.

Unfortunately for Medea, the answer had been "everything."

Salome looked into Medea's brash, hard eyes, her slack coarsened face, and felt a stab of pity as she took the cages.

*   *   *

Sharptooth, who had stayed up far too late arguing online about whether monogamy was a form of bigotry, awoke feeling cramped and achy. She stretched, rubbed her shoulders and the base of her spine, and immediately reached for her phone.

Hi Tumblr friends! Slept on my phantom tail all wrong and now I'm stiff and sore. #kinproblems #wolvesarentmorningpeople

She giggled. She was grateful that she could still act like a carefree little cub sometimes, even though she now identified as an adult.

*   *   *

Dylan stumbled into the kitchen, where his hockey fosterage parents were waiting with embarrassed, punitively Minnesotan expressions. For over a decade they had agreed to house high-school hockey stars who needed to be near their team; this year they'd gotten Dylan. They wanted to file a formal complaint, but they couldn't shake the worry that this situation was, somehow, their fault.

"Morning," Dylan attempted. "How is everybody?" His voice was slurry, whiny, cottonmouthed from the hangover.

The two adults in the room silently moved away from the cabinets so that he could get a box of cereal. He tried to find a bowl but they were all in the dishwasher, so he poured the cereal into a novelty glass (lipsticked girl in pink gear, holding pink hockey stick, under the logo PUCKER UP) and ate it with a fork. No milk: He was in that state where everything was horrifying. The glassy, blue-tinged sheen of the skim milk in its plastic gallon jug, the jug's gooseflesh skin, the white beads pearling on the blue cap with its thin, crumbling crust of dried milk—it all filled him with dread.

"We gave your date a ride home," the man said.

Ooooooohhhh, Dylan thought. *Oops.* "I, uh, I'm gonna make some changes in my life, yes—have you ever heard the term, 'secondary virginity'?"

They did not look impressed.

Dylan tried to remember the girl. Then he did, and things got much worse. She had hooked up with several of his friends. He had promised everybody that he would not take advantage of her obvious familial-neglect issues, despite his own obviously compatible ones. She was known for carrying mace and Rohypnol on her at all times, and every guy got one or the other. Dylan blinked and realized that his eyes were still burning a little, so apparently she hadn't felt that she needed the drugs.

Wow, he thought, crunching shakily on his cereal. *I think I banged a villain. So that's new.* He wondered if he could count this as a "yet"—he'd heard this term when his coach made him go to AA, their jargon for all the bad things that hadn't happened to you yet until they did. A sort of bucket list of poor life choices.

"We're very glad that you'll be moving on," the husband said stiffly.

"Martin!" his wife hissed.

"Moving on—to *better things*," her husband said. "That's what I meant."

"Yes, sir," Dylan said. "After I finish this I'll clean out my room and the bathroom."

The couple exchanged glances.

"If you think that's wise," the wife said. "We were planning to hire someone. Or possibly call—there must be some kind of government agency which deals with these things."

"Martha, I don't think the EPA will come to people's houses—"

"Or maybe Animal Control, if we said we thought the goat might have come back?"

Dylan left them arguing about whether the Army Corps of Engineers would send someone with the industrial-strength cleaning products needed to clear up the disaster area he'd left in his wake. He slunk to the bathroom and threw up. *In the toilet, come on, I'm not that bad*, he thought, with the cereal scratching at the back of his throat. *Still mostly human.*

Chapter 3: How to Make Spaghetti

They were all brought in separately. J. Malachi stumbled out of a tiny rental car, where he'd been riding in the back trying to look competent. This was difficult since during the flight to Philadelphia he'd vomited strawberry-rhubarb smoothie all over his seersucker suit.

The November afternoon was chilly and cloudy: a cottony, mildewed day. J. Malachi tried to pretend that he was "on assignment," which had never happened to him but which seemed much more romantic than being on a reality show about what a fuck-up he was. He walked across the parking lot and noticed a car with a vanity plate that said IPRY4U. It made him feel, briefly but comfortingly, superior.

The show was using a real rehab center, which was set in a pastoral Pennsylvania area between gently rolling hills. It was called Noah's Rainbow. *Didn't Noah have blackout sex with his own daughters?,* J. Malachi thought, but he tried to be positive. The center was a low tan building surrounded by thin, tall pines. A hawk wheeled overhead, and J. Malachi thought he saw a rabbit bolt away from him into the underbrush, although that might have been the DTs. The air was soft and wet and clingy, but at least it carried away some of the smell from his suit.

He went through the glass doors into a big scooped-out lobby. The furniture looked cheap and new and hard. There were cameras already set up to watch the check-in personnel going through their bags.

J. Malachi didn't think it was entirely professional to do a bag search in the lobby, but he opened his bag like everyone else. He didn't want to watch the gloved employees sorting his belongings, sniffing his toiletries to make sure his shampoo wasn't grain alcohol, so he watched his fellow contestants instead. The lights for the cameras made him uncomfortably hot and, he was pretty sure, smelly. He had hoped that he would stand out in the suit but unfortunately he had achieved his goal.

As he came in he thought he heard someone yelling, but it was just the ring tone on the cell phone of one of his fellow cast members. This person was tall, with an oval face, light brown skin and slightly tip-tilted eyes with long black lashes, and clean-cut, golferly good looks. He looked like he had an invisible sweater draped around his broad, muscled shoulders. And his cell phone, in the gloved hands of a security guard, was yelling, "Bastard. Bastard. *Bastard!*"

"We're just gonna keep a hold of this while you're with us," the guard giggled. And then, holding up a Rolex: "Ooh, is this real?"

"It's a real *watch*," the golf-faced man said wearily, as the guard turned it over to reveal a logo that said, BOLEX.

There was a tall, thin woman with just one small bag:

skimpy underwear, skinny jeans, lots of frothy white cloth, maxipads and insect repellent. Emebet—there were name tags set up for them at the front desk, and J. Malachi felt simultaneously annoyed and relieved to see that he was expected to use his first name instead of his professional one— had a soft, pale voice and a shakiness to her movements. Her high-cheekboned face caught the light at unexpected angles, like a bent spoon. There was a pleading and disoriented quality to her gaze. The intake personnel patted her down and then explained that she should go to the "confession booth," where they'd do the first interview.

At that moment the woman patting down Medea— *Medea, really?* he thought—found the airplane-sized vodka bottle she'd nestled in her cleavage.

"Oh, is *that* where that was?" Medea gave a flamboyant guilty look right at the cameras, and flung out a hand as if to stop them from taking her booze. She was a busty woman, with a sag to her face and belly which suggested that she had at one point been slender; she was moon-faced, mixed Asian and white, with a broad nose and lush black hair cascading in tangles down past her shoulders.

A few feet away, a young white woman whose improbable name tag read "Sharptooth" was arguing doggedly that the intake personnel had no right to remove her gray felt tail and pull it apart to search for drugs. "I identify as a wolf! That tail is sacred!"

"My tits are sacred and they're searching *them*," Medea noted.

Medea and the sacred wolf, J. Malachi thought. *Somebody help me, I'm going to rehab in a Greek myth.* And then, sensing his advantage, he turned to the camera and said it out loud.

* * *

"Hey, Gair," Dylan said, squirming so that he was wedged into one corner of the confession booth. He put one foot up on the seat and wrapped his arms around his knee. He was all angles and muscles, hiding his face in his arms for a moment before looking up and grinning at the camera, head cocked, trying to charm it. "They've told us to pick somebody to do these video letters for and Pikachu, I choose you.

"We have already been *thoroughly* ravished, I plan to haunt your lonely nights with the image of me being strip-searched, and now we're going to get to know each other. This is honestly like all the worst parts of hockey—airport security and *teamwork* exercises rolled into one. I'm super positive I don't want to get to know these people, or myself," and he gave a big dimpled grin there. "Not sure what they're gonna make us do. Musical chairs. 'Pin the Needle on the Vein.'" His smile shivered a little but he turned it into a bratty smirk. "'If you were an animal, what animal would you be?' As you know, I'd be a sponge.

"What? It's an animal. Anyway, I did want to say thank you." He had to duck his head for a moment. "Everything's either a good time or a good story, right? I know why you guys wanted me to do this."

He couldn't think what else to say. "Okay, gotta go. They want to blindfold us and have us whack each other with sticks until *secrets* spill out."

He flashed a peace sign to the camera to signal that he was done.

He breezed past Emebet, who was standing outside the

booth waiting for her turn. She looked at him—even in looking at him she was somehow shaky, and he found that he couldn't meet her gaze—and then shuffled into the booth and sat down. She was reading a brochure about their treatment options.

"Can you tell us how you're feeling right now?" Ana asked.

Emebet had her own agenda. "It says here," she said, opening the brochure and pointing helpfully to the place, "that we could die. From simply not drinking alcohol? Does it really happen?"

"Yes, withdrawal for late-stage alcoholics is extremely dangerous," Ana said brightly. "You'll be meeting with a nurse right after we get done here. And we need you to be honest with us about exactly how you're feeling—physically, emotionally. Please tell us if you are feeling any distress!"

Emebet considered this request, and the implicit consequences of refusing. Could it really be so simple—just open her hands and let go? Could she finally stop failing, without having to *do* anything at all? Surely keeping your pain to yourself couldn't be a sin.

"No," she said, smiling. "I don't think I will tell you."

*   *   *

The guts of the rehab center were a few small bedrooms off of a My Little Pony-colored corridor. There was a seafoam green room for the men and a pinkish room for the women. Each room had a bathroom with a shower.

There were a lot of signs. There was a big stained whitish bin on the hallway with a sign saying, PLEASE PLACE PILLOWCASES, SHEETS AND TOWELS HERE. DO NOT PUT DUVETS HERE.

"Now here's something I've often wondered: What the fuck is a duvet?" Medea asked, speaking for many of them. "Pardon my French."

"It sounds like an animal," Dylan said, trying to lighten the mood. He had just answered a series of questions about whether he'd ever had alcohol-induced seizures, hallucinations, or memory loss, and even though most of the answers had been "no," he felt unexpectedly scared and shitty. Nobody had laughed when they'd asked if he'd ever blacked out and he'd used his old line, "Not that I can remember."

"Duvet, a small woodland creature," he suggested. "Like a badger, only nicer."

"It's a bedspread," said the woman who was leading them, a skinny and bubbly Asian named Jen. "But don't put any small woodland animals in there either!" Everyone glared at her.

There were signs in all the bathrooms telling them to wash their hands, with pictures to show them how. There were signs by the plugs, which were covered with plastic tabs, ordering them to ask a staff member to remove the covers before they plugged anything in. There were signs by the toilets saying, PRESS BUTTON FOR ASSISTANCE. There were signs on the popcorn ceilings, not just in the bedrooms but also in the halls, and these were the worst signs: THINGS ARE LOOKING UP! EVERY NOW IS NEW. THINK AND THRIVE.

Dylan tried to distract himself, as he threw his possessions into the bottom drawer of the dresser in the men's bedroom, by coming up with alternate rehab ceiling-sign slogans. He settled on DON'T DROP THE HOPE.

*   *   *

Emebet sat in the nurse's office—a white room, not pastel like the bedrooms—and placidly lied. Lying to uniformed Americans helped to comfort her, to steady her shaking body. It reminded her of some of the happiest memories of her life.

She had first learned that you could lie without guilt when her brother got married. A naturalized American citizen had returned home to Ethiopia and they had been wed, in a certain formal sense, and everybody had danced. All the girls had new clothes, and people put money down the front of the little girls' dresses to reward them for their dancing.

Emebet had forgotten the woman's name; she flew back to Washington the next day and they never saw her again. Everyone had been giddy, the weather had been balmy, the papers had all been arranged, and they were going to America.

When they set out her brother had warned her to pretend that she didn't speak English, and not to say anything to anyone. He had tried to sound threatening, but she had hugged their secret knowledge to herself, glowing with it. Their lies and complicity had bound them together. Nobody really saw her except her brother; everyone else only saw the passport photograph.

He hadn't expected her to be responsible for herself. She was allowed to act much younger than her age, for once. She trotted along after him, pointing out signs and instructions he might have missed, and he shepherded her through all the bureaucracy and only hit her once.

In the airport everything seemed intelligible. Everything was labeled. All the humans and the human things seemed to crowd out the presence of God. They'd had to stay there overnight and as she had slumped across the divided plastic seats, a foreign liturgy buzzed and clanged in her tired head: *Caution! The moving walkway is ending. Caution!*

Sometimes, in the morbid moments when all of her good memories seemed to have become dirty, she wondered whether this conspiratorial sojourn in Baltimore-Washington International Airport had prepared her for a life of dishonesty.

The nurse held out a paper cup of pills and a paper cup of water. "Take these, please."

"I feel fine!" she protested; but apparently her body had betrayed her.

"Let me explain what these are," the nurse began, but Emebet gave up and gulped them down. She was going to get quality medical care whether she wanted it or not.

Maybe it won't work, she thought, trying to stay positive.

*   *   *

Jaymi, Emebet, Colton, Sharptooth, Medea, and Dylan—the inmates, or the talent, in their new name tags—had to set up the room three times for their introductory lecture. The sound equipment kept having problems. So they had to unfold, refold, unfold, refold, and unfold the folding chairs. Medea did Emebet's work for her, partly because Emebet was cloudy and uncoordinated but primarily because she had been told not to. By the end of this exercise Medea felt that she and Emebet had bonded.

Their "sober director" gave the lecture: the skinny one, Jen, who had led them all to their rooms. She was a bright and bouncy thirty-eight-year-old, a tall twig with a mop of thick black hair at one end and chartreuse Crocs at the other. She brought her folding chair over when the rest of them had finished and sat right among them, Jesus dining with prostitutes and Republicans. They looked at her with varying levels of calculation and misery. Most of them had showered, but under the hot lights the room still stank of sweated-out liquor.

Ana, watching from the side, noted which of the talent looked more accusatory and which more ashamed. Emebet kept twisting her hands together. Ana had never seen someone wring her hands before, outside of Edward Gorey books. They were wearing various forms of armor: J. Malachi's pocket square, Emebet's white scarf floating around her shoulders, Dylan's tiny silver cross on a chain, Sharptooth's ears on a headband and tail on a belt.

Jen smiled at them—even her smile seemed bouncy, like hair in a shampoo commercial—and explained the rules. "In a lot of ways your time here at Noah's Rainbow will be just like any other rehab experience. Our day begins at seven o'clock—"

"In the *morning*? Is that a real time? I thought they just stuck that on the clock for symmetry."

Jen directed a quick, bright frown at Medea, who lifted her hands ironically but shut up.

"In the *morning*. You'll have a half-hour to dress and shower, and then breakfast, which includes several healthy options like whole-grain toast, fruit, and muesli."

"Also not a thing," Medea muttered.

"*Also*, breakfast is your only chance to get coffee with caffeine in it. And look, I realize this is a tough new experience for many of you, but we're all in this together," which the expressions of the talent suggested was not a persuasive tack, "so please don't interrupt or this will take much longer than it needs to. In general we don't like to use a reward-and-punishment system, but we can't allow one person's belief that she's special to distract us from the needs of other clients." With this vague threat she returned to the subject of the schedule. Medea hunched in her folding chair like a gargoyle that had lost its cathedral.

"Each day you'll be responsible for chores. Morning chores will involve cleaning the common areas and will be assigned via a rotating schedule; your only afternoon chore is to help prepare your room for inspection before dinner. If you're receiving medication for withdrawal symptoms you *may* be exempt from chores; we'll let you know.

"Lunch is at noon. The afternoon is mostly self-work. You'll each have an hour of individual counseling every day, along with the special therapeutic opportunities that are part of the unique concept of 'Amends.' From four to six you can clean your room and then have free time, unless you're on the roster to help make dinner. Dinner is at six, followed by clean-up.

"You'll also have opportunities to schedule meetings with debt counselors, financial self-help groups, time-management advisors, and other resources."

Jen took a breath, breathily. "Rules about filming: We'll ask you to make confessionals about once a day. You can say absolutely whatever you want. I won't be mad if you complain about me. You do have to provide some kind of material for the camera. Outside the confessional, try not to look at the cameras. We believe that's a strategy for avoiding intimacy.

"We reserve the right to ask you to leave for *any* reason,

and I'll especially call your attention to the rules against unwanted touching of any kind and inappropriate sexual contact."

Dylan raised his hand.

"Yes?"

"What's appropriate sexual contact?"

Amid the chorus of high-school snickering, Jen smiled at him and answered, "If it happens during your stay here, it's inappropriate."

Emebet came into focus long enough to raise a hand and ask, "What about church?" Dylan nodded at that.

"We'll have a sign-up sheet where you can indicate whether you'd prefer to go to a church in the community, have a religious authority come to you, or both. We're striving to be sensitive to your needs. There will also be field trips! We'll go to the zoo and a local park."

She composed herself, and looked at all of them with deep sincerity. "The next thirty days will be the toughest and most beautiful time of your entire life."

The cameras zoomed in on their mistrust and fear.

*   *   *

The pastel bedrooms had harvest yellow curtains, to give an atmosphere of sunlit calm. The confessional room was draped in satiny black and light blue cloth, so that the talent could be posed in front of whichever color would help them stand out.

And the room where they had individual counseling was washed in a soft pink like the inside of a seashell, or like a scar. It had flowered couches, and a table made to look like a trunk with luggage stickers from all kinds of exotic destinations. On a little side table by one of the couches there was a table lamp with a fringed shade, a box of tissues, a box of disposable gloves, and a bottle of hand sanitizer (which was kept in a locked cabinet when the room wasn't in use). There was a calendar on the wall with pictures of baby animals struggling to stand, and an inspirational poster showing a creamy white bar of soap with the word *Love* stamped into it and the legend, "Gets you clean!"

That poster is the thing I will get sick of first, J. Malachi decided, as he watched the camera crew setting up before his first bout of individual counseling. He sat on the flowered couch and tried not to pick at it. His stomach felt twisted, and something which he thought might be his liver was aching dully. The nurse had decided that he didn't need any medical care beyond a painkiller; sour granules of it still coated the back of his tongue.

"Would you like some herbal tea?" Jen asked.

"...Really? Isn't that kind of a cliché?"

"It's soothing," she said severely.

"I guess you could argue that a cliché is the same as a tradition," he mused. "Only cuter." He didn't want tea and wasn't sure he could keep it down, but he believed in submitting to the wisdom of the ages, so he thanked her and took a cup. He blew on it for a long time, but the camera crew had to replace a gel, and he had to take a sip eventually.

When the camera crew was ready they had to film Jen sitting down and offering J. Malachi a cup of tea. They made him repeat what he had already said. This made him bracingly aware of his own try-hard tendencies. It reminded him of a guy on the football team in high school who would respond to jokes about jocks or meatheads with, "Huh? I don't get it," making the joke-teller explain the joke until it collapsed. J. Malachi had fallen for this tactic every time.

After this brief round of humiliation the session began. Jen settled herself and wrapped her legs around one another like twizzled licorice. J. Malachi wished he could raise one eyebrow. *Transference is also a fine tradition*, he thought, and almost felt better.

"Why do you think you're here?" she asked.

"One of my editors said I should do it. I guess I had been sending him rough stuff, things I'd written while I was, you know, not sufficiently sober. I, uh, I wrote a thing where I had this whole extended metaphor about 9/11 and United Flight 93, which was supposed to prove that Congress should loosen standards for how much lead can be in children's toys. 'In the words of Todd Beamer, "Let's roll"—roll back regulation, that is.' Something like that."

Oh my God, he realized, overhearing himself. *I think I just became a reality-TV villain.*

And, a moment later: *That has got to be one of the dumbest rock-bottoms ever.*

"Is that why you're here, an article you wrote? Or is that a symptom of something else?"

"I mean, I know I drink a lot. Too much."

"Have you ever tried to quit?"

"I give up mixers for Lent?" This didn't seem to make an impression. "I've been cutting back! I drink much less than I used to when I'm out with other people."

He also went out much less, but he chose not to mention the drinking-alone portion of his personal improvement project.

"I've been trying to play the game with different rules." He sipped the tea, which was simultaneously watery and bitter.

"Can you be more specific?"

"Like, don't drink during the week, or drink beer instead of vodka. I've switched around a bunch there. You'd think I would've lost weight when I switched from Corona back to vodka, I mean that was the hope, but I guess not."

He felt like the cameras were getting bored with him. He needed to say something sincere and painful or else they'd make him pure villain, no redemption arc at all. Stressed, his speech pressured, he blurted, "I don't think—"

He felt as if he were betraying someone, doing something deeply morally wrong, by saying this sentence. He had to force it out.

"I don't think I could just... not ever drink again. I can't imagine ever living like that." He took a breath. "I could do it for a while, though, I think. I could do better than I am."

"What do you hope to accomplish here at Noah's Rainbow?"

I hope I never have to do anything remotely like this ever again. I hope I can write a book about this experience.

"I hope I can understand myself better and address my problems, including but not limited to the drinking... thing, and be a better person."

And then get hit by a bus as I'm leaving this place, so my parents can believe I was trying.

*   *   *

In the women's dorm room Sharptooth was pulling all the sheets and blankets off her bed to create a den in one corner. Medea had already asked what was up with the tail, giving

Sharptooth the opportunity to explain, "I was born in the wrong body. I'm actually, spiritually, a wolf. It's called being otherkin. It's very important for me to be open about it— coming out transformed my life, and my family. Our dog used to be terrified of storms and postal workers, but I was able to communicate with her, and now she's much more secure and self-grounded. I think of communication as my calling."

"Please don't eat me," Medea said.

"That's a misconception and a stereotype," Sharptooth said dogmatically. "Wolves almost never attack humans unprovoked."

"Addicts do," Medea said dryly, at which point Sharptooth had explained that she had overcome her addiction already and was only participating to help others. The other two women glared guiltily at her.

Now Emebet was lying on top of all her covers, suffering. Her wish that the medication wouldn't work had been partially granted; she was seeing things. She kept murmuring and making the sign of the cross. She wouldn't tell her roommates what she saw.

"It's just DTs, nothing to worry about," Medea said, trying to be comforting. "I always thought they were such a relief. Like, you'd see something and think, 'Oh shit! I have a mouse in here, I hope it doesn't scare the cats,' and then you'd realize it was just DTs."

"These aren't mice," Emebet said stiffly.

Medea shrugged. "What are they, like demons or something? Look, they're *not real*, that's the important thing."

Sharptooth looked up at this, and twitched her nose. "I'm not sure it's a good idea to come up with arbitrary, normative standards for what is and isn't real. If she perceives them, aren't they real to her?"

"They can't hurt her," Medea said.

"They are signs," Emebet said. "I've already been hurt; I have hurt myself. These are visions, they are warnings."

"See?" Sharptooth crowed. "Don't police her religious beliefs."

"What if she starts seeing *wolves*? What if she starts saying they're coming for her, with their fangs all slathering foam and dripping blood? Are you gonna tell me then that the real problem is that her hallucinations are *stereotypes*?"

At this point Emebet herself stood up; it felt like she was filling with dark red water. She wandered toward the bathroom, falling against the furniture, as the other two women watched with interest. She came out again and looked around at them all, lost.

"I look... puffy," she said, and collapsed onto the bed again.

"It's the steam," Medea said kindly. "Everybody looks awful in bathroom mirrors."

"It's a symptom," Sharptooth said. "I don't want to body-shame, but you'll lose weight and your skin will improve once the toxins leave your system! You'll both look much better."

"You know, under ordinary circumstances if a wolf started talking to me I would think that was so awesome. I would do whatever it said and we would go on some kind of amazing wolf adventure. Life is so fucking disappointing when you get what you want." Medea didn't deign to look at Sharptooth throughout this little speech.

Sharptooth wasn't going to be cowed. She composed herself. "Thank you for acknowledging my identity! I hope you know that I acknowledge *your* identity, too. I truly believe and accept that you are an artist."

She curled up in her nest of blankets, folded her hands over her nose like paws, and pretended to go to sleep. It was one way of getting the last word.

*   *   *

In the confession booth, Colton smiled like a Ken doll at the camera. "I do have a plan for how I am going to get through this experience. My plan is to lurk. This is step one." He pulled out a pair of large sunglasses, with lenses shaped like hearts, and put them on.

"And this is step two."

He got up in one fluid movement and moonwalked out of the room, shooting a finger-gun as punctuation.

He was still wearing the sunglasses when it was his turn for individual counseling. Jen got a little bit Shar Pei in the forehead, but she didn't say anything about it. Instead she offered him tea and, when he refused, she fired her first question.

"Colton, were you surprised when the collections agency where you were working asked you to get help for your drinking?"

"Yes, it seemed like a creepily human thing for them to do. Like if a giant lizard-creature suddenly reached behind its head and yanked off its skin, and it turned out to be your cousin."

"That was the only thing that was surprising about it? Had other people confronted you about your drinking before?"

"No, I always cleaned up after myself."

There had been the one time when a friend had invited

him over for an evening-after beer, and asked him if he'd meant it when he'd screamed over and over that all men were assholes and he was going to cut their throats like chickens. That had been a rough moment. In his defense, though, the night-before had *begun* with grain alcohol, fruit punch, and dry ice all mixed together in a giant plastic pumpkin, and at one point he'd been drinking out of a fake skull. It had been a road rash of a night.

"What did it feel like when your supervisors spoke to you about your drinking?"

It was a strange memory. They had seemed nervous. They had acted as if they were the ones getting called out for bad behavior.

"I don't know if it felt like anything. I wasn't paying attention to how it felt."

"You must have felt something. What are a few adjectives that describe how you were feeling?"

"Bad. I felt bad."

"Good."

"Mad."

Jen nodded encouragingly.

"Sad."

She frowned. "I hope you're not deflecting here."

"Oh, gross! I would never do that in front of a *lady.*"

She nodded sharply. "Could you take off your sunglasses, please? The camera people are indicating to me that they're getting a lot of glare."

They're about to get a lot more, he thought. He briefly considered arguing that the sunglasses were part of his identity, like the wolf-girl's tail, but he felt really tired and if he made an effort for a little while maybe they would let him get some rest. He took off the glasses, slowly and sensually, and stuck the end of one of the legs in his mouth.

It was, he reflected, genuinely weird that he couldn't remember any emotions at all from the meeting with his supervisors. He had been drunk, but there was a kind of airless hilarity about the memory; it had felt very unreal. He wouldn't have been too surprised if they *had* reached back and yanked off their skins. *Instead of*, he thought, *sending me here, to unzip and show my monkey on reality television.*

*   *   *

The talent didn't have to cook dinner on the first night. This was a wise choice on the part of the production staff, since some of the inmates had enough difficulty simply digesting food, let alone preparing it. Dinner was mostly yellow, with some brown: macaroni and cheese, corn, summer squash, and bananas. Dylan was the first to puke. He had to be scolded into cleaning up his mess, which he did with a frown so deep it made him look like a disappointed Muppet.

"You can still see the individual *kernels* of corn," Colton commented.

When Emebet also vomited up her food the other women tried to help her clean, but they were shooed away by the staff. Jen informed them that dealing with unpleasant bodily functions was one of the consequences of their addictions. Solidarity, apparently, was not one of the approved consequences.

Once both of the rooms had been cleaned up after their baptism in consequences, Dylan and Emebet had to go to the confessional room and record their reactions to vomiting. Emebet's film wasn't used, even though she puked again right there in the confessional room, because she just kept apologizing and looking around in sallow, exhausted confusion. She seemed dazed and the film editors agreed that it would make "Amends" look bad to show her being forced to get on all fours and clean up her mess by herself, as Dylan encouraged her and offered to help.

For his part he perked up a bit once the nausea had passed. He was determined to look as good as possible in a situation designed to make him look awful, so he was trying to be bright, helpful, and funny. He couldn't quite manage "bright," but he did make it to Eeyore's-birthday levels of buoyant vivacity. His voice was a deadened drawl but he kept smiling.

"Hey, at least they picked food that tastes okay coming back up," he said, giving the camera a smile like bad CGI. "If it were me running this place I'd be so bad. I'd make dinner the first night, like, wings with ranch, tabasco on everything, Kool-Aid for that special 'puking up blood' look. I mean I puked corn through my nose just now and I basically feel okay."

Someday this will be a great story, he told himself. "*You would not believe the crazy shit I got into when I was eighteen.*" *Someday all of this will just be skid marks on the underwear of life.*

Everyone went to bed early that night, but no one got much sleep. They cried and writhed on the beds; they got chills and fever. The nurse came through the rooms and shook her head, and gave Emebet her third round of pills. The rest of them got up over and over to go and beg for aspirin, for mouthwash ("I know I can't have the kind with alcohol in it," Medea said, "but right now my teeth feel like fuzzy dice hanging from Satan's own rear-view mirror"), for more blankets, for muscle relaxers. All of these requests were denied.

"Why can't I have more blankets?" Dylan asked. "I swear to you I spent ten minutes trying to come up with *one* thing that would let me feel part-human, one thing I'm not banned from having here, and blankets is all I could come up with. Fuzzy, warm, comforting, not-puked-on blankets. I promise I wouldn't even use them to build a fort, since I know this is all about breaking down our barriers."

Ana and Bentley stood in the hallway outside the men's bedroom, a little after three in the morning, under the humming and shivering overhead lights. All the cameras and the camera lighting had gone dark. They could hear a woman moaning down the hall, and the smells of sweat and vomit sometimes surfaced in the air despite the tired whickering of the ventilation system. Ana looked up and noticed the posters on the ceiling; a corner was hanging down from the one that said, YOUR MIRACLE IS COMING! GET OUT OF THE WAY. From the men's bedroom somebody shouted, "*Shit!*" and they heard a crash, and then some conversation, then silence. It seemed to Ana that the white light in the hallway had begun to go yellow.

"This is bad," Ana said. She felt smaller than usual. "...Is this unusually bad?"

But Bentley was smiling, a little shrugging grin. She turned and looked at Ana with surprise and some contempt.

"Why is this bad?" And then, as her smile turned inward, she tapped her skull and said, "This is what it's always like in here."

Can that be true? Ana wondered.

The moaning got louder.

"Like this, really?"

"Oh yeah, but with like a guitar solo in the background. Come on, pull it together. There's pizza in the kitchen for the crew, let's go take advantage."

*   *   *

By the afternoon of the second day, a few of the inmates were recovered enough to crawl out of bed and lie saggily in the overstuffed chairs of the common room. Medea, draping herself sideways across one particularly aggressively-upholstered specimen, proclaimed, "We have died, and been reborn into a Chekhov play. Let's whine and suffer and stare at each other." Nobody answered her.

Emebet took an unsteady walk in the courtyard. The sky was a stormy welter of grays and blues. She would walk the ten feet or so from one white stone bench to the next and then collapse onto it and spend several minutes recovering. The courtyard was surrounded by tall, thin pine trees. The grass was a green which looked almost black under the lowering sky. The leaves of the grass were long and flat and slipped unpleasantly against her calves when she strayed off the gravel path, like hands grabbing for her.

She knew she was supposed to be thinking and praying, but her head felt stuffed up and she was overcome with frequent bursts of panic breaking through the numbness. She felt very much like she had when she first came to the United States—the overcrowded, chaotic world outside the airport.

In fact, she reflected, Noah's Rainbow was like America boiled down to its pungent essence: an excruciating place without privacy, without anything familiar, for which she was expected to be grateful. She had felt almost proud of herself for vomiting up the dirty American coffee that morning. Something in her was still Ethiopian, even if it was only bile.

She sighed, and began to trace big coralline curves in the gravel with her toe. She wasn't here to complain, and anyway, what would be the point in complaining? God had no interest in such things.

She wondered if God's interests coincided at all with the interests of the cameras. She was being filmed right at that moment. She wondered what they were hoping she would do. Suddenly she was seized with a terrible certainty. She dropped to all fours and began to heave onto the grass. She brought up only a thin thread of yellow spit, but as she shook and struggled she felt completely abandoned.

Her brother had made fun of her when she was little, because she'd treated God as her imaginary friend and playmate. She would prattle to Him and tell Him stories; she hid from Him, which was a silly game because He never lost track of her. Then, when men had come to her house looking for her mother, and her brother snapped, "Hide!", she and God had hidden together. She always pictured it as if they had been hiding together, under the wings of an angel.

Emebet was born the year before the revolution, a famine child. Her mother was a nurse. Emebet never knew the whole story—she had been afraid to ask her brother, and then she'd been distracted, and then he had died—but she thought her mother had treated someone the Derg didn't want treated. Her father was killed, her mother had sent them to live with relatives, and then everyone told her that her mother had died, but with a covert unsettled look as if the truth might somehow be even worse.

But Emebet had still felt that God's attention flowed through her and filled her; His gaze sustained her even as it sometimes frightened her. She was created by His attention.

And then when she was sixteen they left Ethiopia on the strength of a marriage scam, and God seemed much harder to find. There were a series of scattered memories: lies her brother told her about the lies other people had told him. False promises and delays—leaving today, no, leaving *today*. She remembered a Sudanese man, tall and narrow, who showed them their new IDs: long arms, long hands, and extraordinarily long thumbs that curved backward away from the documents, as if to make an elaborate frame. She remembered those dark, finely wrinkled thumbs better than she remembered anything else about their trip to America.

In the new country, first in an airport bathroom and then with increasing frequency in the high school hallways— anywhere with too many people speaking English too quickly—there had been moments when God seemed to shut His eyes, and she had blanked out of existence. These blank circles became bigger, and she learned to live within them. She learned that inside the blank gray American circles she could do anything she wanted.

When she tried to talk to other people about this slow, draining absence, the guttering away of God, she didn't feel like she could mention His name. She thought probably people would make fun of her. So she tried to describe the feeling in other ways, and the people she asked told her that all she was describing was growing up: the process of learning who you couldn't trust. She began to understand that the blank gray circles were normal life.

And now she had arrived in this aggressively American place, alone before the black muzzles and gleaming, mirror eyes of the cameras. She didn't know if they were satisfied with what she had done; they didn't react.

When she could manage it she got up on her knees and began to mumble a few prayers. She clasped her hands, grained with dirt and smeared with grass, and prayed until she needed to hide her face. The camera crew gave no indication of whether her prayer would get better ratings than her puke.

*   *   *

In the kitchen, Dylan was hunting through a series of packages and jars with the labels removed. Colton was ignoring him and lugging a huge pot of water over to the stove. The camera crew had been instructed to supervise them, but only to step in if they were about to seriously injure themselves. Colton pulled a cutting board from a drawer and used a can of tomatoes to crush a couple heads of garlic.

Dylan stopped to look while he did it. "That's pretty cool, dude. I don't want to eat the papery stuff, though."

"It comes off, that's why I slammed the can on them. Look."

"What are you boiling water for?"

"...The spaghetti, once you find it. For the spaghetti dinner we're supposed to be making as part of our rehabilitation." Colton peeled garlic fast—he'd worked briefly as a line cook in an Italian restaurant called Scent of Venice—and started mowing through it with a large knife.

"Wait, what? Gross. It'll get all slimy."

Colton gave him a look which said, precisely, "..."

"Is this one of those things, like, 'I grew up poor and now I water down the milk'? Because I'm pretty sure you're not supposed to put spaghetti in this huge vat of water. It'll be like eating spaghetti and tomato piss."

"I honestly have no idea what you're—wait, the spaghetti is right in front of your face. In that drawer. Hand me the bag of onions, too." He gestured with his knife, and Dylan yipped and jumped backward, stumbling against a footstool and swinging his arms wildly to keep from falling.

"*Catlike* grace," he said as he righted himself. He crouched and looked into the drawer. "I don't see any spaghetti. You might want to take off your shades, Bro-lita."

Colton took off the sunglasses and gave Dylan a long, tired look. He bent down, grabbed the box of spaghetti, and shook it. "Spaghetti."

He opened it, and Dylan looked completely baffled, like a dog looking into a mirror.

"Pick-Up Stix," Dylan said blankly. He reached out and took one stiff strand, poked the end into the pad of his thumb, and tried to bend it. He looked startled when it broke.

Colton stared at him, and then started to laugh. "Seriously, have you never seen spaghetti before?"

"Of course I have," he said with dignity. "Jemima made it for me all the time."

"Jemima," Colton repeated. A look of horror dawned. "Jemima, your *maid?*"

"She wasn't just a maid," Dylan huffed. "She was part of the family."

"Yeah, the *poor* part. And I bet her son Leroy was your

some-of-my-best-friends black friend."

Dylan turned away, scowling, and bent down to get the onions. "His name was Dwayne, and we were really close, especially when my parents were divorcing, okay? We were, like, blood brothers, we did the thing where you cut your fingers and put them together. So we're kind of related. ...And maybe *actually* related, given my father, but who knows."

"Well I've learned something already. White people feel pain just like normal people."

Dylan turned around and handed Colton the onions, looking casual, though there was something a bit swollen around his nose and eyes.

"Here, I'll show you how to do one and then I want you to do the rest on your own," Colton said.

"I'm surprised they even let us have knives. Shouldn't we have those kiddie scissors? Plastic knives, like on airplanes."

"Maybe they don't think you and I pose a serious risk. Maybe the real hard cases have to clean the bathrooms. It's an incentive for good behavior."

"You're taking off a lot of that onion," Dylan commented, trying to sound innocent.

Colton shot him a level gaze. "I'm taking off the skin. Do you eat candy-bar wrappers?"

"I like the skin," Dylan muttered. When Colton raised his eyebrows, Dylan grabbed a curl of yellow onion skin and put it in his mouth. He chewed. "Mmmm."

"Just like Jemima used to make," Colton said, shaking his head.

*   *   *

At dinner everyone was depressed. They didn't want to look

at one another and they definitely didn't want to look at the limp pasta and overcooked sauce, with its glossy burnt flecks. Blond wood, silver sinks, black cameras on wire-draped stalks, no windows, and a sign that said, GROW BIG OR GO HOME.

Medea lifted her fork and let pasta and sauce glop off the end and squelch back onto the plate. She propped her chin on her hand and stared existentially at the tines. "I am so bored. Isn't television supposed to be interesting?"

Colton grinned wearily. "That's why they're just gonna montage right on through this part when they show it."

"We could play games," Sharptooth suggested. "Get to know each other."

"Sure," Medea drawled. "Anybody know any party games that don't involve alcohol?"

Silence. Dylan offered, "I can do this thing where I put candies in my mouth and pretend I'm a piñata."

"I'm guessing alcohol is definitely involved there," Colton said.

"Yeah, fair enough.... I woke up with two black eyes once. I mean I think that's why that happened."

"We could play quarters with soda," Medea said. "We could play I Never. With—what even is this horror?" She sipped from her plastic cup and grimaced. The labels on the soda bottles had been removed for television. "Is this what Coca-Cola tastes like when it's alone? Is this—I'm getting a bacony undertone. Are they putting bacon in soda now?"

Colton took a tentative sip from his own cup, and a broad grin spread across his face. "Tab! Now this takes me back."

"Tab, do people still make Tab?" Dylan asked.

"Of course! Son, Tab is glorious. Diet Coke wants to be Tab when it grows up. You know Jesus turned Crystal Pepsi into Tab one time. This... this is my grandmama, this is home. This is taking your earring off to talk on the phone, this is dialing with a pencil eraser. This is *old-school*."

"This explains so much," Medea said. "But no, we should play I Never."

"I can never remember the rules," Dylan said. "Do you drink when you have done the thing, or when you haven't?"

J. Malachi stirred himself, like a zombie. "I don't want to," he said. "This show is one big sober game of I Never and that is precisely what I don't want to do."

This dampened everyone else's already soggy enthusiasm.

*   *   *

They were all starting to gather up their scraps of self. Some of them were scrappier than others. Medea spent much of the third day screaming: not quite at random, since the screaming seemed to come upon her most often when she was told to do something. If anyone asked why she was screaming she said she was in pain.

"Where does it hurt?" a valiant technician asked.

"My *existence* hurts!"

Jen was more pointed: "You're in pain? What's wrong with you?"

And Medea, looking her straight in the eye, said, "I'm sensitive to loud noises. Someone's screaming here. It's very painful to me."

Jen said what she would have said no matter what Medea's excuse had been: "I'm sorry that you feel that way." And she *was* sorry; they all were. Medea screamed some more, but eventually she had to stop—her throat started to feel scratchy, and she didn't want to lose her voice.

*   *   *

From the "Amends" thread at Idiotbox.com:

DutyFree: First episode, what do we think? Gotta say, I don't have a lot of sympathy for these people so far. Dylan seems basically like every asshole I went to high school with, "Jaymi" (wtf) apparently wants children to eat lead paint, there's a hot dude who also looks like an asshole, and an actually mentally ill person who shouldn't be there at all. I guess I kind of feel for her, the wolfgirl, except for how she's unbearable.

BessiesGirl: IDK, I thought the hallucinations were really scary. It shows you the dark side of alcoholism. The wolf person was super weird though, I mean, what? Is that a gimmick? Is it maybe a tie-in with "Teen Wolf," some kind of cross-marketing for MTV?

stmorrissey: >*Dylan seems basically like every asshole I went to high school with*

LOLOL inorite? Being a dumb jock is an addiction now?

brunchingehenna: An Ethiopian who has enough spare cash to get drunk every day. Truly, America is the land of opportunity.

BessiesGirl: Defs want to punch Jaymi in his smug fat face.

princedog: OK, unpopular opinion but Sharptooth is my favorite. You can tell that the show wants us to hate her and think she's crazy, but that only makes me like her more. She doesn't deserve to be made fun of just because she relates better to animals.

uberdoobie: @DutyFree the hot one is called Colton. :9 gimme summa that.

dollparts: The food looks really good. I hope they're not going to be coddled and given horse therapy and bullshit like that. At my rehab all we had for dinner was scrod.

Chapter 4: High-Bottom Girls, You Make the Rockin' World Go Round

On the fifth day it was sunny. After morning chores, lunch, and individual counseling, Jen led her troops out to the courtyard.

Colton winced and cringed as they stepped outside. "Oh, fuck a whole *bunch* of the sun," he said; but Jen wouldn't be dissuaded.

She presented them with two hula hoops and announced, "We're going to start today's group with a bonding activity!"

"Dear God," Medea said.

"Come on, everybody, stand in a circle here." They reluctantly obeyed. They weren't looking at each other. Jen put the hula hoops on her own arms and rolled them up to her shoulders.

"Now take the hands of the people next to you."

Only Sharptooth did this as soon as she was told; the others had to shuffle and stare before they capitulated. When they were all holding hands, Jen explained that they were going to pass the hula hoops from person to person without letting go of one another's hands.

This turned out to be less awful than they had expected. With some slight wriggling and high-stepping, they managed to complete their task with limited humiliation and even some tentative laughter.

J. Malachi was distracted by something he noticed for the first time. Now that Emebet had begun to recover from her first days without alcohol, her skin looked less chalky and sallow. In fact, in the sunlight she almost seemed to have a healthy glow, although this was only a trick of the light.

She was directly across from him in the circle. The golden light played over her long nose, strong chin, and high cheekbones; with her sad, knowing eyes, she struck him as a Barbara Stanwyck type, a femme more fatale to herself than to anyone else. She moved through her hula hoops with a certain disjointed grace.

He shook his head, and looked around the group to see if any of the others could be matched with movie stars. It was a way of taking his mind off. Medea was definitely a Bette Davis type, permanently brazen and accused. Sharptooth was only in her twenties, but she had somehow acquired a weatherbeaten serenity, lesbian or lesbian-adjacent: Mary Stuart Masterson? Colton and Dylan were television, not movies, he thought; they both looked like they should be on the CW, solving crimes in high school or being hot vampires. His eyes kept straying back to Emebet, standing in that soft light interlaced with the waving shadows of the pine trees. He thought, *She has a very Pam Grier skin tone and bone structure.*

And then the hula hoops, which had been moving

clockwise and widdershins around the circle, converged on him. Several of his fellow sufferers cheered him on, only half-ironically, as he squirmed and contorted himself. He got stuck more than once, with a hoop wedged around his neck or stuttering between his feet. When he finally got one hoop to pass over the other, wriggled free of both of them and passed them on, he looked up to see Emebet laughing very quietly, with a lightness that made him feel a lot better about being on reality-TV rehab.

Then he had to do the whole thing all over again, because the camera crew wanted a different angle on his face. He felt much less resilient the second time around.

When the bonding exercise was over they all had to fetch white ironwork chairs from the patio and arrange them in a circle. Jen had a stack of index cards, and she explained that each card had a short description of a particular kind of person. For their next exercise, she would read each card and the group would give brief responses indicating what they thought of when they pictured that kind of person. She also pulled a koosh ball from a duffel bag, and said that she would throw it at them if they were disrespectful or talked over other people.

Jen shuffled the cards and picked one with a dramatic flourish. "Okay, we're starting with this one. 'Heterosexual'!"

She looked around the silent circle. "Emebet?"

Emebet made a low, dismayed noise. Her mind was skipping a beat. She hated when her English blacked out like this. "I know this word, I can't remember—in English, I don't always know...."

"It's when a man—it's a man who loves women," J. Malachi

said, looking at her with intense earnestness. "Or a woman who loves men."

She smiled at him, relieved, her lips parted. There was such unexpected sincerity and winsomeness in his voice that the camera crew made sure to get good close-ups of both of them, looking at one another and smiling heterosexually.

"Oh, yes, straight!" she said. "That's what I am." She didn't seem inclined to add anything more.

"*Normal*," Colton said, in a voice curlicued with contempt, and Medea laughed and nodded.

"Normal, but they're always trying not to be normal," she added. "Trying to be cool."

"It's the default," Sharptooth said confidently. She was leaning back on her chair with her arms draped over the seat back, so her hands dangled in front of her like paws. Her tail was tucked carefully around her hips and rested in her lap. "People don't notice heterosexuality until they question it. It's like the old fish who asks the young fish how the water is today, and the young fish says, 'What's water?'"

Nobody seemed inclined to offer more opinions, so Jen read her next card. "'People who have served time in prison.'"

There was a long silence. Dylan said, "I don't know if I think of anything in particular? I mean anybody can go to prison."

"I don't know," Colton said. "Jail is one thing. Anybody can go to *jail*. Prison is a whole 'nother kettle of nasty."

"People who get caught," Emebet said, which seemed inarguable.

"'Evangelical Christians,'" Jen read, and looked around the group. "Dylan, you look like you have something."

He looked down and shook his head, waving a hand as if to dismiss what he was about to say, but she kept her eyes fixed on him.

"Uh... I guess the thing with them is that they mean it, you know? When they say that they love Jesus and they just want you to know the Lord because they care about you. You can pick out all their mixed motives and good for you, you've figured out that they also want to feel superior to you or they want to sleep with you, or they want to prove something to Jesus or their parents, but underneath all of that it is genuine sometimes. They're like Crab Rangoon," he said, grinning. "It's not *crab* in the like dictionary definition of 'crab,' but it's so tasty you can't stop eating it."

And then, more seriously, "Underneath all the fake love is real love."

It was Emebet's turn next. "We have these back home too, the evangelicals, but mostly I've met Americans. The Americans are very... American, *very*. They always want to talk to you. They don't just help. They have to talk also."

Medea said, "They're not very good at art. They don't make it and they don't understand it; they only see it as politics. I'm the other way around."

Sharptooth said, "I don't think people should try to convert others. I don't think that's respectful."

"Yeah, a world without arguing, *that* sounds fun," Medea said. Jen threw the koosh ball at her.

J. Malachi shrugged. "Protestants, man, I don't even know. I'm sure they're good people; maybe that's their problem."

Colton said, "If I were a better person maybe I'd be a Christian. Not a Baptist. My mother was a Baptist every now and then and I definitely wouldn't go back to that, you couldn't pay me. I've done some dirty jobs but I won't do that! But there are some churches where it isn't, you know, the Christian clubhouse, it isn't all gossip and telling you to hit your kids more and sleeping with the deacon. Or the organist," he said, with a hint of a purr. "I think there are some churches where the people are for the most part better than *us*, certainly."

J. Malachi nodded, chastened. "Yeah, we've been pretty judgmental, for a group of fuck-ups."

"Think of it as honesty," Jen said, and Sharptooth nodded. "You have to know where you're coming from before you can know where you're going."

"Years of blackouts suggest that is not true," Medea said.

"'People who cry easily,'" Jen read.

"Maternal," Colton said.

"Manipulative" was Medea's contribution, with which Dylan immediately agreed; "George W. Bush" was J. Malachi's. ("Really?" Jen asked, and he confirmed it.) "Very sad," Emebet said, and Sharptooth thought they were in touch with their emotions.

"Here's the purpose of this exercise," Jen said brightly. Everyone looked at her with varying degrees of dread. "All of these descriptions are things that are true of me!"

After a pause, Dylan said, "Seriously, you've done time? What did you do?"

Jen smiled. "Maybe you'll get that story if you work hard on your recovery. The point of this exercise was to show us how we carry stories in our heads, images of the kind of person we think we are—and the kind of person we think we're not. We can only make the changes in our lives that we think people like us are capable of making. So I want us to work on expanding our imaginations. Up until now we've been a certain type of person and we think that's all we're capable of being."

Medea laughed, but her voice was tense. "Next, on *Rehab Rainbow*." She twisted in her chair. "I think it's great that you *asked* us to judge others and then judged us for judging them. It's very meta."

Sharptooth said, "I don't think we were being judged. I think you're projecting—", at which point Medea shot her a look like Sarah Palin shooting wolves from a helicopter.

*　　*　　*

On day six Medea sashayed into their group session late, wearing huge cork wedges and a red micro-mini. She arranged herself carefully in her seat as Colton gave her a look he'd borrowed from his grandmother.

"Girl, that skirt is so short I can see your *soul*," he said.

She smiled thinly.

The others were more modestly dressed, if Sharptooth's ears and tail were considered prosthetics rather than accessories. Emebet was wrapped in a shawl which she could huddle in when she felt threatened. Jen was modeling a white baby-doll dress, which frothed around her and showed off her skinny, golden limbs. She twizzled herself into her seat, then remembered the cameras and draped herself more gracefully, with her legs crossed at the ankles.

She explained their purpose that day: "For addicts shame is like quicksand. We get stuck in it. For other people sometimes shame can be like a cattle prod. It pushes them forward, gets them to do anything they need to do to stop feeling bad about themselves. But for us it's the opposite; we get stuck. So a big part of what we're doing here, in order to help you guys get ready to make your amends, is to help you get out of that quicksand. We're going to work on the shame you feel for the things you've done, but we're going to start with what might be even harder to work through: the shame you feel for the things people have done to *you*.

"Because we do feel ashamed of being hurt," she said—with a glance at the cameras, and then a quick nervous glance away. "When I was using I would seek out guys who reminded me of my rapist and I'd have sex with them for heroin. They would talk to me like I was a dog and I remember hearing one man say, 'Okay, stay there,' like he was ordering me: 'Sit! Stay!'"

Her voice was light and soapy, confiding, with a hint of humor: deeply unsettling, like a clown. "Even that phrase, 'my rapist': That's how I thought of him. Like he belonged to me. Like he was a part of me."

She paused to let them contemplate that, then continued: "Sometimes blaming ourselves when we're victimized is a way of taking control of the situation." Up at the cameras again: They were still there. She raked her hair away from her face and felt the thin film of sweat. She told herself, *The client is always watching you, and judging. This isn't different.*

"We feel like if we were to blame, then at least we weren't helpless," she said, and was glad that it came out sounding natural and not rehearsed. It was hard to see her clients—*the talent*—under the lights. "If he was *my* rapist then maybe at least I had some control over what happened to me. So here, we're going to try to find a better way to take control. I want you to share the moments in your life when you've felt most helpless, so that by telling your story here, it can become a part of you that you control—not through self-blame, but through self-honesty."

Colton mouthed, "'Self-honesty'?", but nobody said anything. They all looked intensely uncomfortable.

Medea spoke first, smiling with all her teeth: "I bet this gets good ratings."

"The goal here is actually to help you all feel comfortable," Jen said, a bit defensively. "Jaymi, would you like to start?"

"I don't know what to say—"

"You said the other day that it was basically just like I Never," Medea said. "What's the thing you'd say when you want to look especially fucked up so somebody with a fixing-people fetish will take you home? Like, 'I never gave myself a black eye so I'd get sympathy for being bullied.' That's a good one if you want to be the only one who drinks."

"Really, that's so sad, how did you manage to do that?" J. Malachi said; but Jen caught him, and made him take his turn. "Nothing bad has ever happened to me," he said bleakly.

Jen nodded, leaning forward to encourage him. "Sometimes when families are under stress we don't realize it at the time," she said. It was easier to talk now that she could think of it as facilitating other people's talking. "Many of us have these unacknowledged wounds. We feel like our griefs aren't important enough, like what happened to us isn't bad enough. But a child's loneliness, the death of a relative... whatever has affected you in your life is big enough for us to talk about here."

J. Malachi frowned. "It actually isn't. I mean, my grandfather died. But I didn't even know him very well. I grew up in California and we only went back to Illinois for holidays—everybody sitting around eating creamed spinach, glowering at Lawrence Welk. So I think you're not going to find anything here. I'm not a sympathetic character."

Medea put in, "I don't know why people nowadays always assume there are reasons for things. In my great-grandmother's day people just *did* the things—they didn't worry about having reasons! You were just a drunk or a cheater or whatever, and people either put up with it or they sold you and bought a water buffalo."

Jen wanted to go back to J. Malachi, but nobody else seemed to want that—a man behind one of the cameras grimaced and made a throat-slitting gesture—so she moved on to the next person.

"I don't know why we have to do this," Emebet said. She shook her head at the cameras; and then focused away from them and onto the group, as they'd all been instructed. "I had a hard childhood. This is usual! Not special. My country had a famine and a revolution, I lost my parents, my brother brought me to the United States, he died when I was eighteen. It was very hard. But all of this is simply life."

Her words came out under pressure. "I met a man, I became pregnant, and I—" She made a shooing motion with her hand, away from her abdomen.

"You had a termination," Sharptooth said sympathetically.

Emebet looked at her in confusion. "Ah? No, it was—" She couldn't say it, kept shaking her head.

"You terminated the pregnancy," Sharptooth tried again.

"She *had an abortion*," Medea snapped.

"Yes," Emebet said, grateful, staring down at her hands. "This is what it was."

"No wonder you're a mess," Medea said briskly. "Women are meant to give life, not take it."

Jen looked startled. "I don't think we should get into politics—"

"It isn't *politics*—"

"I guess that explains why *you've* got four kids and a Cuisinart," Sharptooth said, waspishly.

"*Everyone*—" Jen tried; but the talent had forgotten the cameras and were focusing solely, sincerely on one another.

"Having an abortion to get rid of a baby is like taking heroin to get rid of pain," Medea proclaimed. "You just end up with dead pain, not no pain."

"That doesn't even mean anything," J. Malachi said; but he saw that it had struck home with Emebet. She was wringing her hands again.

"Hey," he said. "Jesus forgave the people who killed him. Even as they were doing it."

"But they didn't know," she said. "He said they didn't know what they were doing. And I knew."

J. Malachi bit his lip, hard, and imagined how great it would be to muzzle Medea. "Uh, well, but... but okay, let's roll with the thing Medea said. Whatever is dead inside you— *anything at all* that's dead—that will come back to life, right? Jesus will raise everyone from the dead and every part of us that's dead will live again."

Medea laughed out loud. "Oh my God. Do you actually believe that macaroni-picture stuff, or are you trying to get inside her *sacristy?*"

J. Malachi started up from his seat, but Colton and Dylan grabbed his arms and pulled him back down. He fell back onto the folding chair and knocked it over, so that his ass hit the ground hard. But as he got up he saw that Emebet was looking up again, and her hands were still; it seemed like what he had said had helped.

"Let's hear a share from another person," Jen suggested. "Sharptooth?"

"Thanks." She adjusted her posture, sticking her tail through the gap at the back of the chair. "I was a unique and imaginative child, and I was bullied because of that, both at home and at school. For example, my mother wouldn't allow me to read my fantasy novels at the dinner table, or at her garden parties."

"You were bullied by *manners?*" Colton muttered.

Jen gave him a warning look, but Sharptooth was a veteran of group therapy. No cross-talk could shake her. Without even noticing it Jen relaxed, feeling herself in the paws of a master analysand.

"My only refuge was my mind," Sharptooth said. "My body never felt right. I always knew that something was off—I could hear sounds that no one else could hear, I had an unusually keen sense of smell, and I preferred peer groups with a well-defined alpha and beta dynamic."

Seeing their blank looks, Sharptooth explained, "The alpha female in a wolf grouping is typically the only female who mates. So in our peer group, when we'd pick which member of N'Sync we were going to marry, the alpha would get Justin Timberlake. ...I always got J.C. Chasez, representing my position as a beta in that particular pack. In college I first began to explore my identity. My college mascot was the Bears, and rooting for the team felt good, in a way I'd never felt before. I began to go to a lot of the games, and I even became a mascot, although I knew that the bear wasn't quite the right animal for me. My first game as Bubba the Bear was—" and she groped for a comparison that would capture her joy and fulfillment—"it was everything my mother said my first cotillion would be.

"It was while I was an athletic mascot that I began to drink. It started with beer, of course, but that was awkward because I'd have to take the costume off each time I had to visit the powder room. So I tried switching to hard liquor, and then I started abusing prescription painkillers, and eventually heroin. I liked the way it made time disappear, as if I was caught in an eternal present, always 'now,' just like a wild creature. It made my body feel unimportant and it gave me a good, warm feeling, like I was curled up with all of my pack mates. I had to drop out of college, but by that time I didn't care. I was starting to realize that ordinary human pursuits didn't interest me.

"In college I'd become involved with feminist activism. I know we're not supposed to talk politics, but I believe so strongly that women's addictions are often a way of coping with our oppression. And one of the big wake-up calls that I had was at a meeting at the campus women's center. I had gone there drunk, even though I wasn't a student anymore, and I was using oppressive language."

She looked down, and shifted uncomfortably on her seat. She always did that when she reached this part of her personal narrative; it was always genuine. "I suggested that a sophomore who identified as homoromantic agendered demisexual was probably 'really' gay. It was totally erasing. I was escorted from the safe space. Uh, after that, I was angry, and I went and scent-marked the door of the women's center," she said sheepishly.

"You peed on it?" Colton asked.

"Yes, but that wasn't the point! I was marking it, asserting dominance. I got a citation from the cops."

"Those pigs," Colton said.

"I don't think we should use language that denigrates other species," Sharptooth said. "Many people identify as pigkin, you know. ...Anyway, at this time I was beginning to understand that I was a wolf. It took me a while, in part because I was sidetracked by the bear thing. So I struggled to figure it out—I knew that I was having phantom sensations in my tail, and I knew I was a pack animal. Even when I was using I always tried to form a pack connection with my dealer. But I wasn't sure if I was a gray wolf, a red wolf, or a timber wolf."

"What about a Mexican wolf?" Medea asked. "You gonna discriminate?"

"I knew that I was not a Mexican wolf! It wasn't discrimination. It was *personal insight*, and a spiritual experience that I had. Anyway Mexican wolves are just a subspecies of gray wolves. And they're smaller than my type of wolf."

"You just so happened to be an all-American wolf. Not one of them immigrant wolves, coming here and sniffing the butts Americans won't sniff."

"Medea," Jen said. "This is Sharptooth's share. It's not yours."

"Why do they call it a *share* if only one person gets to talk?" Medea asked sulkily, but she subsided.

"I finally found my identity when the San Diego Zoo brought a special exhibit on wolves. They set up a microphone, so you could howl into the mike and it would play in a wooded area inhabited by wolves. If you sounded enough like a wolf, then the pack would howl back and welcome you as one of its own. Nobody else there took it seriously," and she was clearly still indignant. "They were just, like, 'Owoo!' and then they'd laugh. It was so human-centric. It was like blackface for wolves."

Colton got a very loud look on his face, but he didn't say anything.

"But when I got a chance to use the microphone I tapped into my deepest spiritual nature. I spoke to those wolves. And they spoke back."

She smiled. Usually when Sharptooth smiled it was like lightbulbs clicking on around a mirror, but in that moment it was more like a sunbeam appearing from behind a cloud.

"They told me that I needed to get clean and sober. They said I was betraying my true self by using man's drugs. We talked for a long time, and the security guards had to come and order me to move away from the microphone—even though I was the only one using it for its intended purpose! But I went straight from the zoo to the hospital and asked for a drug and alcohol assessment, and I've never picked up since that day."

She paused, as if waiting for them to clap.

"Now I'm an advocate for otherkin and addicts," she said, when nobody applauded. "And for people who live, like me, in the intersection of those two identities."

"Are there a lot of addicted wolves and things? Does heroin even work on wolves?" Medea asked.

"You'd be surprised," Sharptooth said. "We don't often hear about them because traditional addiction treatment is oppressive to otherkin identities. When I was in detox my beliefs were totally disrespected. And a lot of otherkin have had people say things like, 'You need to deal with reality,' which is defining reality in a totally speciesist way. Or, 'You need to learn to handle your problems like an adult.' I don't think I need to point out how problematic *that* is!"

The faces of the rest of the group suggested that maybe she did need to point it out, so she clarified: "It's so ageist! That kind of language *assumes* that dealing with your problems like an adult is better than dealing with them like a child. And it also takes a very human-centric perspective, as if everyone goes through the stages of childhood, adolescence and adulthood in the same way, at the same rate. Many species have a very different life span, and some of those terms aren't appropriate for 'kin at all—we may think of ourselves as being in a larval stage, rather than adolescence."

"I am definitely going to use that with my coach," Dylan contributed. "'Sorry sir, I'm going through kind of a larval stage right now.'"

Sharptooth frowned. "You shouldn't appropriate other beings' identities."

"Define 'irony,'" Medea said softly.

"Okay, I think I get it," J. Malachi said. "Recovery is about transforming your emotional problems into a spiritual belief."

"You know, religion is so strange," Medea mused. "I think something in it calls to us. I was obviously raised without any kind of superstition, but I used to think I was possessed by a demon. I called her Restlene. Like the word 'restlessness,' but without the double 's'es. It was cool because none of the other kids were possessed. But later I figured out that the thing I'd thought it was, was actually a yeast infection."

Nobody quite knew what to make of this. "I think I'd like to be a demon," she concluded, meditatively.

"It's your calling," J. Malachi muttered.

"Or else a ballerina."

*　　*　　*

J. Malachi cornered Medea after the session. He held a folding chair in between them as if he was trying to tame a lion. "What the hell is wrong with you? I thought you liked Emebet—she said you'd helped her!"

Jen started toward them, but Ana took her arm. "Let them talk it out," she said. "They need practice in handling disagreements." Jen was skeptical, but everyone on the production side nodded sagely, so she backed off.

"I am helping her," Medea said. "We're here to learn to be honest. This isn't a dating service."

Ana and Bentley talked to Jen, who was keeping a worried eye on her two charges. "We loved this session," Ana said. "It was raw, it was confrontational—and *educational.* The one thing is that we do hope you'll work to draw out Dylan a little more. The athlete."

I know which one he is, Jen thought, and spread a smile over her irritation. She had a hard time keeping it steady when Bentley added, "Yeah, he's great on camera. Every time that dimple pops out on his cheek I hear a tiny little *ka-ching!*"

Ana turned her head sharply and cocked it, widening her eyes and frowning, like a mother disciplining a wayward child. The look Bentley gave her in return was thoroughly adolescent. She, too, was going through a larval stage.

*   *   *

Slumped on his bed, J. Malachi ruminated on his exchange with Emebet: that brief respite when he'd completely forgotten the cameras.

Abortion was not an issue (he thought of it as "the abortion issue") he'd thought much about. The arguments on his side seemed to be based in science and human rights, two things J. Malachi neither understood nor liked; or religion, which he liked but feared.

He was a connoisseur of political slogans which predated his birth. He'd often referred to his haphazard Lenten discipline as "getting clean for Gene," and on sleepless nights when he was more than usually aware of his drinking problem he'd sometimes thought, *In your guts, you know you're nuts.* He had never expected to find himself troubled by a woman who had lived through two-thirds of the case against George McGovern: "acid, amnesty and abortion."

We have met the social issues, he thought uneasily, *and they are us.*

And Medea had been right to guess that the language of Christian resurrection didn't come naturally to him. J. Malachi was an Anglo-Catholic, by which he meant that he enjoyed evensong and sherry. He loved the Book of Common Prayer, and praised it even more than he loved it; he sometimes confused it with Shakespeare or even Kipling, and had once cited "They also serve who only stand and wait" as an example of the simple, grave music of the Pauline epistles. Belief in a personal resurrection struck him as a touch inartistic, even presumptuous—a bit low church.

His sudden religion had been a put-on; but then, he was against authenticity and in favor of affectation. He'd developed a theory that affectations were a form of aspiration: Shouldn't everyone strive to be wittier, more tasteful, more genteel and cavalier than they really were?

So he wasn't surprised that in group he'd acted better than he was. He was surprised that he'd acted better than he'd wanted to be.

*   *   *

While J. Malachi was investigating his fit of religion, Emebet had to go a few rounds in the confessional. Ana prompted her, asking her what she thought of J. Malachi.

"Who?"

She in fact had not been thinking about him at all. He was a blurry American piece of furniture, an attribute of the rehab center, like the duvets. Then she remembered, and made herself think about him.

"He seems sad," she said, surprising herself. "He's like me. He knows that he deserves... the things that happen."

From then on he was a puzzle to her and also a person. She took an occasional interest.

*   *   *

From the "Amends" thread at Idiotbox.com:

brunchingehenna: Episode two: I enjoy the camera's

decision to linger on the silent hockey pinup. Nary a thought nor a feeling disturbs his creamy surface. Long may he wave.

BessiesGirl: I don't get these people. Usually with these shows you understand why the addicts are the way they are, but here you could tell that they were reaching for sob stories. Even the Ethiopian one probably has a better life than ninety percent of people where she comes from. Everybody else was either totally spoiled or just normal life. My parents divorced… I was poor… My parents used an egg donor???

My parents split up when I was seven, and there were a lot of nasty custody battles, I was kidnapped a couple times, but I never used alcohol or drugs to solve my problems. Most people don't. What's next? "I'm a crackhead because when we played Monopoly, I always had to be the boot"?

namewithheld732: The one I really can't deal with is Emmabet. (sp?) In my experience people who talk about God and their faith all the time are trying to distract attention from something about themselves they don't want you to notice.

In her case I might blame the show itself though, more than her. Anybody who reacts so strongly to a normal medical procedure that she can't even say its *name* needs serious psychiatric care, not exploitation on TV. That's not religion, that's mental health issues.

uberdoobie: @namewithheld, wait, is Emabeth Catholic? She's from Ethiopia, right? I thought they were mostly Jewish there.

DutyFree: Do we even know for sure that she *had* an abortion? She's an alcoholic on a reality television show, which is like the perfect storm of bullshit. I'm sure many of these people would fake some kind of tragic history.

princedog: I know you guys are going to laugh at this, but I thought Sharptooth's share was really moving. The part that hit me was when she said that heroin made her feel like she was in an eternal "now," like a wild creature—because isn't that what we all wish we could do? I'm always so anxious, everything is always the bad things that might happen or the bad things that happened already, and there's no space to just be in the moment. She's trying to find a drug-free way of living in the now, and that's the hardest environment for a human being. So maybe she felt like she had to stop being a human in order to bear it.

I went to the Washington Monument one spring and all the cherry blossoms were out, and the tourists were crowding around taking pictures of them. I remember being so judgmental, thinking, do you have to be taking photos? Can't you just live in this moment when the cherry blossoms are blowing? But I feel like most of our lives are spent taking photos of cherry blossoms, or looking at old photos of them. In fact, isn't this show kind of a photograph of cherry blossoms? It's trying to capture the moments of clarity in these people's lives, so of course they don't make sense from the outside.

Sharptooth manages to live not even "one day at a time" but one moment at a time. The "now" is big enough for her. I wish I felt like it was big enough for me.

I wonder if she's single. Does anybody know?

DutyFree: Whoa there, tigerkin.

82Camaro: I just have no sympathy for people who make bad decisions and then regret them.

Chapter 5: Higher Powers

The rest of the first week was mostly unphotogenic. The talent did a lot of snuffly crying. Colton, Emebet, and Medea admitted that they'd had sex with someone because he was paying for their alcohol.

"Did you prostitute yourself?" Jen asked, as kind as tweezers, and Medea said, "I would say that I occasionally spend time with men. I consider it field research." She held her face completely still for a full minute as the camera tried to make her cry.

She did cry at several other points in her counseling. She found herself disappointed in Jen: She had hoped that this was her big chance to project all over her counselor—who was even Asian, a major bonus. She was looking forward to accidentally calling Jen "Mom," the way she'd done with the nurse at horse camp when she was sobbing her way through an explanation of that yeast infection. Instead she found herself with boring old transference. She loathed Jen and couldn't stop thinking about unhooking her bra. She found that sexual attraction did not conduce to self-honesty.

"Now, I know you grew up in a nontraditional household, because of your fathers being gay," Jen said, in a lotiony voice.

"Actually my upbringing was quite traditional, insofar as I was frequently reminded that I was a disloyal and ungrateful daughter."

This was an exaggeration, but a deliberate one: Medea felt that exaggeration was the only way to be true to the outsized emotions of childhood. For her it was a question of genre.

"Can you talk more about that?"

"Why?" Medea asked. "Do you need evidence?"

"Uh—no, just, let's work on identifying the situations in which you were made to feel shame."

"Oh, but that was the whole point: that our family had nothing to be ashamed of. If I told the other kids that my real mom was Camille Paglia—and surely *that's* a sign of problems in the home?—Dad would explain very carefully that there was nothing wrong with our *family*. So I was a 'storyteller,' which is how helicopter parents say 'liar.'"

Medea, grinning tightly, swiped a hand across her eyes. Her shoulders were up defensively and her smile hitched to the right, and she tried to look directly at Jen but she kept having to do these slow, liquid blinks.

"You would get in trouble—?"

"No, no, they always reminded me that I wasn't in trouble. So that was another thing to be grateful for."

Then there was the session when Jen wanted to talk about her coming-out experience.

"Was it hard to come out at school, or with friends?"

Medea laughed. "School was fine. My friends were great. My parents were the problem." She met Jen's gaze, and her eyes were bright and angry. "Things don't always happen the way other people expect them to."

"Your fathers disapproved of your preference for women?" Jen tried to look as if she believed this.

"Well, no," Medea conceded. It had been more complicated than that.

At first her parents had reassured her. Henry, her more lenient father, had said, "You know, sweetheart, you don't *have* to be gay. We won't be disappointed if you want to date boys!" They thought of her coming out as an adorable play for parental approval. Then they met her girlfriend.

Janna was studying communications at a local college. (Medea, by contrast, was in the tenth grade at an Episcopalian private school.) She enjoyed bondage and discipline; worse than that, she smoked.

"Do you think we should take her to a specialist?" Henry asked.

"Why, is there medication for being a teenager?" (That was Bastian, her less-lenient father.)

"You think it's just teenage rebellion."

"Look, if you think therapy will help her, by all means get her to a shrink! I don't want my daughter dating an unemployed dominatrix from a state school."

"I don't think it would be better if she were employed."

Bastian shook his head. "Do you have mental instability in your family? I mean, your mother is very tightly-wound. Do you think that's where she inherited it from? It's not as if she could get it from me."

This discussion went on every night. Medea yelled that five years wasn't a huge gap, "I'm not dating a sexual predator!

And even if I were, maybe I like being sexual prey!"

Her case for her own ability to make good choices was not helped by her outfit: peach tutu, ripped fuchsia stockings through which you could see her leg hair, and a purple t-shirt with orange lettering that said, SHAME IS SEXY. Bastian pondered genetics and tried to advise her on color matching. Henry considered therapy for all of them.

And meanwhile what Medea remembered about that year was that Janna had very cold hands. Medea would press the long, knuckly red fingers between her ardent palms to warm them, and they would stand like that for a moment, leaning toward one another but not kissing. Then Janna would laugh, unlace her fingers from Medea's, and go to get her gloves.

"You make me feel shabby," Medea had murmured against her ear, into her hair, where the scent of cigarettes and spray paint lingered. They'd sprayed sloppy graffiti on the sides of warehouses, and Medea's heart still shook when she remembered the rattling sound of the aerosol can. They'd never been caught, which meant that Medea had to endure an unglamorous end to her criminal career when her girlfriend decided that graffiti was cliched and immature. Janna reached the same conclusion about Medea herself a few months later.

Janna had felt like a part of her life which she could keep completely separate from her family: a secret garden. Instead her fathers had managed to get their hands all over her experience, explaining it to her and—worst of all—turning out to be right.

And so Medea found herself blowing her nose with a TV-rehab Kleenex, wiping her eyes and muttering angrily, "It's not about my *parents!*"

"I've always known that my fathers loved me," she said acidly; "they're just afraid that other people will think I'm their fault. Rest assured, I am a self-made woman."

* * *

They began to learn to perform their various household tasks. J. Malachi had to be shown how to mop away a tough stain by leaning hard on the mop handle and bouncing up and down a little as he pushed. Jen said, "Let me give you some advice which you can use in many different life situations: Sweep before you mop. Do the *next* right thing, not the thing after that."

Sharptooth got out of a lot of the chores. She couldn't wash and put away the dishes because the clinking of the forks and plates sounded too much like bottles, and triggered her desire to drink; she had an allergy to most of the cleaning products. ("It's not 'undiagnosed', it's self-diagnosed! I've personally diagnosed it. Self-knowledge.") She made up for it by working especially hard to give useful advice.

Dylan found himself surprisingly soothed by cleaning toilets. He enjoyed being praised for doing a good job with them. He tried to hide it; but after Jen came through and inspected them, lifted the seats and peered at the bowls and told him, "Great job!", he would grin, lift his arms in a cheer and make the "haaaaaaaaa" roar-of-the-crowd noise with his breath. "America wins the gold!" he'd tell himself, before moving on to the shower stalls. He liked cleaning everything in the bathroom, but the toilet was the best because of the comforting noise it made.

"Listen to it!" he urged Emebet, pushing down the handle to make the newly-bleached toilet flush. "*Shoosh.* It's so pleasant, like the ocean."

She nodded at him dubiously and suggested that he could do all the toilets then, and she'd mop the floors and clean the mirrors.

"Why do we even have mirrors here," he wondered. "We all look like shit. I guess it's for that movie thing where you stare into a mirror and have a big revelation. Well, I am going to *exhibit defiant behavior*. If I have a revelation I am gonna have it looking into a toilet."

Emebet was surprised and pleased. "Me too!" she said. "I have had many visions in this position," indicating being bent over a toilet throwing up.

Dylan considered this. "I guess there's a reason it's called the Porcelain God," he said. This intercultural exchange left them both feeling affection for one another, but also confusion.

Emebet was also good at cooking. The others, for the most part, were not. Sharptooth was vegan, so she got to make her own pristine little meals, which provoked a great deal of resentment. Medea spoke for many of them when she asked whether wolves could be vegan.

"Identifying as wolfkin is only one part of my belief system," Sharptooth said. "Many 'kin believe that our identities bring us closer to the natural world and to all other animals, not just the ones we identify as. So we choose not to eat or exploit our brothers and sisters in other species. Anyway, we're discovering new species all the time. It's entirely possible that vegan wolves are an unrecognized subspecies, which appear only in otherkin. We may be pointing the way to enormous scientific advances."

"Why do I get the feeling that what you call 'species' the rest of the world calls 'mental illness'?" Medea asked.

"I know you're just trying to deny my identity, but actually, I do have certain mental illnesses. I prefer to think of them as giftings. I'm gifted with OCD, which manifests through certain rituals, like I always need to smell my bras before I put them on. I think that's also a sublimated marking instinct."

"Is there such a thing as Wolf-B-Gon, I wonder," Medea said.

"Once again, by the way, you're calling attention to my identity in order to *distract* attention from the fact that your cooking lacks serenity and balance."

"She has a point," Colton put in. "You cook like you were raised by neglectful vegetables."

This was the night of the clingy chili. It had gotten stuck to the pot, and the cornbread had to be scraped out of the pan. They began a game—Medea started it, but the others joined in enthusiastically—of finding the perfect comparison for the taste of their dinner. It started with the chili, as Medea scraped her fork against her teeth and then proclaimed, "This tastes bitter and mushy. Like being forgiven."

Like new parents, they also spent an extraordinary amount of time discussing digestion and excretion. They were amazed at how difficult it had become to take a shit. "Seriously, I was grabbing my belly, massaging it, I started talking to my poop," Colton recounted on Day Five. "'Come on out, little man! Come and see the big wide world!'"

"Why can't we have laxatives?" Medea asked. "It can't be entertaining for viewers at home to look at a closed bathroom door with a lot of grunting coming from behind it."

"It's easier if you prop your feet up a little," Sharptooth offered. "You want to be in almost a birthing position. And don't strain! Remember, 'Easy Does It'!"

Medea got a visit to the dermatologist, since her eczema had broken out on her upper arms. She handed around her medication at the dinner table so the rest of the talent could longingly read the labels.

"When I was diagnosed," she declaimed, "the doctor explained that eczema is like being allergic to yourself. *How true*, I thought. *Even my skin is on-the-nose.*"

The others didn't fully grasp this. They also didn't care; they were all getting used to Medea saying incomprehensible things in a leopard-print voice dripping with doom.

"Good thing you don't play sports," Dylan said. "These are steroids. They could screw you up in doping."

"I play the sport of life," Medea said. "I maneuver the ball of dreams past life's great dismal goalie." And then, somewhat defensively, "I also play badminton."

"Is there a lot of steroid use in junior hockey?" J. Malachi asked.

"I wouldn't know!" Dylan said. "Give me some credit. I've never used a performance-*enhancing* drug in my life."

On Saturday Jen raised the delicate subject of a Higher Power. "I don't want you guys to feel like we're pushing religion on you," she said.

Several of them looked eager to have almost anything pushed on them, though Jen would not have been their choice of dealer.

"When you think about your Higher Power I want you to think of it as the guiding force in your life. What has that force been up 'til now? What do you want it to be?"

She paused in case they wanted to think, and then continued. "True freedom doesn't mean doing whatever you want all the time. True freedom means figuring out which Higher Power you want to serve."

J. Malachi perked up at that. "'You gotta serve somebody,'" he said, "in the unexpectedly-conservative words of Bob Dylan."

"*Leaving politics aside*," Jen said, "that's right. You know, we say that a bartender serves alcohol to people. But the person who really serves alcohol—is the alcoholic."

Medea, mittened for her own good, scratched elaborately at her shoulder. "Yeah, I'm gonna go ahead and say that the worst part of rehab is the wordplay."

"Sometimes people choose an element of nature," Jen said. "You could pick a majestic tree," and she spread her arms up over her head like swaying branches, "which lasts through the storms, takes in what it needs to sustain itself and puts out oxygen to provide for us all. You could do a lot worse than to model your life on a big sycamore."

She brightened. "I got a dog! When I was just getting clean I got this great shelter mutt. She was my rescue dog and I was her rescue person. She was my motivation, she got me up in the morning. Before I gave my life to the Lord she was my Higher Power."

"Oh, you're dyslexic!" Medea exclaimed. When Jen looked at her blankly, she said, "I get it now. When you want your *drug of choice*, you just remind yourself that Dog has a plan for your life."

"Now who's playing with words," Jen murmured. She was

looking at the cameras less that day; she felt more confident. It was doing wonders for Medea's hate-sex transference. Jen felt they were really making a connection.

"Can I pick a light switch, please?" Medea asked, husky and smoldering. "I've heard that you can have a light switch as your Higher Power and I've always wanted to know what that's like, to turn your will over to a light switch."

J. Malachi manfully suppressed the urge to say that he would keep her permanently flipped to "off."

"One guy I knew said he was his own Higher Power," Jen continued.

"Come on now, what is that?" Medea said. "Did he marry himself, too? That's not how that works."

"Seriously," J. Malachi said, and then felt annoyed with himself for agreeing with her. Still, he was pretty sure that the whole point of a Higher Power was that you weren't it.

Jen observed, "I'm glad we all feel so comfortable sharing our opinions, from our *experience* of sobriety."

That shut them up.

Jen said, "Some people find that the sense of empowerment they gain from taking control of their recovery is more self-centering for them than the concept of surrender which gets used in a lot of recovery circles." This took all of them a moment, so she said it again: "It's okay if you need to center yourself in empowerment rather than in surrender. You don't need to *surrender* to your Higher Power, a lot of people find that to be very negative language; you can think of it more as a 'way,' a guide for living."

Emebet waved her hand shyly. "I don't understand," she said. "You need to have self-control in order to surrender.

Don't you? Do I not understand it?"

She looked around at the others, searching their faces. J. Malachi tried to look helpful even though he wasn't sure what she was talking about.

"I was not able to surrender to my—to God, if this is what you are calling a Higher Power—because I didn't have self-control. This is what I need to work on: giving up." She lifted both hands shakily, as if making an offering, and then let them fall.

"We don't think of it as giving up," Jen said. "We think of it as *getting* happiness."

"I don't want that," Emebet said.

"Good for you!" Medea cheered.

"I don't want to be a person who gets," Emebet explained. "I want to give. To give myself up to God, like how they say in television, he gave himself up to the police."

"That's really countercultural," J. Malachi said warmly, and was gratified when she appeared to notice him.

*   *   *

The confessionals were supposed to be their chance to speak their minds, but most of the talent felt unusually inhibited in the little room with nothing to look at but the cameras.

Colton, back in his sunglasses, gave the production crew some advice. "You're not gonna get inside me here. If you want to catch us off-guard you should put cameras on the back of the toilet seats."

They spoke with the kind of politeness associated with answering one's parents, or the cops.

"She's definitely come up with a creative solution to the problem of late capitalist alienation," Medea said when the interviewer asked her to talk about Sharptooth. You could almost hear the next sentence: *Would you pass the pork buns, please?*

*   *   *

"*Oh* my *God*," Bentley moaned, propping her head on her fists like that photo of Aleister Crowley. She and Ana were celebrating the second week of filming at a bar called Bargaining, which was attached to a restaurant called Acceptance. Bentley was wearing a t-shirt that said I'M OVER IT, and she was complaining about Jen. "That woman has a voice like *knitting*. I look at her when she talks and all I can hear is a ponytail."

Ana ordered a sloe gin fizz, and Bentley made a face.

"Oh, does it bother you, is it okay that I'm ordering alcohol?" Ana said.

"It's not okay that you're ordering *that*. What is wrong with your generation? 'Oh, I'd like a sloe gin fizz. I'd like a brandy Alexander.' What the hell did bourbon ever do to you? At least people used to be ashamed to order appletinis."

"Maybe you're focusing too much on your self-image and not enough on your self-care," Ana said.

"This from the supposedly codependent. A codependent drinking a sloe gin fizz, this is now my life."

As Bentley kept whining in an unusually blowsy voice, Ana noticed that her words were coming out a little too quickly, as if they were under pressure.

"Can I ask you a personal question?" Ana said. "Although I guess it's also a work question."

"Part of my recovery is being of service," Bentley said, straightening up again and trying to look like a grown-up.

"Do addicts in general have a need to be better than other people? Because I've noticed a need to be better than other people, in many of the addicts we're working with."

"I don't think I'm better than other people!" Bentley did mutter, "I'm better than a sloe gin fucking fizz, though. ...Anyway, I dunno. Maybe we compare ourselves more to other people, than other people. Is that like a self-fulfilling statement? I remember the first time I went to NA I felt like such an amateur. There were all these people like, 'And then I decided I was just gonna wrap the car around a bridge support and end it all,' and I was like, *That is hardcore. Respect.* I felt like I was a fake, a cute little college chick who pretended she was a junkie so she could make friends."

"Do people without drug problems enjoy making friends with junkies?"

"Hey, fuck you, junkies are some of the best people. — Wait, no, I *do* have a drug problem, maybe you make a good point. I'm right though. I think we have insight—occasionally, anyway. Maybe that's what you mean when you say we think we're better than other people. You would not believe the number of times I've been standing on, like, a grocery line, and some guy is having a huge entitlement meltdown, screaming at the poor cashier who's from Botswana or wherever, because she rang up his carrot juice wrong. And I've been like, *You need a meeting.*"

"Does Jen have insight?"

"Ahhhh, Jen. I love that her name is 'Jen,' you know? Anybody can be a Jennifer but only some people can be a Jen. Like, if you're in recovery but you're still all fucked-up or really fun, probably you're more of a Jenny. I brought her in because she was like a competent version of me, and I thought, *It'll be good for my recovery*. Good for my sobriety to learn to like her, or however you're supposed to feel. Now I think that was not a good idea."

Bentley shook her head; and then shook herself all over, like a wet dog. "No, she's great though. She's such a cheerleader. Like a cheerleader that grew up into a guidance counselor. ...You know cheer is a real sport, right? It's athletically demanding, those girls have muscles like," and she put three fingers of her right hand together and kissed them, then made a little "explosion of confetti" motion. "I bet cheerleaders have a lot of resentment about that, how people think of them as little pink princesses and mean girls and shit, when they're actually major athletes. They're a stigmatized group in our society."

The server brought their drinks. Bentley thanked him and began tearing open sugar packets and pouring them into her iced tea, while drinking it. She used her mouth to stir it with the straw. When she'd built up a snowfall of sugar on all the ice cubes, and a little pile at the bottom of the glass, she stopped sucking the straw and said, "It's good that you ordered that thing." She nodded to herself, psyching herself up. "Because I have literally no cravings for that. Seriously, you could probably pour heroin right on top of it and I'd be like, 'I don't know, I can take it or leave it.'"

"Was that your drug of choice?" Ana felt that it was important to learn new things.

"Ah, everything was my drug of choice. *Drugs* were my drug of choice. I ate nutmeg once, just to see."

"Nutmeg?"

"It's a hal-*lu*-cinogen. Hallu-*cin*-ogen? Anyway. You know what time you *don't* want to be hallucinating? When you're puking your guts out. I saw fucking Vietnam flashbacks in that toilet bowl, I'm telling you. Don't take nutmeg."

"Okay," Ana said.

"I can't even eat pumpkin pie now. Nutmeg is the worst. But these days I tell people that *life* is my drug of choice. Humility and service, bitch! I should get that on a t-shirt. Anyway you almost do get a kind of high from it, from being good to people, making amends, being of service. I mean it's a kind of shitty high, like Robotripping but without the headache if you've ever done that—no? okay—but you get a little warm feeling and it takes you out of yourself for a while. Kind of neat."

*   *   *

Medea was trying to eat a hamburger with mittens on. She did not look like she was accepting the things she could not change.

"How come you get to use your thumbs?" she whined, pointing the crumbling hamburger at Sharptooth. "Wolves don't have opposable thumbs. Don't you feel like you're being an assimilationist here, taking on the traits of the oppressor? I mean they shoot your people—excuse me, I don't mean to use speciesist language—they shoot your *kin* with those thumbs."

"I find it interesting that whenever you're unhappy about something in your own program of recovery, that's when you bring up my identity," Sharptooth said cattily.

"I find it *interesting* that your identity only matters when it makes you special, not when it would make it hard to eat french fries," Medea snapped. "You have a few rehearsed little scripts that allow you to function in the world, play dress-up and pretend it's activism, but beyond those scripts you don't have a lot to say. Same thing over and over again."

Her eyes lit up. "I don't think you're 'wolfkin' at all. With your rehearsed tapes and your—your *opposable thumbs*," she spat. "I think you're Teddy Ruxkin."

There was a pause while this sank in. And then Colton and J. Malachi, who were the only ones who had any idea what she was talking about, began to cackle helplessly. J. Malachi glanced at Emebet, who was looking confused and slightly miserable, and felt badly about himself, but he couldn't stop laughing. Colton felt no shame whatsoever. He felt that he had earned a few laughs on somebody else's tab.

And anyway, Sharptooth could take care of herself. "I'm sure that's an awful insult, for someone of your generation," she said. "I'm not sure what it means, but then I'm not sure why we're having a fight about opposable thumbs."

"Ooh, she called you old," Colton laughed, slapping the table. "It is *on*."

"She's much older than me in wolf years," Medea replied. She lifted her chin. The insult had helped her compose herself and rise to the occasion; even in mittens, eating a hamburger in reality-TV rehab, she was able to regain her dignity.

She didn't mind being called old. Ideologically she was in favor of old women. Besides, an ex-girlfriend had told her she had an "old soul," meaning that she was unusually insightful and wise, and because it wasn't true she had believed it.

*   *   *

That Sunday they had the option of going to church. J. Malachi, Colton, and Dylan went to a local Presbyterian church that turned out to be white in every possible way. They huddled together looking startlingly alike: looking like refugees from rehab. Colton felt that he was learning a whole new way to be a goat in sheepworld.

He went there in order to make his first amends, ahead of schedule. The exchange with Jen and J. Malachi about evangelicals, out in the courtyard, had shaken loose a few bad memories. In his troubled youth he'd stolen from the collection basket: those twenties sticking out of the old ladies' envelopes like a little kid sticking her tongue out, daring him. He was pretty sure he'd bought his first six-pack with money he'd stolen from church ladies—which, in retrospect, might have been a bad sign.

They didn't have any money on the show, but Colton was familiar with the barter economy. So in that cold church, in the pale, narrow rows of pale, narrow people, he slipped the Bolex off his wrist and let it slither into the collection basket. He was startled to find that his heart was beating faster; he felt like he was about to get caught, like he wasn't allowed to try to put things right. The watch glinted, his cheap and pretty shame, as the basket passed on.

"Not actually a church, I think," he said loudly to the other two as they left. "More like the box a church came in."

But he felt lighter. That watch had never really suited him.

Emebet was driven to an Orthodox church, and came back quiet and saddened. J. Malachi followed her out to the little courtyard surrounded by pine trees. She was sitting on one of the benches with her shawl wrapped around herself, looking miserable. He sat beside her and didn't speak for a little while. They watched ragged clouds drifting high above, in a disaffected sky.

"How was it?" he asked, inching closer to her.

"Church? I didn't understand what was happening. I don't think they found a right church—I think that it is a Greek church. I took off my shoes and they said that was wrong, I couldn't come in like that."

She shook her head and started to get indignant all over again, which strengthened her a little. "'No shoes, you can't come in.' Is this church or convenience store? And when we do kiss of peace, to kiss and give peace, it didn't happen, nobody turned to me."

J. Malachi sat there under the hangover sky and thought he could not possibly have been given a better opening. *Learn to do the next right thing*, he told himself; and, not looking at the cameras, he took her hand gently, lifted it, and kissed it.

She looked at him like he'd just puked on her.

"No," she said. "Not like that. We do like this," and she bowed at the waist, which was awkward since she was sitting down, "to show that we are giving one another Christ's peace. I went to them but they turned away. And then the priest told me that I should not have brought people with the cameras. But we're not allowed to go anywhere without them!"

He was still holding her hand, limp, totally unattended to. She didn't seem to realize he was still touching her. She was much more concerned about having been called out by the priest.

His own cheeks were burning. He felt thick and lumpy. He tried to figure out whether he should put her hand down, and how he could reassure her.

"It's not your fault," he tried. "It's the rules."

She noticed that he had possession of her hand, and she

took it back. "Where can I go next Sunday? There's nowhere I can go."

"One day at a time," he beseeched her. He heard one of the camera operators muttering to another one.

That night at dinner they were more glum than usual. They ate in near-silence until dessert was brought out. This was apple pie, with a sandy crust and a filling so punishingly sweet that Emebet, who needed major dental work, gasped in pain when it hit her broken back teeth.

"This pie tastes like *Sunday*," Colton said with feeling, and they laughed until Emebet was banging a fist on the cafeteria table.

"Why did you do this? I have had pie, I have had Hostess pies. It is not pie," Emebet said, with giggles breaking through her words.

"I'm sorry, you guys!" Dylan held up his hands in surrender. "So the thing I thought was sugar was sugar, which is great, but the thing I thought was salt turned out also to be sugar."

"What were the things you thought were *apples?*" Medea inquired. "There's a kind of... a kind of sinister undercurrent to this pie. A hidden agenda."

"Aw, it's not *that* bad," Dylan said. "I'll eat yours if you won't."

"Recovering addicts and alcoholics need to be very careful about sugar," Sharptooth said. "We crave sweetness, especially in early recovery."

"This is the real damage of addiction," Medea said, pulling her pie away from Dylan's questing fork. "It turns you into a bad metaphor for yourself."

Chapter 6: How to Change the Weather

At the start of the second week their individual counseling focused on concrete, indisputable facts. "According to your very first answer here," Jen told Medea, "you drink more than ninety-nine percent of women."

"Hey, high score!"

Jen asked them to list five things they had lost due to their drinking. Colton wrote in swift, dismissive cursive, *Keys down elevator shaft, shitty exterminator job, cell phone, other cell phone, shitty clown job*. He thought he would get out of this exercise relatively easily. But Jen took him through each item.

She couldn't do much with the keys, although she did note that his building management had had to help him get them back, maintenance had been called, and everyone who worked the night shift had seen him stumbling drunk, which was embarrassing. "Have they seen that before?"

"They've seen everything before," he said; but for some reason he remembered the Ghost of Christmas Past with his white python, and he shuddered. He looked up and away, trying to hide his emotions and buy time to think, and Jen scolded him for rolling his eyes.

She also asked if he had applied for any other jobs when he took the shitty exterminator job, or if he'd just taken the first thing he was offered. She asked if it had felt like too much work to look for work.

"It seems to me like behind each of these items you've lost there's something bigger. Which you also lost."

"Yeah, I like losers," he said, trying for a casual purr. "I *love* losers. You know in high school I promised the whole football team I'd do 'em and go *through* 'em, if only they would lose the big game."

"So then, you must love yourself a lot."

Walked into that one, he thought, and tightened the screws on his smirk.

She made him add up the amount he spent on alcohol in a typical week, month, and year, and come up with alternative things he could have spent the money on. In two weeks sober he could have gotten his bike fixed. After a month, he could have gotten cheap plane tickets.

"Which is especially useful when you don't have anywhere to go," he pointed out. "Are these tickets after I get my bike fixed, or instead of?"

After a year, she informed him, he could buy a pet sloth, and care for it for six months. He gave her a startled look, and stopped chewing on his sunglasses long enough to laugh.

"I feel like me owning a sloth is a little too much like those Russian dolls," he said, but he couldn't take back the laughter. She made him cut a rough sloth shape out of brown construction paper and pin it to a cork board in the men's bedroom.

They were all supposed to pin up these little emblems and discuss, in counseling, how the cork board made them feel. J. Malachi put up a picture of Veronica Lake, which he claimed represented the woman he could get if he pulled himself together. He told Jen the photo made him feel hopeful. In fact, of course, Veronica Lake's photo had never made anybody feel hopeful; it made him think longingly of Emebet. It made him wish it were her photo, wish he could just be honest about what he wanted. Actually wanting to be honest about something was a new experience for him and so maybe, in a convoluted way, Veronica Lake made him feel hopeful after all.

Dylan's emblem was a trophy cup. He'd secretly made a little champagne-bottle shape out of a twist tie, and every night before he went to bed he'd tuck the bottle into the cup. He'd remove it and hide it every morning.

"A man's gotta have his pride," he told the confessional camera, to explain this tiny rebellion. "If 'pride' is the word I'm looking for."

He told Jen that looking at the cup made him feel guilty, and he was telling the truth there.

She tried to use objective evidence against Emebet. She read off Emebet's police record: breaking and entering, public urination, solicitation, public intoxication, trespassing.

"I'm homeless," Emebet pointed out. "Half of this list is things that are only illegal because I'm homeless. Wherever I go, this is trespassing! If I had a bathroom to urinate in and a bedroom to intoxicate in I would not have these problems."

"What about the solicitation?"

"I don't remember that," Emebet said stiffly, holding onto

her dignity with both hands.

Jen's most effective trick was a question she deployed against all of them: After she'd gotten them to give some of the more degrading details of their drinking, she'd ask them, "How long do you think you can keep doing this?"

It hit them pretty hard. They looked at her, at the cameras, caught; they stared and tried to come up with some kind of comeback.

J. Malachi tried out, "Just long enough to reach the ground," but his voice lacked conviction. He wasn't surprised when the episode aired and he saw that the editors had cut his line and just showed him looking at Jen like he'd taken a softball to the face.

The only one who wasn't fazed by the question was Medea, and that was only because Jen messed it up: She was afraid that her line was starting to sound overpolished, so she tried to manufacture authenticity by changing the phrasing. "How much more of this do you want?", she asked, and Medea spilled bustily forward and said, "Wait, do you *have* any more of it? How much more do you have?"

Group was much less intense. Spreading Jen's (and the cameras') attention around all six of them seemed to diminish the pressure on each. Jen would start the session with a brief introduction, laying some easy-reader wisdom on them: "There's only one place where nobody will tell you 'no,' and that's the cemetery." These needlepoint phrases stuck in their heads, making their insomnia all the more miserable. They were supposed to stay put in group no matter what happened; but storming out looked good on camera, so it wasn't penalized. They referred to it as "LIH," Left In Huff.

They were recovering enough to notice their surroundings, and judge them. Specifically, they had all noticed Ana's clothing choices: the pill-bottle dress, for example; and a white sheath dress with a dramatic black neckline and a front-pointing hem, which was intended to represent a syringe.

"What is with her?" Medea asked, jabbing her spoon at a gloppy bowl of oatmeal. "I've put together better outfits drunk."

Colton snorted. "Amish people on rumspringa have put together better outfits drunk! I mean, a necklace made out of beer tabs. I just want to know *why*."

They resented Ana because she ran the confessionals. She asked them how they felt about one another. Even Medea had decided that these questions were just shit-stirring, and refused to play along; they were all ornately polite. They exercised empathy and felt like they were getting away with something.

Ana liked to ask about Medea.

Colton's verdict: "She's a gay man trapped in a lesbian's body."

And Emebet's, after careful consideration: "She's out of place in this world. She is homeless in her *heart*."

Emebet knew as she was saying it that this line was trying too hard; it was pushy and soggy. She was using her own miserable situation to put one over on Ana. But the viewing public thought she was profound. The AV Club used "She Is Homeless in Her Heart" as the title for their review of the relevant episode. And anyway, underneath the sogginess there was something hard and sincere.

Ana asked them all these tweezering questions: How did

they feel about the activities, what were they learning? She made them chew and re-chew the cud of their experiences.

They were expected to peel off their skins and display the anatomy of their desires, while Ana stayed hidden. She was a Potemkin longing; all her insights were on her outside. She wore somebody else's heart on her sleeve.

"Whatever she paid for that dress, it was too much," Colton said.

And from Medea, in a more metaphorical key: "I would say whatever she paid for it wasn't enough."

*   *   *

J. Malachi suspected Emebet of insisting on sitting out in the courtyard, even when the Pennsylvania late fall weather shifted from clammy to cold, solely because the camera operators would have to follow them outside. He sat on the stone bench watching the wind whip the tops of the fir trees. She sat close, but facing slightly away from him. She was listening to the firs' unease.

He could taste the threads of her long curls where the wind drove them between his lips. He could smell her, warm and golden, in the blue scent of the coming rain.

She started to talk. Pressured, unsure of what to do, she stumbled through the story of the slow blanking-out of her faith in God. She expected him to tell her to pull herself together and try harder.

Instead he nodded and said slowly, "I've always liked how in the Anglican Church they make a big deal about Ascension Day. It's not much of a holiday in this country. But the English celebrate—or they used to—the day Jesus went away from us into Heaven. Almost a day to celebrate feeling like God has left. Maybe the point is that that's a normal part of Christian experience."

She didn't know what to do with that.

"We call it Ergete," she offered. "But I don't know if we think about it the way you do."

"I don't know if anybody thinks about it the way I do," he admitted.

She wanted some space to think her own thoughts for a little while, so she asked him to talk more about Anglicans. Happily he unbuttoned himself on the subjects of Candlemas and Whitsuntide while her mind tunneled back, against her will, to her abortion.

She had been counseled against it. She sat in a pink counseling room, with posters on the walls showing black men and women cradling their babies, as two white women talked to her about her pregnancy. She had squeezed the hand sanitizer bottle over and over, rubbing it into her hands until for days afterward she thought she could smell it. The older woman had talked about oxytocin, which Emebet confused with OxyContin; the younger one showed her pink and orange pictures of life in the womb, the tiny glowing fingers.

"I can tell from talking with you," the older woman said, even though Emebet had barely spoken a word, "that you are a warm, loving, good person who just wants the best for herself and her baby." It sounded weirdly like a pickup line.

When she said she was going to have the abortion anyway the older woman said, "Oh. I have seen so many women go through that and regret it, but maybe it will be different for you. I'm sorry you've chosen to view your choices this way." She stapled a smile on the end of that. "Please read through this legal disclaimer and sign here."

Then Emebet went out to the waiting room and looked through the pamphlets.

Was the Sex Worth It?

STD: Sexually Transmitted Depression

Jesus Was a Bad@$$: Meet the Man Who Raised More Hell Than You Ever Could

You Wouldn't Do It to a Puppy. Why Would You Do It to Your Baby?

Choosing Life on a Budget

Having His Baby: What a Lovely Way to Say "I Forgive You"

There was one which promised, The Ultimate Morning-After Pill. Emebet flipped that one open and learned that the Ultimate Morning-After Pill was Jesus. He could take away all the consequences of her sin. (The baby would still be there.)

Afterward she went out into the frigid night. A homeless woman was sleeping right outside the door, under a pilly gray blanket. Emebet, who was heading back to the apartment she shared with the man she was in love with—the one who had told her that an abortion was "maybe not the right thing, but it's the smart thing to do"—shivered and felt a wave of disgust and fear. She was used to giving to beggars, but this time she didn't try to tuck money into a fold of the blanket.

She wondered later whether if she had given charity, she wouldn't have made that appointment at the clinic. She wondered too, when she lost her man and her home, whether this was punishment not for the abortion itself but for her callousness toward that sleeping woman. But she had felt so deprived; the whole world seemed hard, and as she clutched the bills in her pocket, they seemed to anchor and protect her.

"King James II was the last king to personally wash the feet of his poorest subjects on Maundy Thursday," J. Malachi chattered. He couldn't see her face.

*   *   *

"Do either of your parents drink more than you think they should?" Jen asked Medea.

"God, I wish. No, my Dad—Bastian—has a glass of wine every night with dinner and gets *giggly*," she said, her voice dripping with contempt. "For someone so bulky he is quite a featherweight. And the only way you can tell when Papa's been drinking is that he tells you, 'Oh, I'm pretty drunk!' And then expresses his annual emotion."

She examined the lipstick prints she'd left on the teacup. "Usually about his mother."

"Did he have a difficult relationship with his mother?" Jen asked.

"Doesn't everyone," Medea said.

She got through individual counseling by treating it as a two-woman writers' workshop. The exercise was to come up with the perfect metaphor for floridly excessive drinking. Jen encouraged her; Jen seemed to find these metaphors poignant, while Medea found them exhilarating, a sheaf of self-justifications.

"When I was very little I had a picture book," she said, "with pastel nature paintings. The beach, the forest, the meadow, things like that. The paintings were on little interlaced paper wheels, with a loop of blue ribbon sticking out so you could pull the wheel, and as you pulled the seasons changed. The slats of the wheel slipped over or under, so the blossoming pink and purple meadow in springtime became the lush green meadow in summer, and then the yellow meadow in the fall, snowy white in the winter. Et cetera.

"That's drinking. When you're bored with your internal weather, when you want the sun to come out or a huge thunderstorm to start, all you have to do is pull the ribbon and the seasons change."

"When you're unhappy with how you feel," Jen said, which wasn't quite what Medea had said. "Do the slats ever get stuck? And what do you do when you pull the tab and it's winter? "

"Well, yes, life is poorly-constructed. But even instant winter is a new set of problems, at least, for when the old ones have become depressing. I mean you've got to make things happen, don't you? Be the change you want to see in the world."

"Yesterday you said you loved drinking because it was so unpredictable and risky. But this pull-tab thing seems like a desire to control how you feel. It's as if you want to control *when* and *why* you're out of control."

Medea rocked backward, then forward again, her whole upper body nodding in surprise like a sprung jack-in-the-box. She wasn't sure it was fair of Jen to win one of their exchanges—she'd been like this in actual writers' workshops too, which is why she'd been disinvited from so many of them—but she was interested, which a step toward humility.

*   *   *

"So what do you like about hockey?"

Dylan, who had been jabbing his thumb into a hole he'd picked in the flowered sofa of the counseling room, looked up at Jen with a startled grin. He'd been expecting another humiliating interrogation—about his suspensions or his grades, maybe, or his relationship with his mother, or the nine weeks he'd spent living at his father's office, which he was sorry he'd even brought up.

He'd only mentioned it because it was funny. His father had briefly ended up with custody, but the new girlfriend had "declared her house a Dylan-free zone," as Dylan always put it. So at age seven he'd spent a couple months sleeping in the corner of the supply room by the copier (where it was warmest), reading the receptionist's stack of *Cosmo*, eating from the vending machines, scootering through the carpeted corridors on the dolly, stuffing his t-shirt and underwear with the packing peanuts, and stamping himself RETURN TO SENDER. He'd figured out how to use the guillotine paper cutter ("learned that one the hard way!"), and he picked up a bit of Spanish after he became the pet of the custodial staff. He saw almost nothing of his father, but the cleaning ladies let him ride the vacuum.

He'd described this lost idyll to Jen and she'd looked very concerned.

But this question should be a gimme. "I like everything!" he said. "I like—"

And then he stopped. He had never bothered with this question before. Hockey wasn't something he liked or disliked; he didn't feel like he was in any position to have emotions about it. He wanted to say he liked everything: the roar of the crowd when they won; the endless drills where he pushed through exhaustion out of sheer cussed obedience; getting grabbed and hugged by his teammates, punched and slammed into the boards by his opponents, or yelled at by his coach when he needed it. He loved all of it. The sound of blades scraping the ice came to him as he was falling asleep, like the sound of waves.

But when he tried to describe even one of the rough-edged pieces of his joy in hockey, he found that the words kept turning into lies. Winning never satisfied him. He hated how lazy and frustrated he got in drills. Gair was one thing, but he was always surprised at his emotional distance from the rest of his team. The adrenaline of taking a punch was fun for a while but he was often scared and sick before games when he knew rough play was likely, and then later his jaw would hurt when he tried to eat a Ho-Ho. And nobody genuinely *loved* being yelled at by their coach, no matter how much he wanted to be the kind of person who would. He wanted to love it. He loved what he imagined hockey to be—what he thought it probably was for all the others.

"I like the uniforms," he finished lamely.

"The uniforms."

"Yeah," he said, warming to his subject. "They've got your name right on the back, you can't miss it, so if you black out and you wake up in like another country or something, and you don't remember who you are, you just have to look at your clothes. 'Okay so... I'm a hockey player, my last name is probably Hall.'"

She got that look on her face again.

"That sounds so frightening," she said. "I'm sorry that's happened to you."

He was startled and about to reassure her, and even felt bad for making her worry about him, when he thought: *Wait, am I being trolled by my therapist?*

*   *   *

Matters had progressed to the point that Emebet was wearing J. Malachi's coat as they paced around the courtyard. He felt that his ensemble of argyle sweater and college scarf was dashing, but a bit shivery. The weather couldn't make up its mind about rain. Occasionally a spatter of droplets would hit his head and shoulders; they clung and glinted in Emebet's curls.

He asked her what she thought of America: "What's surprised you?"

She considered it. Before they'd left Addis her brother had procured a guide to American business etiquette, originally written for Russians but translated and annotated by an Ethiopian. She could still picture the subject headings.

Greetings: "When an American asks, 'How are you?', the correct response is, 'Fine, and you?' Answers involving medical conditions or feelings are incorrect."

The Color Line: "Ethiopians are black to white people and white to black people. The exception to this rule is that when somebody wants something from you, you become a part of his race."

Food: "I cannot describe an American supermarket. You *must* experience it for yourself." *Tipping*: "Never call it bribery in front of Americans."

In the Workplace: "Do not treat American businesswomen as women. Don't flirt, don't compliment, don't kiss, don't ask if she is married. But don't treat them like men! It's best to

131

pretend that you and your coworkers all belong to a newly-discovered alien species without the normal desires, which reproduces via fax machine."

Emebet told J. Malachi a few of these—not the racial one—and then added, without rancor, "People are not so friendly here. And everything has to be done exactly the right way, even if it is not possible. It has to be according to the rules. You need so many pieces of paper to do everything! You need a piece of paper to get your piece of paper. And if you miss a step along the way it's your fault, don't complain, you must be positive!"

She laughed a little, shaking her head. "They will help you *less* if you are suffering, because suffering is not being positive."

"The power of positive thinking. Yeah, I have to admit that's one of our bad inventions, like the A-bomb."

"*Yes.* But I like Americans," she said, with a sigh. "Everybody likes Americans. You have to. It upsets them so much if you don't."

Chastened, J. Malachi shifted the subject. "How old were you when you came here?"

"Sixteen."

"That must have been hard."

She cocked her head, and pulled his big coat more tightly around her body. "Well... I don't know. It wasn't easy for my brother. He had all the responsibility, because he was two years older than me. I just accepted what was done to me. Maybe I was lazy."

She shrugged, and paid little attention to J. Malachi's murmured reassurances. "It was hard at school because my

English wasn't as good as I had thought. People asked me questions and I couldn't tell if they were joking: 'Can you ride a camel? Do you have a pet lion? How many goats does it take to marry you?'"

(Emebet alone in a crowded hallway, with a group of boys asking her, "Do you speak African? Speak some African!" And the tallest and most confident of them saying, "Fool, there ain't no language 'African'! You think they speak one language in the whole damn continent? She Ethiopian, she speak Ethiopian. Y'all *ignorant*.")

"I felt really stupid, frustrated," she said, "I was always wrong. I would try and try and not understand."

"If it helps," he offered, "that's basically how I felt when I was sixteen too."

"Well, I hope you didn't cry as much as I did. Because you would have been hit a lot in the face."

He didn't know what to say to that. They walked through a cold, prickly little rainshower. The clouds above them were high and slaty, with darker edges where the cloud cover met the pines.

To his surprise, Emebet chose to keep the conversation going. "We've been two weeks. How is your recovery coming?"

"*My* recovery?"

"Yes," she said, with a thin steel wire of amusement in her voice. "From your addiction to alcohol, which is why you're here."

"Uh, right," he said. "I... I guess I haven't placed that terminology on it. Yet," he conceded. "I just—something's keeping me from using that label. Which is odd when you think about it, since ordinarily I like labels. I mean, I approve of them. Everybody always says, 'Oh, I don't believe in labels,' as if we're all individuals, but labels create group loyalties and obligations, you're responsible to the other people with whom you class yourself—they bind people together. They're inherently good."

She snorted. "You've lost me."

"Right, sorry. Just—the one time I went to AA—or not strictly speaking 'one time,' I went a lot for a couple of months, but it was all in the same period of my life so I always think about it as one time—but whenever they wanted me to introduce myself I couldn't do it the way they were doing it. In spite of my general desire to conform. I ended up saying stuff like, 'Hi, I'm Jaymi,' or if I was really pushing myself I might say, 'I'm Jaymi, and I guess I'm worried about my drinking,' but I couldn't just say," and he took a breath, and watched her face very closely, "'alcoholic.'"

He was relieved to see that she didn't seem offended.

And the next day in group he made sure to start a sentence, "Speaking as an alcoholic...." It came out sounding confident and natural, even jaunty, but he felt distanced from it. He felt as though he were watching someone much like himself saying the words. The moment had a stylization, a performative quality, which made him suspect that he had actually managed to do the right thing for once.

*   *   *

The bouncer didn't believe Bentley's ID.

"You're nineteen?" he asked, lifting just one eyebrow. "Is this one of those shows? Am I on 'Punk'd'?"

"Mentally," Bentley protested. "Mentally, spiritually nineteen. Look—just do the X's on my hands and let us in, okay? You can't get in trouble for X-ing me." So he laughed and stamped their hands, crossed Bentley's stamps out with magic marker, and shooed them inside.

"Does that ever work?" Ana asked. She was dressed tonight as a beer can.

"What do you mean, does it work? It worked tonight! But yeah, I mean, sometimes it gets me discounts and stuff."

Bentley overheard herself and for the first time wondered about the propriety of profiting off her fake underage ID. She'd gotten it as a joke, and then it had proven useful for making her feel safe in clubs—she got the X's on the backs of her hands and felt like the decisions had all been made for her—and then occasionally she'd found that there were fringe benefits. She made a mental note to stop taking advantage of those benefits. She liked this feeling, the occasional yank she gave to the corset lacings on her character.

Ana nodded and tried to stay on the bar stool. Her beer-can dress was Mylar over a cylindrical crinoline, stiff and shiny and very fashion fast-forward. Very slippery.

Bentley ordered a Fresca and turned to Ana. "So what do you think of Philadelphia?" she asked. "Wait, no, I take that back. I'm sorry. I'm trying this thing," Bentley said, in response to Ana's confused look, "where I don't have opinions. I'm trying to just experience stuff, you know? And not have to *evaluate* and *judge* and have thoughts about them.

"Like with this Fresca. Ordinarily I would be like, 'This literally tastes like less than nothing, when you wish you'd never been born this is what you're wishing you were, it's like those people who are shallow on the outside but then even more shallow once you get to know them.' But I don't have to be that way. I can just accept it as... a drink." She looked at the polka-dotted can dubiously. "Of sorts."

"That sounds like a good spiritual practice," Ana said. She thought it might be good to have a boss with fewer opinions. "I accept Philadelphia."

"But so," Bentley said, suddenly turning intense in that predatory way Ana didn't like, "not asking for your opinion but for a professional judgment. What do you think of 'Amends' so far?"

Ana nodded. "I accept 'Amends.'"

"Oh, God."

"Our challenge is to be watchable but also medically sound, I think. We have to simultaneously give the audience what they want, and give the talent what they *need*."

Bentley looked at her for a long moment. She wondered if it would help her recovery to stop having opinions about her show. Bentley needed "Amends" to be good, morally good not aesthetically, and she never liked how it sounded when she tried to justify her needs. She had to feel that she was helping other people, because hurting others was very stressful for her.

"It'll be better after Family Day," Bentley said. She nodded hard, as if to underline it, but truth seemed to leach out of it the longer her sentence hung in the air.

"Family Day will be great television," Ana said, and thought she was agreeing.

Chapter 7: The Human Heart Is Gross to Lick

In the third week they took a field trip to the zoo, where Medea judged the animals' marital habits. They stood on a weighing platform which told them what kind of prey they could eat if they were predators. Emebet by herself could only eat rabbits and field mice, but when J. Malachi jumped onto the platform with her, she could take down a whole gazelle. Jen urged them all to get on the platform together, at which point they were capable of downing a wildebeest.

They were all making progress. Emebet taught Dylan how to make a potato salad with lemon, sauteed onion, and hot green chiles, and he replicated it so successfully that even Medea chewed thoughtfully and pronounced, "This salad tastes like... *food*."

"Tastes like victory," Dylan cheered.

They did some role-play: "Let's practice parties. I'll be a party girl and you can be a sober individual," Jen said.

"Oh, can I really?" Medea muttered.

Jen started with J. Malachi: "Jaymi! Great to see you, old pal, it's been ages. Let's do a round of shots!"

"Uh... let's do a round of... 'not's?'"

Jen, undeterred: "Okay, Jaymi, let's try that again. Maybe not so hard this time."

For Colton she went with, "Hi, great to see you! Want a drink?"

He licked his lips and drawled, "None for me, thanks. I'm pregnant."

They had a night of beauty therapy in which Jen, a licensed beauty therapist, taught them all to make mud masks. Colton insisted that there was a right way to do this, which involved cucumber slices and white towel-turbans, and J. Malachi went along with him because he believed tradition should trump expert opinion. So the two of them lounged and glared at the cameras in their turbans, cucumbers blanking out their eyes, covered in therapeutic mud. They looked like a cross between *La Dolce Vita* and video-game monsters. Their journey of recovery had brought them deep into the Uncanny Valley.

They had a talent show. Emebet came out in her church clothes and said, in a shy husky voice which piqued J. Malachi's anticipation unbearably, "This is a dance from Ethiopia called 'eskista.'" She stood awkwardly for a moment, leaning forward, feeling that she needed to say something else but unsure what there was to say. Then she shrugged and clicked the mouse to start the music.

Her whole face changed. She flashed a huge, thrilling, crowd-pleasing smile as she started to jerk her shoulders and hips in quick syncopation. She stamped her bare feet and held out the ends of her white headscarf, which she'd tied around her waist. It frothed around her rhythmically jerking body; the softness of her smile and the flowing scarf contrasted to the sharp, almost industrial-age working of her elbows and hips and neck. The dance was like a stylization of laughter— her shaking shoulders, her lowering and lifting torso—and a stylization of repetitive, manual labor. Her curls bounced and her small breasts jogged in her loose white dress. Dylan yipped out a few startled "Woo!"s, and J. Malachi tried to clap in rhythm and didn't much mind when he kept missing the beat.

When the music cut off abruptly her smile lingered for a moment; then she covered her mouth and bowed. Everyone cheered, and Colton called out to her, "It works if you work it, girl!"

She could still feel the music rippling through her. It reminded her a little of the way her body had jerked and shivered in withdrawal. The last time she'd danced like that, she'd been drinking in a church parking lot with the man she loved and two other couples. He'd strutted and flowed around them all, the most boisterous, the best, stretching his arms out like he was going to grab all three of the girls. He'd swung his arms at them fast and hard so they'd had to duck, laughing, and he'd yelled, "Freestyle! Woohoo!" as the late-night churchgoers shook their heads.

Emebet, sitting on her folding chair, felt grimy and frustrated that her good memories had soured. But she looked around at the surprised, happy expressions of the others and tried to warm herself with them.

Colton performed a little rap about a man who gets inspiringly drunk one night:

He's got a lot on his mind
He's got a hat on his feet

He can't be beat

...Ooh, he just got beat.

He thinks he's on the run, but he's really on the nod—

Son, your dick's too short to fuck with God.

"I'm pretty sure I dated that guy," Jen said when he was done. "He was so suave, he couldn't even stand up. He just oozed along the ground, being smooth. 'Be cool, girl. I got it.' I think he was trying to tell me he had the clap." For a very brief moment, everybody liked her.

Medea's talent was theatrics. Nobody else wanted to act in her silent adaptation of the myth of Persephone, but she exercised the virtue of perseverance and decided to play every role herself. For six minutes and forty-three seconds she flung herself around the room: sneaking up on herself, kidnaping herself, remonstrating with herself, and releasing herself into her own care. She also portrayed the fields and meadows shivering and shedding leaves in the winter and blossoming again in the spring. She had several costume changes per minute, and she battled herself so enthusiastically that she gave herself a split lip.

Colton was reminded of his childhood pet, Boss Man, a disturbed tomcat who would not only chase his own tail but catch it. The cat didn't seem to grasp that the front part of him was attached to the back part, so he would roll across the floor rump over head, alternately biting his feet and kicking his face.

Colton was surprised when nobody laughed at Medea— and then surprised all over again to realize that he was touched, and a little bit proud of them all.

They endured another Sunday, another bout of church. It

was just as bad as the first one.

Emebet's views continued to evolve in the confessional. She told the camera, in response to yet another pushy prompt, "I do like him. He makes me feel good about myself."

"What does he do to make you feel that way?"

"Well, he's very, really a mess! He is a disaster, he is as bad as I am, but he's lived a very easy life."

This wasn't what Ana was hoping for, and she frowned, but Emebet was nodding intently.

"I've often wondered, 'What would I be like if life was different?' If I did not do—the things I did, if I were from a different country, if I had someone else's life. And now I look at him and the way he thinks, the way he feels so sorry for everything and does nothing about anything! And I see now that maybe I would be just as bad if I was an American or a rich person or a man. Only I would be fatter."

This perceived symmetry between them gradually became a part of the mythology of their relationship, the willful fables which made the gears turn. Emebet chose to look at the truth with this side up, the side with their similarity; it had another side, which they were both aware of, but she chose to lift the side that made things easier. This was the greatest kindness a girl had done J. Malachi since his sister Armistice let him know she'd found the stash of *Firing Line* tapes under his bed.

*   *   *

And then they learned that it was time for Family Day, like a bug learning that it's time for a windshield. They all sat in a circle and Jen handed them each a manila envelope, in which they would find a photograph of the family member or friend who would participate in their on-camera treatment.

Everyone smiled tensely.

The cameras swooped in over their shoulders as they opened their envelopes and reacted. "Oh my God, I'm America's next top model!" Dylan cried, as he'd planned to; but then he saw that his photo showed Gair Cupek, not any of his parents or stepparents, and his face went in several different directions at once. After an emotional six-car pileup, he managed to say, "Well thank God for that," and sat down abruptly.

Sharptooth's mom had a photo she could send to casting agents. She was plump and petted, in a blowout hairdo with blonde highlights. Colton's sister, by contrast, looked like the Dust Bowl edition of *Vogue*—she stood in a sepia-tinted urban wasteland with a baby on her hip and a grim pout on her face, with her lumberjack shirt undone almost to her navel, in skinny jeans and giant wedge heels. She looked like sex and blame.

Both of Medea's dads were coming, and both of J. Malachi's parents. She met this news with a lockjaw grin and he wrung out a miserable little smile.

J. Malachi asked Emebet who was in her photograph. "I don't know who this is," she said, angry and helpless. "I don't know."

An edge of disappointment came into her voice. "I thought it would be maybe one of my relatives who are still in Ethiopia—maybe they could even get a visa? There is a lot of pull, I think, with these television shows. Or I thought it would be—him, my—the person I—"

J. Malachi nodded and made a cooing sound to tell her she didn't have to finish the sentence.

"But I don't know who this is! Maybe there's a mistake?"

"No mistake," Jen said, bobbing over to them. "You'll find out all about your visitor on Family Day, but I can guarantee that he's an important person in your recovery. I believe making an amends to this man will help you move forward in life."

Emebet looked at her with a certain immigrant superiority.

"Even if it isn't anybody special, uh, that's good too, right? It can kind of teach you to deal with disappointment," J. Malachi attempted.

"Yes, I'm sure that in my daily life in America I will often need to deal with disappointment of being lied to by a television show," Emebet said. Her voice was so calm and level that J. Malachi didn't realize she was joking at first; when he got it, he grinned for real, and gave a high hysterical giggle like a cartoon hyena.

They spent the rest of that afternoon in canine therapy, which was a decent distraction. Medea kept ordering her spaniel, "Heel thyself!", and then cackling when it wouldn't. Sharptooth's German shepherd loved her, and they rolled on the grass together and played tag. Sharptooth could move surprisingly fast on all fours.

J. Malachi disliked dogs, but he ended up with an old and sweet-tempered poodle who was content to sit and be petted and watch the others, which turned out to be soothing. It was pleasantly, humiliatingly childlike, he thought, sitting there feeling happy to be petting a dog in the cool sunshine. The poodle drooled on his battered seersucker and he didn't even mind. "I've done worse," he reassured the animal, fondling her soft ears.

At dinner, though, the specter of Family Day returned, like the bad memories you only have when you're drinking. They ate disconsolately and too much. In the morning everyone felt sick, and people tried to beg off on the grounds that they were "coming down with something" (Dylan) or "going through extremely post-acute withdrawal" (Sharptooth). Nobody was reprieved.

Jen explained how the day would go. They'd sit in a circle, with two chairs pulled forward facing one another, and the family members would enter one at a time like pro wrestlers. The talent would sit opposite the relative (or whoever) and listen silently as he or she laid out resentments and grievances. Then the talent would have a chance to talk, to apologize and also to register complaints. Last of all the group would be allowed to offer feedback to both parties.

Once the cameras and the lights were all ready, Sharptooth went first. Her mother came into the room, looking very looked-at. Her face was powdered, her hair was blown out, and her eyelashes looked like they were wearing little fur coats. Sharptooth, with precise little movements, adjusted her tail and draped it over her lap.

Her mother frowned. "Shayna. You're wearing your— headband." She indicated the fuzzy gray ears. "Why do you have to embarrass me like this in front of *television?*"

Sharptooth, waving her hands in front of her mouth, mimed that she wasn't allowed to talk. She pointed at her mother—*You talk!*—nodding with big-eyed, big-eared enthusiasm. Several of the others snickered.

Sharptooth's mother, who was named Mical, turned to Jen with a look of exasperation. Jen said, "I think we should focus on the bigger issues. This is your chance to give voice to any frustrations you have toward your daughter concerning her behavior, any resentments—"

"I *resent* the fact that she is being allowed to parade around here looking like a mental patient."

"We are in a mental-health facility," Jen said softly. "Anyway, is this our purpose today?"

"Tchah. *Fine.*" Mical flicked her eyes around the room so that her sabled eyelashes swished like feather dusters. She said, "Shayna, I resent that you are living with me and Ronald as an adult, and that you are not earning a living. You spend all your time with talking animals on the internet."

Sharptooth looked scandalized, but kept her mouth shut.

"What can you put on your resume? Howling at the moon and not shooting heroin isn't a job qualification."

"Is that everything?" Jen asked, encouragingly.

Mical thought. "Do your own laundry!" she snapped.

The others pondered this example of honest communication. On the one hand they were gratified that Sharptooth wasn't as successful as she'd implied. On the other, howling at the moon *and* not abusing substances was one thing more than most of them could manage.

"Okay, Sharptooth. Do you have anything to say to your mother?"

"I am a counselor on the internet," Sharptooth burst out. "I help people!"

"You help people who think they're *giraffes*," her mother said.

"And I'm discriminated against in the workplace, you know that. I've told you that most human workplaces are a hostile environment for me. But I could do the laundry," she conceded. "I'm sorry I'm difficult to live with, as I pursue my calling."

"I need you to move out or start paying rent."

"I don't believe in money! Are you turning into some kind of capitalist?"

"You never believe in anything that would require you to act like an adult! Being a layabout living in your momma's house is not a part of anybody's religion!"

"You know, I think *you* have an addiction, too! You're addicted to this image you have of the perfect family, and you're sacrificing your real family to feed your habit!"

"Asking you to pay rent is not exactly blood sacrifice. Nobody is gonna tie you up, cut your throat and make brisket from you."

"You see, you see this violent language she uses. This is very triggering for me."

Oh, I get it now, Medea thought. *She doesn't understand what a metaphor is! This explains everything.* She sighed. *The American educational system has so much to answer for.*

"I help out around the house," Sharptooth said mulishly. "I taught the dog to stop barking at the mailman, and I keep her calm when there are storms. I'm good with dogs, obviously, because of our family connection."

"Well maybe the *dog* should come to Family Day, then," her mother said. "And honey, the dog went deaf. That's what happened. You were gone for a few years to *shoot heroin*, and the dog went deaf. That's why she doesn't bark at storms and mail carriers anymore. It's not because you used your sparkle powers."

Jen broke in, "Let's remember to speak with love and respect." Jen had grown calmer as the mother and daughter became more agitated. She said that they both needed to make concessions. Sharptooth had already agreed to do more housework; her mother could agree to use less "graphic" language. They could both seek family therapy. And Sharptooth could volunteer at an animal shelter or a crisis hotline, and use those experiences to build her resume. With these suggestions, Jen opened the floor to the rest of the group for their comments.

Colton, who found the Miller family's genteel dysfunction exotic, raised his hand slightly and was surprised when Jen called on him.

"Against my better judgment I'm gonna try to be helpful here," he said. "Pretending to be a wolf isn't the worst thing somebody could do. She got herself clean. She isn't stealing your money. *You should be grateful*," which he said with the relish of someone who had heard it too many times himself.

Mical held herself still, her chin tilted slightly upward. She wore an unwavering bless-your-heart smile.

Then he turned to Sharptooth. "But I don't get you, Miss Big Bad Wolf. You could be grateful your own self. You may not be stealing from her, but you are not contributing. If I had a wild animal living in my home, *who didn't even pay rent*, I would call Animal Control! You don't need a resume to go ask for a job washing dishes, bussing tables, call center—believe me, the world is full of shit jobs. Just go and talk with the owners. Don't inform them of your *species*, that is like rule number zero, the rule that comes before the rules. I can't believe no one taught you this! I blame the parents."

He shook his head. "Think of it like your secret identity, you know? Be Clark Kent. Don't be Superman. Clark Kent was not discriminated against just because he had to wear his glasses, that is not how that works."

"Anybody else?" Jen asked, but for once, not even Medea thought she could top that.

*   *   *

It was Dylan's turn next. They had a brief break while the lights and cameras were checked and adjusted. There were cookies set out and bottles of water, and Mical made a show of dabbing at her eyes. She stayed far away from Colton, and regarded Sharptooth with a certain wariness; mother and daughter circled one another like two predators from different species, unsure who had trespassed on whose territory.

Dylan sat nervously on the edge of his plastic chair, waiting. He twisted a hand in the chain of his little cross necklace and felt like an asshole and an idiot for wearing it, but he thought taking it off on camera would make him look like a melodramatic teenager, so he didn't. Then the door opened and Gair came in, looking as pale and shaky and determined as he did before a big game. He looked around and then made a beeline for Dylan, pulling him up out of his chair and into a huge evangelical hug.

"Hey," he said, holding Dylan at arm's length and looking at him. Dylan looked away.

"Hey, Cupcake." Dylan snuck him a little grin, and got a much bigger grin in return. They sat down.

Gair had a sheet of yellow lined paper, which he smoothed out. "So I'm supposed to, I think, tell you stuff that I feel resentment about, which—I guess is honesty? I feel like it isn't, uh, really kind, but I guess you need to know. I'd like to know if it were me, so like, 'Do unto others,' I guess. Anyway you'll get a chance to do unto me—" and then he blushed and his eyes widened, and Dylan *really* felt bad about having all of this on camera, but Gair laughed at his own embarrassment and shook his head. "So to speak. You'll get a chance to tell me anything you think *I* need to hear, so it's not just one way." And then he grinned and added, "We'll be switch-hitters," and Dylan was startled into a big, stupid donkey laugh.

"So," Gair said, looking down at his paper. "I wrote out a bunch of stuff but honestly I don't care about most of it. Like, okay, you stole some traffic cones and trashed a lot of hotel rooms trying to make party decorations, and you stole that goat which is kind of animal cruelty, but whatever. And there was the time you got the whole team kicked off that plane because you stole one of their little bottles of vodka from first class and put it up your ass, I guess because people get drunk that way or something? Only you forgot to open it because you were *already* drunk."

"No, I—" Dylan remembered that he wasn't supposed to talk, but he looked around and nobody stopped him, so he grinned and went on. This wasn't so bad. "I didn't put it *up* my ass. I was holding it between my cheeks. Lovingly, like a butterfly cupped in the palm of a hand."

"But *why*," Gair said, charmed against his will and trying not to laugh. He was still willing to play along. Dylan felt like this whole experience might be survivable, like most of his other experiences.

"You know, I'm not sure? I think I wanted to find out if my butt was prehensile."

"Did you drink it afterward?"

"No, I wasted it. Of course I drank it! Well, I didn't find it until the next morning, to be honest. But yeah, I'm trying to learn to be thrifty."

"So," Gair said, returning to his purpose. "All of that is just... whatever. You hold the junior hockey record in suspensions for off-ice behavior, by the way, I looked it up. Which is kind of scary since hockey is not exactly ballroom dancing to begin with. I have no idea how you have managed to avoid a DUI."

"Because I put my car keys down the disposal," Dylan said.

"...Oh. That's why you're always trying to get rides from me?"

"No, the car ride thing is because I'm lazy, but yes, I got rid of my keys because I didn't want to total the car on a lamppost or whatever."

He suddenly overheard himself. *If anybody else said that to me I'd think they had a serious problem.*

He was still processing that thought as Gair continued. "This isn't a thing I'm resentful about, obviously, but I'm worried that you were genuinely trying to quit drinking last year when you were doing AA. I know you said you were just trying to get the coach off your back but... I got the impression that you were taking it seriously, for months. And you couldn't do it, you kept going back to it."

Dylan looked away.

"That night when you were throwing up blood was during the time when you were trying to quit drinking."

"I—look, I was throwing up and also bleeding. I wasn't

throwing up blood." Dylan felt like the rest of the room wasn't taking this distinction seriously.

"And there was the whole thing with the NHL lockout."

"'Lockout With Your Cock Out,'" Dylan reminisced. "Now that was glorious."

"You were like a wildlife preserve for endangered social diseases. Do you even remember coming home to a card on the door that said, 'This season, give the gift of crabs'? You used my credit card, which was really bad, I can't believe you made me explain to my parents why there was a charge from Desperate Housesluts, although creepily enough I think they might have been sorry it wasn't me. And you've obviously peed on a bunch of things." He sighed. "But the big thing was when my grandma died."

Dylan took a quick breath and nodded, looking down. He knew he had this one coming.

"I needed you, dude. And you couldn't be there for me because you were drunk, and I remember thinking to myself, *What did you even expect of him? You know what he's like.* And—I can't imagine being that person. The person somebody thinks about like that, somebody who cares about you."

He glanced over at Jen. "That's basically it. I know it isn't dramatic."

Everyone looked at Dylan. He wanted to play a hard defense—he had liberated the goat because that other team wasn't treating her right, and he was still planning to pay Gair back for the credit card charges. But he couldn't argue about the grandmother thing.

"I'm honestly sorry about that. I meant to come over and

cheer you up but when you called I was already, uh, pretty wasted, and I didn't want to inflict that on you so I just... didn't. I'm sorry."

Gair looked confused. "Wait, what are you apologizing for?"

"For not coming over when you called me?"

"Oh," Gair said, in a small, compassionate voice, a little Kleenex of a word. "You did come over, though."

And Dylan felt a very familiar sinking in the *oh, shit* part of his stomach.

"You came over, even though I told you not to because I didn't want you to drive drunk—this must have been before you ruined your keys—and you were loud and you said all this stuff, like my grandma had been kind and baked cookies and knitted afghans, when you never met her and in fact she was basically the Republican Party platform in human skin. If she ever knitted anything it was a gun cozy, and I think she thought kindness was a Communist plot."

Gair wasn't looking at him as he said, "And then you peed in the fridge, *again*. And crapped in my mom's ficus, which was just unnecessary." He shook his head. "I don't know, cleaning up after you did distract me, I guess, for the rest of the night. And then I took you home."

"Wow," Dylan said softly. "I'm learning so much about myself here."

"So that was the big thing."

Dylan found it hard to think about this and figure out what to say. It felt like there was some obvious way to respond but it kept getting away from him. "I'm sorry. You know I'm sorry, right?"

Gair didn't answer, and Dylan realized that you weren't supposed to ask people to reassure you while you were apologizing for pissing all over their horrible grandmother's memory and also their refrigerator. Of course Gair's beloved grandmother was a horrible person. Gair had a talent for loving the unlovable.

"I don't know what to say. I'm sorry. I'm really trying here, I promise, I'm trying to learn how to be better."

Gair's face didn't change at all, like he knew that when Dylan said "I promise" he meant it with all his heart, briefly.

"I don't know what I can say that you can believe," Dylan muttered.

"I don't know what you can say that *you* can believe. I know you can do this, I know it's hard but you're a lot tougher than you give yourself credit for." Gair tried to cheer him up: "You have the mind of a toilet seat, the stomach of a garbage disposal, and the *heart* of a hockey goon. And you will take your—your drinking problem and break its nose, date its girl, and steal its goat."

Dylan gave the kind of maudlin laugh he usually only managed when he was thoroughly trashed. "I'm sorry I'm such a shitty friend," he said.

"You're worth it."

Dylan laughed a little more genuinely then. "You're not even gonna try to argue that I'm not that shitty?"

"Well, you are," Gair said. "It doesn't matter to me though. The whole point of friendship is that people don't get what they deserve."

"Somehow I feel both reassured and scolded!"

"Maybe that's why they call this Family Day," Gair said.

He paused, and then grinned. "Do you remember when we went to the medical museum in fifth grade, and you licked the heart?" He turned to the others, smiling, open and enthusiastic, the youngest person in the room. "We were on this school field trip, and the guy running the museum was showing us various horrifying things they kept in jars. It was seriously the coolest thing ever. And he brought out this actual preserved human heart on a tray. And Dylan, because he is crazy, darted forward and stuck his tongue out and *licked* it. Actually licked it."

"How did it taste?" Medea asked.

Dylan thought. "Kind of... pickly? And it felt sort of hard and tense. Like that stuff you made last night that was supposed to be pasta sauce."

"Ooh, that's hitting below the belt," Medea laughed.

"I thought you were the coolest person in the world," Gair said. "I was like, *Let's be friends forever.*" And then, more theatrically, "The human heart is hard to lick. Yours especially."

"The human heart is *gross* to lick," Dylan said. "And you have a bizarre method of choosing your friends."

He was smiling, but looking a little bit past Gair, over his shoulder.

There was an unsteady little pause, and then Gair remembered something else he wanted to try. "I wanted to ask you if, when you get out of here, you'd come to my church," he said. "I think it would be good for you, you'd get support, you could come to Dinner with a Sinner—"

Medea laughed out loud. "I am so sorry," she lied, "what?"

Dylan rolled his eyes and tried to explain. "It isn't what it sounds like. I mean *they're* the Sinner, the person from Gair's church. They call it that because we're all sinners but only Christians know it, I think is the idea? Or maybe the idea is that you can't even sin before you know Jesus."

"Oh," Medea said, disappointed. "I thought it was some old-time, Savonarola stuff, not this fifty-proof wine into water Jesus. Just the usual Christian plea-bargaining, then, where if you admit you killed God you get off with a lighter sentence."

Jen intervened: "I think we should all respect one another's spirituality."

"I think we should not push religion in rehab," Medea shot back. "God, they're like *toddlers*, whatever question you ask them the only answer you get back is 'Jesus.' Oh, you can't have a whiskey and Coke? Well how about a *Jesus* and Coke! Spraying it from water-guns strapped to their tits like bar girls. Open your mouth for some Jesus! Put a dollar down the cleavage of the ministers of hospitality on your way out!"

Dylan was trying to suppress his giggles. "She's, uh, this is Medea," he tried to explain to Gair. "She's like the me of TV rehab. Like imagine how I look compared to the rest of the team, that's how she is with us. So you know it's rough."

Medea smirked.

Dylan shook his head, shaking the grin off. "But I do feel like... obviously you're a better person than me and I want to learn. I just—"

"Oh," Gair said, suddenly unhappy with himself. "Sorry. I get it. I didn't mean at all that I was a better person. I know I'm not. You're right, I shouldn't make it sound like I'm the teacher and you're the student, I have just as much to learn from you if not more. You've probably learned so much here, about humility and—stuff I obviously still need to learn."

"Oh yeah, I have so much to *teach* you, my naughty little student," Dylan purred. "See me after class. Wear something... extracurricular."

"You're a dick," Gair laughed, but he felt both scolded and reassured.

Dylan grinned at him, and his dimple popped out like a beer-can tab flipping up. "All my life I've been waiting for you to say those three little words, the three words I dream of—"

Gair yelped, and his eyes skittered toward the cameras. "You are *such* a dick!"

"You too, man," Dylan said, and they looked at each other with sudden, intense gratitude. "Seriously, you too."

Well, at least it'll really hurt when I fuck this up, he thought.

*   *   *

Medea was next. A small thrill went through the group.

Her fathers came out and took their seats. They were both short and a bit rounded, one of them hairy and cudgel-faced and the other intellectual with a faint air of purse-dog. The hairy one, glowering, reached for the doglike one's hand. Medea sat very still, with her back straight and her hands tucked under her thighs, like a dissident being interrogated. She had erased all expression from her face; she looked like a papier-mache of herself. But her cheeks and ears were very red.

"What happened to her lip?" the intellectual asked Jen, in an accusatory voice. "Is this a safe environment for her?"

"She had a small accident during a theatrical performance," Jen said soothingly.

He considered this, and nodded. "That definitely sounds

like our little girl."

Jen went through her spiel. The intellectual, Henry, began: "Deedee, we love you and we support you. I don't think we have 'resentments.' We just want you to be happy. You're very angry, we can see that, but writing plays about how you never knew your egg donor isn't helping anybody. And it stigmatizes our family." He sighed. "We're hoping that you can learn coping skills. I know you're a warm, wonderful, resilient person."

Medea, speaking for everyone, snorted.

"You're our dream child, our perfect little girl, and you always will be."

Bastian, the hairy one, broke in: "I was incredibly hurt when you called me a 'butter vampire.' You know that I'm watching my weight!"

Henry frowned. "I don't think this is the real issue—"

"She also said I had 'Sasquatch arms.'"

Jen invited Medea to air her own concerns, but she declined: "I get paid to write up my resentments. I'm not gonna give them away on television for free."

Henry began, "Maybe anger management approaches would help you—"

"Fuck you!"

He appealed to Jen. "Is there some way we can help her? Wait, is that a codependent question?"

"Don't you get it?" Medea asked, soaring to the heights of the Lifetime actresses she'd idolized in childhood. "I don't want to be less angry. I don't want to be better, I don't want to be resilient, I don't want you to win!"

She had never learned that you shouldn't let the actresses

write their own lines.

J. Malachi raised a tentative hand, and Jen called on him. "I feel like everyone here is caught up in their own images. You all want something unbroken and you aren't going to get it."

"Our family isn't broken," Henry said testily.

"*Okay*, but your kid is."

"I don't think negative judgments like that are helpful," Henry said.

Medea gave an elaborate sigh. "Oh my God, this is where we all have to use 'I' statements and we're not allowed to have actual *beliefs*, just feelings," she said. "I'm fucked up, it's fine to say it! I want to hear what else this seersucker has to say."

J. Malachi gave her a judgmental look, out of gratitude, and turned back to the two men. "You don't have a perfect kid. But you've got someone who is unique and outspoken and passionate."

"So was Hitler," Bastian muttered. J. Malachi ignored this.

"She's wonderfully imaginative," Henry said.

Medea writhed on her chair and snarled, "I practically write nonfiction! You think every emotion you don't like is a product of my *wonderful imagination*."

Bastian was eloquently silent.

"Oh hey, speaking of imagination," Medea said, as J. Malachi tried to break in. He gave up. "Remember that girl I was dating, how you told all your friends that she was a lesbian agitprop artist who made political postcards for an underground resistance movement? So glamorous. Yeah, I told you, that was her Etsy shop. She was a waitress at a TGI Friday's. But you told everybody that your daughter was dating basically Andy Warhol and Valerie Solanas combined. Secondhand glory for you, total embarrassment for her if she met any of your friends. Who *does* that?"

Bastian looked indignant and Henry pitied her. They looked uncomfortable for her sake, not their own, as if she was willfully ignorant about her exotic ex-girlfriend or maybe just mistaken.

J. Malachi tried again. "Medea. A lot of the stuff you want to talk about, I think maybe you won't ever understand. It won't ever make sense, why people do what they do. I mean, why do you do what you do? Why do I fuck up so much? Maybe the past—" and here he meant, *your parents*— "is one of those black boxes they put in airplanes so that they can retrieve it from the wreckage and figure out why the plane crashed. But sometimes the crash may have been so spectacular that nobody can open the black box anymore. Maybe a lot of what you want to resolve is a black box nobody can open, from a plane crash that will always go unexplained. Could be faulty wiring or terrorists, or a gremlin on the wing, but at some point you have to accept that you will probably never know.

"I mean, putting all the parental stuff aside: You seem really caught up in your own big idea of yourself. It's like you won't give them the satisfaction of getting better because it's *cliched*. Like oh, she was a drunk and now she's sorry, how boring. Also I think you're worried that if you get sober and make amends then your writing will be dull."

She was listening, intent and predatory, a cat imagining what it might be like to be a mouse.

"Which is a huge cliche itself, by the way. All of these fears, writing because you're angry at your parents—all of that is really played. A real avant-garde artist would break through the cliches by writing better sober. I mean humility is practically a built-in punchline, if you were able to take the punch."

"I thought you were a conservative," Medea hedged. "How are you suddenly on the side of the *avant-garde artist*?"

J. Malachi laughed; he knew this one. "Conservatives and the avant-garde are symbiotic on one another. They always have been. This is like our whole job, what I'm doing with you right now, keeping your side from lapsing into its own sentimental cliches. So often you guys replace old sugary cliches with new saccharine ones."

"I'm not sure what the relevance is of this writers' workshop," Henry said. But then he sighed. "We haven't always understood you, Deedee, I know that. But we've always loved you."

She looked suddenly, acutely nauseated, and as her rehab compatriots reared back in alarm, she choked out the words, "I love you too." She took a deep, shaky breath and spewed again: "I always have. I couldn't find an original way to say it."

"You certainly found an original way to *show* it," Bastian murmured.

"I can't believe it if it isn't original," she said.

"That's an excuse," Bastian argued.

But J. Malachi cut in. "That is so American," he said. Medea looked stung to the quick.

Jen, using her most thoughtful eyebrows, said that Medea was trying to fix her past rather than her present. "You need to take life on life's terms," Jen said.

Medea lunged for the opening. "No I don't, and I won't.

I don't believe in that. That's something oppressors say, just lie back and accept it!, and—and mainstream literary realist novelists. 'I'm just taking *life* on *life's* terms.' That's a hack phrase. My job as a poetess is to imagine new ways of being—to make life take me on *my* terms." (Sharptooth, to her dismay, found herself nodding at this.) "I am not a mainstream lit realism character."

Most of her audience looked bored, baffled, or (in Bastian's case) slightly disgusted by this, but J. Malachi just grinned. "Fine," he said lightly. "So don't have a mainstream lit realism recovery. Have an expressionist recovery. This is a problem with an easy fix."

The others turned their boredom and bafflement and slight disgust on him, but Medea held still and thought about it. She chewed on a knuckle, even though the action made her split lip hurt; she thought it was picturesque. She put one foot up on her seat. She tilted her head. She performed "thinking about it" perfectly, even going so far as to muse out loud, "'An expressionist recovery.' Huh."

Jen, feeling that the session had gotten out from under her, said brightly, "Good job, everyone! Let's break for cookies."

*　　*　　*

From the "Amends" thread at Idiotbox.com:

DutyFree: Family Day, part one. Go!

BessiesGirl: Sometimes I worry that I'm doing something wrong by watching this show. Doesn't anybody care about privacy anymore?

AnitaTucker59: I have a female relative whose son is an alcoholic. We love her dearly and it's always good for us to spend time with her, although it doesn't happen often. But I think it's even better for her to spend time with us, because frankly, I'm certain that she needs role models of appropriate parenting. She behaves very well and is very quiet and calm while in our company. I hate to think of what her life is really like, but I can imagine, having watched many programs of this kind. It's always so hard to watch someone you love reap the consequences of their actions.

DutyFree: @BessiesGirl I care about privacy for normal people, sure.

brunchingehenna: I just don't feel sorry for them, or whatever we're supposed to feel. Which makes the experience a bit unfulfilling. I feel like I'm doing something wrong by being bored.

82Camaro: The whole concept of the show seems gross to me, actually. They say they're sorry, they feed this little coin into the forgiveness vending machine, and get what they want. Meanwhile the people they hurt have to say, "Oh, it's okay! I would've done the same thing in your place! We're all sisters under the track marks!" Sorry, that's just not true. If you're the kind of person who hurts others because you'd rather be drunk or high, just own it! Don't try to have it both ways—don't try to get all the fun of being an alcoholic *and* all the self-respect of being a good person.

I like Medea because at least she knows who she is. She's totally free of bullshit.

CheeseSniffer: I feel bad for the gay hockey one whose boyfriend came to family day. That's one where you wonder why they drink so much and then you realize he has total gay face and it's like, OH. Now I get it. His boyfriend seems nice though.

dollparts: I've been in recovery for twelve years and I can tell you that this show is total BS. The one guy, Jamie, is clearly not an alcoholic at all. Nobody in rehab is going to be showing any kind of sexual interest in the first few days. His whole showmance with the Ethiopian woman is basically "reality television" at its "finest." Sure, sex happens in rehab, but they've set it up like he starts flirting with her in the very first week—when they're all still sick and shaky. Then they have this weird, very conservative kind of Jane Austen "affair" where he kisses her hand? Come on. The idea that these two people would ever get together or even look at each other seems so farfetched to me that it makes every aspect of the show impossible to trust.

DutyFree: I don't have a lot of sympathy for people whose biggest problems are narratology and shit in a ficus.

*   *   *

Bentley was on set, drifting around astringently in the background like the smell of bleach. Today her t-shirt said, I CONQUERED ATHENS ONCE. She bared her teeth whenever anyone looked at her.

She came over to menace Ana a little, and stole a Chips Ahoy. "I fucking love Medea," she said, shoving crumbs in her mouth with the heel of her hand. "Totally unfilmable, this whole part is a train wreck from a commercial standpoint, but she's my favorite."

"She's horrible!"

"I know, isn't that what I just said?"

"Did you understand what she was talking about?"

"Whatever, I understood why she was talking about it, which is more important. I liked her crazy 'I'm gonna make life take me on *my* terms!' shtik, that's classic addict bullshit. Half of these people think they're gonna change the world, right after they finish up this bottle of Popov."

"She's so ungrateful!"

Bentley's face softened, and she stole another cookie. "Yeah, poor kid, that must be so hard for her. ...Anyway I thought you were a codependent, you root for the villains, right? They just need to be loved!"

Ana admitted, "I think maybe I'm just codependent with men."

Bentley sighed. "Yeah, you and literally every other heterosexual woman in the world, ever."

Jen came over to them. "Okay, we're ready for Jaymi's parents and Colton's sister."

Bentley was still mopey. "Boo, boys and their families. I'm going to wander off now."

And she caromed out into the corridor in her unevenly-worn heels, shedding a spray of crumbs.

Chapter 8: The Berenstain Bears Go to Hell

"'I am a *counselor!* On the internet!'" Medea was hovering at the snack table, scooping up handfuls of gorp, picking out the chocolate chips, and dumping the rest back into the bowl. She didn't seem hostile, just amused.

Sharptooth was in no mood for it, though. "I'd rather be a counselor on the internet than a troll in real life," she said crabbily.

"I am trollkin, it's true," Medea replied.

"Stop bogarting the chips, dude," Dylan chided her.

"Give me *one good raisin* to," she said, and giggled.

"Oh my God, I want to die," he said, and swiped ineffectively at her. "Anyway you don't have to take life on life's terms, or whatever that even was, but you do have to take gorp on gorp's terms. That's like the whole point of gorp, you take the good with the bad, the chocolate chip with the yogurt-covered raisin."

Meanwhile Emebet had four cookies on her paper plate. J. Malachi was shadowing her, hoping for a chance to bring her some Gatorade or fruit punch. She considered him.

"I didn't understand that, what happened with Medea," she admitted. "But you were helpful there."

He nodded eagerly. *I helped you, too, didn't I?* he thought. She didn't give him any more praise, but she did carefully take one sugar cookie from her plate and hold it out to him. He cupped his hands and let her drop the cookie into his palms.

"Now you have to be *helped*," she said, with the irony of a comrade in arms.

The PA waved them back to their seats. J. Malachi took the hot seat, feeling like he'd just lost a game of duck duck goose. He felt flop sweat spring out on his forehead.

His parents came into the room together. His mother was tall, in a blue denim dress and clogs, with the tired face of a public defender. His father was shorter and a few years younger, with a narrow face, bushy eyebrows, and keen eyes: a helpful rodent in a Disney film. They were named Mary and John, which explained how Jaymi's sisters got the names Urgency and Armistice. He had been raised on homemade "Mor-eos" made of circles of brown bread filled with apples and peanut butter (later renamed "End War-eos"), and picture books like *Sebastian and the Magic Pamphlet* and *The Mermaid Who Wished for Pants*.

His mother took her seat and waited patiently for the cameras to get ready. Then she hand-cranked a smile onto her face and began, but she couldn't bring herself to specifics: "Well, we wanted to not get too much into your life or be pushy, to let you make your own choices and have a relationship with you that was on that basis. Adults. But I think you know, we're just, I felt that we should, to see if we can make the best of this process. If you're ready."

It was like being scolded by oatmeal.

His father stepped in, mousily direct. "This whole setting of the television show is not ideal from our perspective. But you're not happy. We can see that. And we're not always happy. We're supposed to talk with you about events, things which have gone wrong, and obviously you remember last Thanksgiving. When you came four hours late, with some girl's—some woman's—excuse me, some *person's* underwear in your jacket instead of a pocket square, and you said that the only consistent result of attempts to improve social equality was bad customer service, and then you fell asleep with your hand in the sweet potatoes."

He sighed, and glowered at the cameras. J. Malachi felt deeply ashamed that, as a result of his alcohol issues, his father had submitted to having his bald spot powdered.

"We're very proud of you," his mother attempted.

"God, *why?*" he said, and they frowned as if he'd belched at a solidarity fast.

"Is there some kind of—pain in your life?" his mother asked, "We've always been skeptical of the 'politics of meaning,' but if it helps you—or there's a Unitarian Church just down the street from us—"

"I want to act better, not feel better," he said. Against all his ideology he was trying to conceal nothing for the sake of social conventions. This, he consoled himself, was in fact the social convention of reality television; he was adjusting his manners to the situation. When in Rome, bang your slaves and vomit.

"I do want to stop being awful to people. But I don't believe in feeling good. I have—the Russians used to call it 'civic grief'—I guess you could call it 'survivor's guilt'—"

"What have you survived?" Jen asked gently.

"No, but—*everything!* I mean people in the world have terrible things happen to them. Kids are bullied, people get—I don't know, mugged, their houses are destroyed in tornadoes. I don't even have the moral legitimacy of the survivor because, as you're implying, I haven't survived *anything*. Or you could say I've survived everything."

He glanced involuntarily at Emebet then, and his nose turned redder than his upbringing. "Nobody deserves to live completely unscathed."

"And that's why you drink?" Jen said, switching from encouragement to skepticism.

"Yes! ...Well, partly. I should've known you wouldn't understand the complex mechanisms of cosmic justice. I don't expect understanding."

"Does any kid get not-bullied because you got drunk?" Jen asked.

J. Malachi glared. "I believe punishment is justified even if you know it doesn't have a deterrent effect."

"That's a rationalization—"

"*You're* a rationalization!"

Everybody looked at him.

He sighed and looked away from them. "I have *civic grief*, okay? Just let me have it."

Emebet raised her hand, and Jen called on her. "You want to be Jesus," she said, with intense disapproval. "But you want to do it on your own terms. It is much more fun to get *crucified* on cheap vodka; it doesn't require a real sacrifice. You are hugging yourself and telling yourself this is the same

168

as punishment, and punishment is the same as penance."

"Wait, why isn't punishment the same as penance?" he asked, humiliated and—or therefore—interested. "Is this a language issue? In English—"

"No," she said; and she was surprised, herself, by the complex mechanisms of cosmic justice. "Punishment just makes you feel bad. Feeling bad isn't making any amends to anybody. It isn't connected to anybody else; it stays inside you. It is self-centered, one hundred percent. Even in English."

Her voice gentled a little. "I see it all the time, you know. The people who won't look at me, even when they're giving me money. I'll still take the cash, but I can always tell the difference between somebody who gives me ten dollars because he feels bad about himself and someone who gives me ten dollars because he wants to help *me*. To the first person, I could be a dog."

J. Malachi looked taken aback; she tilted her head and shrugged at him as if to say, *No hard feelings.*

He shook his head and gave a bitter, world-weary smile, like a hippie in the '70s.

"How can you people have such a clear idea of what *I* need to do when you can't run your own lives?" he asked. "This is less like group therapy and more like dramatic irony."

Jen grinned. "If somebody bakes you a delicious muffin, do you complain because they didn't also chew it for you?"

"'Stop whining and be grateful' isn't a delicious muffin," he said, although his resistance lacked conviction. "It's one of those shitty blueberry muffins made of corn subsidies and blue dye. It's a misery muffin."

"It is the only muffin you are going to get," Emebet said

severely—and then, shyly, "Unless I'm not understanding. I don't know why we're talking about... food?"

"No, you're right," he said. And then, because she had been rough with him, "Thank you for helping."

Jen nodded, and turned to his parents. "I think it would be good for both of you to have some clarity on what you can and can't control here. You *can't* chew the muffin for him—"

"This metaphor has passed its sell-by date," J. Malachi said.

"You can give him a chance but you can't take it."

With this advice, their time was up. J. Malachi went toward them and they stared at one another for a while before all of them converged in an extraordinarily awkward hug.

"I'm gonna eat the muffin," he promised, feeling like his life was degenerating into an Aerosmith song.

He looked around the room and saw that everybody else who had already had their turn looked like he felt: uncomfortable, dirtied. They didn't seem like people who had experienced the cleansing power of forgiveness.

His mother sighed. "I hope you eat it. We know that you can throw away this chance. But everything that's thrown away can be recycled. We will compost your muffin," she said bravely, "and it will return to you in a new form, when you're ready for it. Maybe as broccoli."

*   *   *

Colton was up next. He arranged himself in casual angles on his folding chair, practicing a startled, misplaced elegance. He rubbed the place on his wrist where the Bolex had rested. He had to look up in surprise three times before his sister finally blew into the room.

She came in big, inescapable, like an unwanted insight. She strutted right through the circle dressed like drunk texting, in yoga pants with HELLO MY NAME IS on the back of the waistband and BOOTY printed across the ass. Her hair was bouncing and misbehaving. She hit her mark in the center of the circle and stopped, pivoted, and gave the cameras a look with big eyes and parted lips, a look that said, "the night before the morning-after pill."

"Hello, Rian," Colton said. "Nice audition."

She held her body completely still and swiveled her neck so she could look at him. "Nice *chinos.*"

Having won the first round, she retreated to her corner, and settled on her folding chair with her legs spread wide. Colton crossed his.

"Resentments," she said, glaring at him like she was trying to win the Cold War through chess. "I resent that you didn't act like an older brother. You were supposed to protect me. Instead you was suckin' on a bottle like a baby. *I'm* supposed to be the baby of the family! You taught me that men were unreliable—"

"Dad taught you that," Colton said, but Jen waved a teacherly hand at him.

"I had to take care of Mom and I had to take care of myself. And I did it. And I didn't whine or cry or become a alcoholic."

"You were bulimic all through high school."

"I was responsible though! I handled my shit!"

"Yeah, taking laxatives twice a day is definitely one way to achieve *that* goal."

"Sometimes I think you would've been a decent big brother if you'd just stopped making promises. Promise me the rest of your Coca-Cola and then say oh, no, you can't have it, that's just for boys, because you forgot and put Jack Daniels in it. Promise me a birthday cake. Promise me things will get better. You promised to buy me a dress for the prom and I thought right then and there, *I'm gonna end up going naked.* Dressed in nothing but your promises, and a bow on my ass."

"You're seriously still holding a grudge because I didn't get you a prom dress? I didn't get you a horse, either, you want to cry about that?"

"You spent the money for the dress on pot and then you wouldn't even share the pot! I had to go in a dress I borrowed, it had *ruffles around my boobs,*" and her voice rose in unforgotten anguish. "And my date's mom stood out on their porch and wouldn't speak to me, and all she said when he took my arm and put the corsage on was, 'Use protection and use it right.'"

"Wait, I thought you went with Kenny White? His mom liked you!"

Rian laughed like a door slamming shut. "She did like me. She *liked* golden retrievers, but she wouldn't let her son pet one if it hadn't had all its shots."

"I still don't think this is the sinking of the *Titanic* over here."

"He wandered off from me around midnight and I had to go look for him. I found him with some of his friends, sniffing on something which I would bet money *you* sold them, and all of them started pushing up on me and trying to kiss me and saying, 'Who's gonna ride the ruffle bus? We *all* gonna ride the ruffle bus!' I started crying and they were pushing me around and grabbing me, and I called you, and you said you would come pick me up but it sounded like you were already blackout. And you didn't come. And I wouldn't even been wearing those fucking ruffles if you'd just bought me a real dress!"

Her voice cracked a little. "And then I guess they rode the ruffle bus, a few of them." She stared at him, or through him. "'It was sad when the great ship went down.'"

Colton's face was very still, and his voice was thin and tired. "Those guys were and *always* were assholes. You could've been wearing a coat made out of Beyoncé and they still would have fucked you up."

"I thought maybe you would protect me."

"I sold them overpriced shit cut with baby powder, does that count as protecting you?" He shook his head. "Every time I tried to talk to you about those guys you blew me off. You said you could take care of yourself, you'd call me names and even hit me, but I bet you don't remember that."

"What *names* did I call you. Yeah, you tried to give me a whole lot of life advice, in between puking in the sink. And I hit you like once and it doesn't count when girls hit guys."

He whooped. "Oh, suddenly you discover chivalry!"

But he stopped and tried to direct his anger somewhere else—somewhere new, instead of all the old home targets.

"What I'm telling you is that I did try to protect you, more than once. But the only protection you wanted came with ribs for her pleasure. Remember that teacher you slept with freshman year of high school? Yeah, you guys met cute when he told your European History class that the Protestant reformers believed that the Bible should be available to everybody, 'Just like Rian Rodman!' He was more of a trapper than a keeper. If you ask me. But when I said you should have more self-respect, you told me I could go respect myself, you were old enough to perpetuate your own cycle of abuse."

"So what," Rian said. But she was listening.

"So I cornered him while he was buying Capri-Sun *as a fucking mixer* and told him I'd report his ass if he laid a hand on yours. To which he replied that he'd plant drugs on me at school and fuck up my probation. He said, and I quote, 'I will mail your monkey ass to Leavenworth in a little plastic baggie if you fuck with me.'"

Colton allowed himself to pause for breath, and emphasis. "*The Berenstain Bears and the Racist Child Molester.*"

Rian took a shaky breath, and tried to wipe away a tear with the tips of her jeweled nails. "For real?"

"Would I lie to you for no reason?"

"That would be a pretty fucked-up kids' book," she said quietly.

"...Yeah."

"I bet you and me could do a whole series. *Call a Cop on Pop. Little Meth Lab on the Prairie.*"

"That one's for middle-grade readers. You gotta start them out with picture books. 'Would you, could you, in your ass? Would you, could you, for some grass?'"

"*Oh, The Places You'll Puke!*"

"*The Pokey Little Needle.*"

"*The Tale of Peter Touch-It.*"

"Damn, girl. I don't even want to know what you'd come up with for *Pat the Bunny.*" He suggested, with a gentleness that sent his compassion account way into the red, "*Lady and the Boys Who Called Her a Tramp.*"

They were both grinning a little, these unsprung grins, twin used mattresses that yielded too much. Everybody could see the resemblance now, in the big punchable chins and the sky-high, stupidly hopeful cheekbones. Rian shook her head. "We'd tell everybody it was a true life story and nobody would believe us."

"They'd give us the Newbery Award for fiction and tell us to say 'thank you,'" Colton agreed. "'Colton Rodman and his sister Rian have crafted a unique portrayal of a teenage dystopia, a young adult novel that reads more like an adult magazine.'"

"'Rian Rodman and her brother,'" she corrected him. "And who the fuck buys an 'adult magazine' anymore? We are living in the future now!"

He felt like he was seeing her the way somebody else would see her, from a long way off. Just another face at a streaky fifth-floor window, mostly covered by the air conditioner you had to buy yourself; just another trail of smoke. He felt a swollen tenderness like a big purple bruise, the kind of deep and true emotion he usually only felt when he was drinking. When he was drinking he could picture her perfectly, his gone-away sister, and she looked like she did right now.

"You seeing anybody?" he asked.

"Me and this guy, we talkin'."

"You want me to beat him up for you?"

She laughed. "Don't you fuckin' dare. I know you." She sighed. "He's okay. I guess. You gotta start somewhere, right?"

"Entry-level is a philosophy for jobs, not dating," he said. "They are not the same thing."

Colton Rodman had felt since early childhood that he

was living in a constant yesterday: the time you'd look back on, from your unimaginable tomorrowland of mercy and success, and say something like, *Back in the day, right? Before all the real things happened.* Or, *I got where I am today by being smarter and stronger than the rest.* Or, *How the fuck did I survive?* Now, as he and his sister collided in a painful hug, chins jabbing shoulders, he felt like time was finally catching up with him. The long dark yesterday, the bar with no clocks and no windows, was finally sending the bouncers around; it was last call. But he had no idea how he would pay, or where he would go.

"Is Emebet the last one?" he asked, as he settled back down into the circle.

"Emebet's next," Jen said, which wasn't an answer.

In her white scarf and her terror she looked more like Elsa Lanchester than Veronica Lake. She moved to the lonesome folding chair like a wave coursing toward its inevitable crash. She took her seat and stared, bolt upright, waiting for her mystery date.

Chapter 9: The Lizard's Tale

This is the story of how Emebet Gebremichael became internet famous: A dapper motherfucker of a man sidled into the room, a long tall pour with the harsh corners of bottom-shelf vodka. He had too much smile on his face, and when he walked past he made Dylan's heart skip a beat. Dylan wondered for an instant if he might actually be gay after all, before realizing that it was the guy's smell: spilled drinks and stale cigarettes.

He settled down in his folding chair, pinched the creases of his slacks, and introduced himself. "My name is Evelio Platero, but I know you don't remember me. I tend bar at the Lizard's Tail on U Street."

The whole roomful of alcoholics was sharpening their attention on him. They were rapidly developing a complex and melodramatic relationship with him, based solely on job title and smell. Colton, noticing how intensely he suddenly disliked this guy despite also wanting to suck his dick, wondered if the dislike was a sign that he was developing a healthier sense of self. J. Malachi wondered why he was suddenly feeling all Klingon in a roomful of Tribbles.

Evelio Platero then told the story of Emebet's big night out. She had come to the bar already drunk, but the men were buying her drinks anyway; he figured she wanted bad company. She started to stab her wrist with the toothpick handle of her little cocktail umbrella. When she jabbed hard enough to draw blood, one of the men called Evelio over, and Emebet explained that she was trying to give herself tetanus. He took her umbrella away.

Then there were more drinks and she was stealing sugar from other people's tables, tearing the packets open and rubbing them on her teeth. "I asked her the rationale for that and she said that she thought she might have an abscess in one of her back teeth and she wanted to make it worse. She said you could die from it; apparently she believed that the teeth were connected to the brain."

He barely moved his lips when he spoke, just this slight curl of the lip to show a fang. "I said, 'Lady, I don't care if you want to commit suicide by tooth*pick* or tooth*ache* or tooth*brush*. Hell, I don't care if you floss yourself to death! But don't do it in my bar.' So I went to get the bouncers. Next thing I knew she was over by the window pretending to be a television set. Holding her hands up next to her face like a box and telling the other drunks, 'If that bartender comes over tell him I'm a television.'"

"Creative," Medea murmured. "Very postmodern."

"How did you need bouncers for her, bouncers plural?" J. Malachi wondered, softly enough that Jen only waved a hand to shush him. "A teddy bear could bounce her, a giant foam finger could bounce her. *I* could bounce her."

Emebet was very still. *I'm on television for real now*, she thought. *Maybe*, with a thin self-lacerating smile, *maybe I am a prophet.*

The barman didn't seem to like the interruptions. He felt the story starting to topple away from him, and he grabbed at it: "She disappeared then, and I thought somebody had taken care of her. Or she was a ghost or a vampire and she'd turned into mist and just misted her ass away. But then this lady came up to me yelling about a crazy person in the bathroom, and sure enough when I got in there she was shrieking at the mirror like some kind of Japanese ghost story. She tried to break the mirror with her face and then she tried to jam her head up the paper-towel dispenser. We got her out of there before she tried suicide by tampon, and one of the bouncers tased her and dumped her out in the street."

He chuckled and shook his head. "You ever seen somebody get tased? Their faces get all scrunched up like little rat faces, and they go *brrrr*—" he shivered in a way that probably got him laughs most of the time— "like they got cockroaches crawling all over them. Wigglin' and wrigglin' and jigglin' like Jell-O."

He looked around the room like he owned it and saw that although the talent were mostly scowling, the camera crew were giggling a little and zooming in on his face. He figured they at least were listening.

"Didn't see her again until we were closing up. I was checking the bathrooms. I always do the ladies' first because let's face it, you *need* a couple after-work drinks in you before you can face a men's bathroom. Men are pigs."

And now he's stereotyping pigs, Sharptooth thought.

Medea mused, *This guy is such a hole-punched condom of a person.*

And then Evelio described finding Emebet in the men's room, curled up like a kind of urinal cozy, hugging its curving base. He pulled on his gloves and tried to wake her up, but she wouldn't go anywhere. She went limp and started to vomit on his shoes. So he let her go, poured ice into the urinal, and let her sleep it off underneath the makeshift waterfall. This was how she had awoken, around five a.m., when she'd stumbled out and went away.

"And she didn't even say goodbye to me," he said, spreading his hands in mock hurt. "No manners, people these days."

There was a long silence, and then Jen said, like a parent coaxing a child, "Emebet, do you have anything you'd like to say to Evelio?"

J. Malachi stirred in his seat. He felt itchy all along his arms, and he was pretty sure his face and neck were red.

Emebet looked at the camera behind Evelio's right shoulder and said, in a remote voice, "Thank you for trying to help me. I'm very sorry to have inconvenienced you."

"Seriously?" J. Malachi burst out. "He left a helpless drunk girl lying under a urinal! Anything could have happened to her! Do you tell this story often, sir? Does nobody ever notice that you're the villain?" (This "sir" was trying too hard, sitting on his words like an indignant little fedora, but he couldn't help it.) "How is she apologizing to *him*?"

"Whose fault is this story?" Evelio asked.

"Whose fault is the *story*? The story is your fault! You're the one telling it!"

"No," Emebet said. "I have to take responsibility. That's

why we're here. To take responsibility and gain—and gain humility."

"And what does he gain?" J. Malachi said. "He's doing you the immense favor of helping you gain humility. Are you helping *him* gain humility?"

"What do you think would be most helpful for Emebet at this moment?" Jen asked him.

That gave him pause. But he snapped, "I think it would help her to know that not everybody thinks this story is funny. Or fair."

Emebet laughed, then. She asked him, "Do you often hear stories that are fair?" Suddenly the misery and humiliation which she had been struggling to accept seemed to transform into something lighter. "You have high expectations of the world and very low expectations of me, I think," she teased. He shook his head, uncertain.

Emebet turned back to the bartender and said, in a much warmer and more lived-in voice, a scuffed and gentled voice, "I am really sorry, sir." (The little "sir" sat more comfortably when she said it.) "I made your job more difficult and I could easily have hurt you or caused a legal trouble. It is something I'm here to try to fix."

And Evelio felt the weird sense that the floor had tilted under him, or he was in some kind of Alice in Wonderland situation, as if he were getting smaller and she were getting bigger. All of a sudden he wanted a drink more than he ever had in his life.

Sharptooth and J. Malachi each took one of Emebet's hands, Sharptooth easily and J. Malachi awkwardly. She squeezed both hands.

"We can't enable or make excuses for one another," Jen said, trying to slap a lesson on the top of this moment, but everyone just nodded and smiled at her and paid her no mind.

*   *   *

Nobody had much to say after that. Evelio wandered out of the room once the cameras were off. He had lost the slinkiness he came in with, and the others found themselves watching Emebet more than him, making sure she was okay. She felt strangely satisfied, as if she had ruined the punchline of a joke at her expense.

This turned out to be a false impression. Although she didn't know it at the time, viewers wouldn't have the same perspective she had. And so when the show aired many months later Emebet went viral.

She became famous as "Urinal Girl" or "Urinal Hair Woman." Her face was photoshopped—the bright, eager smile she'd worn during her eskista at the talent show, with her curls haloing out around her—first into pictures of urinals, then into pictures of any kind of embarrassing or disgusting situation. She popped up in the litterbox of a hairless cat who had also become internet famous, covering the crotches of celebrities who got out of limos in insufficient underwear, in beer ads to imply that the beer tasted like piss. A satirical artist used her as the model for a Urinal Hair Magic Barbie; people coaxed their friends to go to bed by saying, "Dude, you are one jello shot away from Urinal Girl." "Don't go home with her, bro, I get a real Urinal Girl vibe off of her. She is a rickety bridge over a river made of snakes." "Ah fuck it, I got Urinal Girl wasted last night. I was wigglin' and wrigglin' and jigglin.'"

Emebet's feral internet image was the breakout hit of "Amends." Nobody else captured the public's attention. Bentley would bring up "Urinal Girl" again and again as she fought to get the show renewed for a second season.

But nobody knew about that, in the moments of exultant solidarity after Evelio left. The talent stretched, inspected their nails, fluffed up their hair, and made other elaborate shows of unconcern.

Colton broke the companionable silence: "'Family Day,' huh. What crack-ass dictionary did you look up 'family' in, show people? When y'all say 'family' do you just mean, 'anybody you hurt, disappointed, or mildly inconvenienced'?"

"That's definitely what *I* mean when I say 'family,'" Dylan said.

"Child, the whole human race is not your family," Colton said easily. "So that's it, right? Can we go? Do we have to do some kind of confessional, or bonding activity, like Telephone where we sit in a circle and whisper our darkest misdeeds to one another, and pass it along until it comes back saying that we raw dogged a chicken in a churchyard?"

"Telephone to Hell, that would be great," Medea said. "I want to do that one."

"There's one more," Jen said; and the whole room tensed back up.

"Who's got to hold the hot potato?" Colton asked. He had a bad feeling about this—a childhood Christmas-morning feeling, where one foot wrong would cause disaster.

"You," Jen said simply. She gestured toward the empty chair, still pulled forward and away from the rest of the circle.

Jen could sense the bruisy tension in the room. She felt a cool, sweet sadness for them all—she thought, *I've been where you are*, a sentence which is never really true. She pulled away the chair the friends and relatives had used, since they wouldn't be needing it.

From outside the open door they heard a dull whirr, and a wave of artificial floral perfume rolled into the room. It was followed by a white woman in a mechanized wheelchair. She was missing a leg. She took her place across from Colton, and her air of regal distress dissolved into confusion. She peered at him through big old-fashioned glasses, with lenses shaped like the bottom leaves of a four-leaf clover.

"Are you the one? I thought you were Irish," she said querulously.

The penny dropped, and Colton groaned inwardly. In a boneyard voice, he said, "Top o' the mornin' to ye."

The woman frowned. "My name is Barbara Gleat," she said, in a shaky voice—a *too* shaky voice, a voice with too much sense of its own undeserved unhappiness, a little blind white kitten of a voice. It was a voice bad people wanted to kick, and Barbara Gleat knew it.

The spindly voice strengthened as she told her tale of woe. It began when she was living in Missouri, with a roommate who ate Barbara's peanut butter from the jar with her fingers. (People were always doing things like this to Barbara Gleat.) This roommate had been responsible for paying the utility bills, but when she proved unreliable, Barbara had done the right thing and taken over.

She eventually met her husband, married, and moved to North Carolina. More than ten years later she began to receive letters and then phone calls from a company whose name she didn't recognize. She believed that she was being stalked, and reported this to the police, who were not interested. Eventually it became clear that her Missouri utilities company had given the company for which Colton was working the task of collecting an unpaid bill from the Clinton administration.

Colton, pretending to be an Irishman, had persuaded her against her better judgment to accept a payment plan which allowed the collection agency to take her car if she didn't make her payments on time. She lost, in succession, the car, her job (to which she could no longer arrive reliably on time), her health insurance, her leg, and her husband.

"I could not get treatment until my condition had become too dangerous. I was diagnosed," she said, as if reading off her imperial titles, "with Type 2 diabetes, arthritis, a storage pool disorder—which is a blood disorder, and chronic flatulence. And that's because of you. I let you take my car. I didn't know that you would take my life."

Colton kept his jaw clenched and waited for her to finish.

"I'm a taxpayer. I'm a good person," she whimpered. "And my life was ruined because of some *drunk*."

"Well, that's what we're here to address," Jen said smoothly. "Colton, do you have anything to say, as part of a mutual healing process?"

"Really? I was doing my job! So I could pay *my* bills. You gonna bring in a bedbug next, and have it tell me how I murdered its whole family?"

Most of the room cringed at this. Barbara seemed to swell with rage.

"I was doing my job."

"You were just following orders?" Barbara snapped. "Like Hitler?"

"Lady, Hitler didn't make you sick or take off your leg or pay your bills late, and neither did I. Are you seriously expecting me to make amends to this woman because she has chronic flatulence? Ma'am, this is America! Your farts are your fault!"

"Would anyone else like to contribute?" Jen asked.

"I actually agree that this isn't his responsibility," Sharptooth said. "It's the system's fault, not his. He doesn't need to be ashamed of the choices he made to survive under capitalism."

Medea nodded reluctantly. Colton felt insufficiently reassured.

Dylan chipped in. "I mean, okay, like, it's the system, fine," he said, waving a hand in the air. "But is this how you want to be? Is this how you want to handle things?"

"Oh God," Colton said, "this is what happens when we teach rich people to walk upright and use tools. Settle down, son, you can talk to me when you've had to work for a living."

Dylan reddened and made a "shutting up now" gesture over his mouth. He squirmed in his chair and wouldn't look at anyone. Colton could feel the room withdrawing from him, like lips pulling away from bared teeth.

"Wow," Medea said slowly. "I always side with the unsympathetic characters, but... wow."

Colton was overwhelmed with a desire to get this over with. He knew they wouldn't let him out of his chair until he apologized. He had no idea how he could "make amends" to this woman. She seemed proud to be affronted; from his perspective it looked like she had already gotten everything she wanted from this encounter. But she wasn't going away, so he would have to grovel.

"Ma'am, I am sorry that I hurt you," he said, hoping that each slender word stuck under her fingernails the way it did his. "It was a time in my life when I was really messed up. I'm here to clean up my mess."

"I hope you mean that," Barbara said.

"I am really sorry."

Her desire to be magnanimous on television warred with her desire to be the sorriest person in the room. At last she said, "Well, I hope you're sorry. I know that God has given me this chance to show you true Christian forgiveness. And I will pray that your children do not take after you." She glared around at all of them and then let Jen guide her out.

The air of relief and unexpected self-confidence which had blown through the room after Emebet's bartender left had dissipated. The talent felt grimy and displeased with themselves, small disappointments which added up to a desire to drink or to die, to *get away*. Jen felt that she had failed on some level also; she could feel tears coming, and she resented the talent for it. These twin ghosts of failure and resentment had haunted her through her whole career, and yet she was always surprised to see their long, weary faces again.

The talent went back to their rooms glumly and the first ones in, J. Malachi and Medea, instantly occupied the showers.

This left Colton and Dylan sitting alone on their beds, not looking at anything. Finally Dylan said, "Fuck it," kicked his shoes off, and got under the covers. He pulled them over his head.

"Hey," Colton said, after a long pause.

"I'm sleeping, dude." But Dylan sat up and looked at him warily. They could hear both showers going at once, in a dull arrhythmic spatter—the showers were completely depressing, lacking in water pressure, so that even if you really tried to clean yourself you'd still end up coated with a thin slick of soap scum. Medea called them the metaphor showers.

"I'm sorry about what I said to you," Colton said heavily.

Dylan looked at him, obviously trying to figure out if he meant it. Colton felt immensely tired of everyone using a Breathalyzer on his words.

But Dylan decided to trust him, and in fact his face got cartoonishly pleased. The dimple popped out like a meerkat sticking its head up to check for predators.

"Thanks, dude. Seriously, I appreciate it. Anyway I should be apologizing to you—you were right, I need to, like, keep my eyes on my own paper, and not think I can run your life any better than I can run my own."

"You probably could," Colton conceded. "Anyway, I'm sorry I was a dick."

"We're all dicks here." Dylan leaned back against the headboard of the bed and flopped his arms around goofily, trying to get comfortable. "No joke, it means a lot to me that you'd apologize. Even though you don't really have to. I mean I feel like I always have to be the one apologizing, and nobody ever apologizes to me because I'm always the one fucking up. It's fair, you know? But it feels so shitty. You feel like you always owe everybody a lot of money. So it really does mean a lot to me that you, I don't know, felt like you had to say that to me. I'm super grateful."

"Maybe too grateful. I know everybody is here because we've messed up our lives. But they push us to grovel, and I don't think it's necessary or right. Not that I was in the right today, *obviously*," Colton said with effort, "but you don't have to say, 'Thank you,' every time somebody decides not to kick you."

"No, I think actually here we're supposed to say 'Thank you' when they *do* kick us!"

Dylan was still grinning, though, and seemed to feel like things were easy now between them. Colton felt weirdly protective of him. He had that Rian look, the too-young look of a kid who wanted to forgive you, who felt guilty when you hurt them.

"That's what I hate about this twelve-step bullshit," Colton said. "They kick you across the street and say they were just helping you to fly. Free rehab, but you best believe you'll be paying them back in *gratitude*."

"How else are we gonna learn to walk upright and use tools?" Dylan asked, teasing. "Gotta crawl first."

"Only because they want to see us crawl. They fuck with us, and then blame us for being fucked up."

"'They.'"

When Colton looked away and didn't answer, Dylan added softly, "I'm just sayin', man." And then, "For what it's worth, you're hilariously good-looking but I have no personal interest in seeing you on your hands and knees."

"I am startlingly handsome. That at least is fair."

"The glory of your face is totally unfair. I'm thinking about filing a formal complaint. Although I think I contracted away my right to complain about being compared to the summit of sheer masculine beauty—I think I had to sign a thing, right under the part where you say it's okay if they waterboard you."

"Excuse you, I believe you'll find it's called water *therapy*."

J. Malachi came back into the room in time to hear this.

"Waterbilitation," Dylan said.

"Are we discussing the showers again? I have a theory about them," J. Malachi said.

Colton grinned. "No doubt you do, my friend. No doubt you do."

"You ever hear the thing about how turkeys won't come in from the rain, they'll just stand out there in the field staring up at the sky, trying to figure out why they're wet? And in fact drown themselves in the rain, by looking up?"

Nobody responded, so he shrugged. "We've gotten away from our agrarian roots, as a society. It's this kind of folk wisdom that used to protect us from our own self-will. Anyway, my point is that I get the impression that the people running this place believe that we are exactly as dumb as turkeys, which: possibly they have a point. So they made the showers so weak that we could not possibly turkeycide ourselves. Hence also the skid daisies."

Colton gave a cheerless jack-o'-lantern smile. "They don't want us to—*break our contracts*."

"I'm gonna go out and ostensibly wander around, but actually look for Emebet," J. Malachi said, with an off-center little grin. "Yes?"

"Go get 'em, cowboy," Colton said. "Hey, tell her she did good today. She made us proud—not that that's something to be proud of."

He waved Dylan toward the bathroom, but Dylan after-you'd him; so he didn't even get the drizzly, lukewarm penance of the last shower.

He peeled off the body mike and dropped it unceremoniously on the floor. He wanted to give it a good kick. There was so much the cameras couldn't capture: the dull hum of the fluorescent lights in the hallways. The way the cereal bowls were weirdly heavy, so you had to use more effort than you expected just to get your breakfast. The way the humidity from the shower suffused the bedroom with a fog of guilt and grief.

He shook his head. *You're letting them get to you*, he thought. *Stay strong, keep your head down and get through this. Someday this will be the kind of story you tell when you want to scare the good guys away and reel in the suckers. YOLO, thank fucking God.*

Something seemed off. He went through a mental checklist: He'd taken off the mic, he had the soap right there in his hand, his towel was hanging over the door to the stall. He was defensively soaping his back when he realized that he didn't have his shower beer.

He refused to accept that this meant Jen and her minions had a point about him.

I know I'm wrong, he thought, *but that doesn't make them right. Everything happens for a reason, and sometimes the reason is that other people suck.*

In his case there was a more immediate reason—at least for the reappearance of Barbara Gleat in his life. At some point during the pre-show negotiations his former employers had realized that "Amends" might not portray them in the most flattering light. They agreed to continue working with the program, and even to feed it the appetizing morsel of Barbara Gleat and her story, on the condition that their name, logo, or other identifying information was never used on the show or in any materials relating to the show.

The Lizard's Tail had asked for the same deal, and in fact when that segment aired Evelio Platero's mouth was blurred when he named his place of business as if he'd started cussing, but enterprising internet detectives figured out which bar he worked at and its business received a slight but noticeable boost: Urinal Girl slept here. The sleuths didn't bother to try the same techniques on Colton's employers.

The show hadn't initially planned to confront Colton with one of his "clients"; but decadent late capitalism called to decadent late capitalism, like autotuned mermaids lip-synching each to each.

Chapter 10: Retail Therapy

On the morning after Family Day, Medea resolved to do a good deed. She went and found Emebet, who was haunting the courtyard as usual.

Medea sat down on a stone bench and patted it. "Hey," she said. "I want to have a word."

Emebet, apprehensive, sidled over to her and settled down. Medea leaned forward and she leaned back.

"I want to talk to you about your 'boyfriend,'" Medea said, making quote marks with her fingers.

"Yes," Emebet said, a bit defensively. "What is it?"

Medea shook her head and gave the other woman a look of pure bafflement. "Do you *like* him?" she asked. "I mean, first of all, he is a wordy piece of work. Words words words. A glazed Hamlet," and she giggled.

"This is his job!"

"It's the most boring thing a man can do with his mouth. In his case, maybe the second-most boring."

"It's your job too."

"Let me ask you: when you look at him. Do you wanna *do*

it with him?"

Emebet opened her mouth to answer, when Medea clarified: "I mean sex."

"Oh. Okay. I thought you meant talking."

"No. Now come on, do you want it? You can't, it's not possible. It's dystopian. I mean, look at you," sweeping her hand to indicate Emebet's narrow person, "you're more or less a good-looking woman. Not a ten, but maybe like an eight for people who go for small tits. Some prefer a woman with smaller blossoms. You're seriously gonna give it up for somebody who looks like Colonel Sanders and the Pillsbury Dough Boy had a baby?"

"I don't know what that is," Emebet said, in a slightly chilly voice.

"What I mean is, he looks like a marshmallow! Do you plan to get personal with that?"

"Oh," Emebet said, nodding. "I see what you mean. Yes, he is pillowy." She sounded quite content.

"'Pillowy.' Pillowy! When I was a little girl we used to *practice* kissing on a pillow, but I would not fuck one. How can you affix yourself to a man who looks like a home furnishing?"

Medea shook her head. "This thing is fine for rehab, I mean, you need something to keep you going, I get it. But he'll think that you're for real."

"I am real. It is real."

In tones oddly similar to the ones with which J. Malachi himself had asked his parents why they were proud of him, Medea cried despairingly, "But *why?*"

Emebet shrugged. "I never laughed at a man before. I like

it. He listens to me. He makes me feel safe—not safe from other people," she said, conceding the obvious, "but safe from him."

Medea shook her head. "That is a low bar."

"This is the kind of bar I like."

Emebet didn't want to talk about the rest of it: their shared sweet tooth for nostalgia and self-blame. The way he gave her advice but then apologized when she explained why she couldn't take it, instead of blaming her for being unhelped. The way he remembered things she'd said and brought them up later, to offer her a present of her own opinions. The way he looked when she laughed at something he had said. The way he asked her about her recovery and, by asking, made life a little more interesting to her than death. She didn't want to talk about any of that on camera.

And, thwarted in her best intentions, Medea had to let it go. "Leave her to Heaven," she muttered as she retreated back inside, still shaking her head, heavy with advice like an unmilked cow. "There's a delusional lid for every moon-mad pot. But... for *real?*"

*   *   *

Jen opened the group session that afternoon by saying she had a thought experiment for them. The veterans of Family Day glared at her. They felt sufficiently experimented-upon already. But she grinned and said, "Let's say that a terrible disaster happens, and a plane crashes on the border between the US and Canada. Where do they bury the survivors?"

They considered this, sucking at cups of gritty decaf. "Where they came from," Emebet offered.

"Yeah, wouldn't they send the bodies home?" J. Malachi said.

"What if they don't know where the survivors come from, where do they bury them then?" Jen asked, and nobody could figure it out. After their long and mistrustful silence, she said, "This is what you guys aren't hearing: Where did they bury the *survivors?* You don't bury survivors. They survived!"

Dylan laughed. "Oh shit, it's one of those things they did with us in third grade! Why doesn't the bus driver stop at red lights and stop signs? *Because he's walking.* I literally never once got one of those right."

"Tunnel vision," Jen said. "We're so concerned with sorting through where we come from that we don't even notice that we survived. We don't have to be buried in a bottle or a baggie. We can walk away. But we'll only see it if we can think differently about ourselves."

"Where did they bury the survivors?" Medea said. "That's a terrifically creepy question. Premature burial. The survivors breaking their fingernails against the coffin lid."

"That's how you guys have been living. So think about that, while I explain your amends opportunity for today."

The very slight relaxation in the room immediately returned to DefCon Three. The talent glowered at Jen.

She didn't seem to notice. "The hardest thing for an addict to deal with is personal trauma like a death in the family or a car crash. The second-hardest thing is an ordinary Wednesday. So today we're going to exercise our patience muscles. We're going to learn to handle a basic working day, including relating to other people and putting others' needs before our own."

"By 'we' you don't mean you," Medea muttered.

"We'll be going to a local supermarket, where you'll all

have opportunities to work the register, clean up, and deal with customer complaints. It's a different kind of retail therapy!"

This announcement was greeted with mixed reactions. Medea, as the child of leftists and a denizen of the theater world, believed that The Workers were plucky, wise, and prone to fits of song. She looked forward to joining their ranks, and hoped that she would get one of those uniforms that didn't button quite right, so you could see her bra. She'd always appreciated those uniforms when she was on the grabby side of the counter.

Dylan had the adventuresome and willing look of someone who had never had a job that wasn't paid for in sips from his mother's glass. ("If it's your father, tell him I'm not here.") Sharptooth and J. Malachi were registering various levels of social anxiety and determination.

Emebet was skeptical, but resigned. She'd done a few required programs like this, usually as a condition of probation. These programs had names made out of big foam bricks: career rehabilitation, skills assessment, work awareness enhancement, and now retail therapy. The names were meant to disguise the fact that as far as the outside world was concerned, a job training program was the opposite of a job.

And Colton looked like if his skin got any tighter, he'd split. He didn't say anything as they picked up their vests and name tags (Medea was disappointed) and piled into the bus that would take them to the store. His face looked calm until you noticed that his expression didn't move at all; it was a placid rictus.

"We should really sing when we're in this thing," Medea said, not for the first time. Last time she'd persuaded them to sing "On Top of Spaghetti," which only reminded them of their own terrible cooking, and then "There Was an Old Woman Who Swallowed a Fly," which they all felt hit a little too close to home. This time she taught them a song about a yodeling ostrich. Dylan and J. Malachi joined in first, followed by Emebet's slender, tarnished contralto. Then they got to a verse about a St. Bernard and dissolved into morbid musing on its barrel of rum.

"Hey," Dylan said softly, poking Colton on the arm. Colton jumped about a foot in the air, and glared at him. "Sorry! Sorry, guy, I was just—this could be fun, you know? It isn't real work. I mean they can't fire us, I don't think."

"What is the worst you have ever been injured in the workplace?"

"Whoa, okay," Dylan said. "Uh, I've actually never had a job? Which probably shows. But... does hockey count? I mean I've had most of my face broken up pretty good at one point or another."

"I'm gonna go ahead and say that sports don't count."

"Okay, fair enough. What about you?"

"I worked Walmart on Black Friday three years in a row. The first year I got pissed on. By a small child, but still. The second year a man dislocated my shoulder while I was trying to carry a home entertainment system to another customer. The third year a woman broke my nose in front of her kids because I told her we were out of PlayStations."

"You broke your nose? Hey, me too, we're like Eskimo brothers."

"Actually *somebody else* broke my nose, let's attribute responsibility where it belongs. That is, after all, supposedly what we're here to do."

"I'm just saying that wow, it healed up well. I would never have guessed."

"We've established that I'm an Adonis. That's not the point."

"You are kind of magical. But—right, more to the point, that stuff isn't going to happen today. They'll protect us."

"Oh?" A lifetime of hard-earned and well-resented knowledge uncurled in that syllable, two letters carrying the sound of pool cues being set down on tables and chairs being kicked back. "All three years I had to stay at the store through closing. I was *allowed* to go to the bathroom and wash my pants with hand soap, or hold my head back until the bleeding stopped, and then I had another six hours of work with whatever disgusting smell or injury I'd received from our valued customers. Oh, and because it was after Thanksgiving, keep in mind that this whole time they are playing Christmas music."

"That's awful," Dylan said; and then, unable to help himself, he added, "You shouldn't hold your head back when you have a nosebleed. You end up swallowing blood, it's really bad for you. You need to hold your head forward and pinch your nostrils shut."

"Well, actually I just poured vodka over it and hoped for the best, but thanks for the advice."

"Hey, but if you get injured on the job today I bet they'll give you painkillers. Maybe even the good drugs. Look on the bright side."

"Have you never watched a Lifetime movie? They don't let addicts have painkillers. We might not use them for their intended purpose of separating the deserving from the undeserving."

Dylan bit his lip. "Okay. Look—how about this. I don't know if they'll let us do this, but I'm a hockey player, basically what they call a goon, you've probably seen it on TV. I pretty much occasionally get into fights for a living. Or not a living, I'm in high school, but you know what I mean. So I'm not that afraid of physical stuff." This wasn't strictly true, but it was true enough for his purposes. "So I'll keep an eye on you, and come over if you have a customer who's getting in your face. And if you start feeling crazy or overwhelmed you can call me and I'll sub in for you. Okay?"

"And then you'll earn your Boy Scout badge?" Colton's speech was pressured, melodramatic and unnatural. He didn't like how he was acting, but he also *definitely* didn't like this conversation. "Is this the thirteenth step, helping the poors?"

"The thirteenth step is sleeping with people in your group, everybody knows that," Dylan said, nettled. "Whatever," he said, turning away from Colton. "I'm still going to look out for you. Call me if you need me. Fuck you, though, for real."

*   *   *

In the end they all did badly. Emebet was probably the best. She had worked retail twice before, at a convenience store and a Hallmark outlet, and she was good at impersonating a blank greeting card. She genuinely did not care at all about the customers or what they thought of her, and so she was able to project, without trying, an air of competence. She didn't seem anxious or strained, because she was convinced that the retail-therapy exercise was pointless; she was looking forward to arguing with J. Malachi about it. Customers responded to this fatalism as if it were leadership quality. She had the serene nihilism of a fluorescent lighting fixture.

J. Malachi did his best to make the cash register into a game: something like Memory or Operation, which rewarded mindless concentration. He only remembered after several excruciating hours of apologizing, in increasingly abject terms, that he had always been terrible at those games.

Sharptooth was trying on her Clark Kent disguise of basic human normalcy, but it was working depressingly well. Nobody treated her like a freak or a puzzle. She felt painfully unoppressed. She wondered if she could let out just one low growl to salve her conscience, which felt that passing was a betrayal of her 'kin. Glumly, she rang up a kumquat.

Dylan was doing pretty well until a junior hockey aficionado recognized him. When the customer asked why an up-and-coming hockey champion was ringing up groceries in Pennsylvania in front of TV cameras, he said flatly, "It's a condition of my parole."

The manager attempted tact, though he was starting to feel brittle. Talking about parole did not increase consumer confidence.

Medea was probably the worst at it. At first she laughed and said that she was terrible on the register because she couldn't do math and paid no attention to detail: "It's a political statement, I'm challenging Asian stereotypes." But after the first fifteen customers she was hunched over and snappish. She knew she was supposed to laughingly accept her incompetence and she couldn't, which only made her more angry and ashamed. It was like the time she'd tried to go bowling.

She hated trying to do things and failing; she thought of this as one of her unique characteristics. Ordinarily she just wouldn't try—in middle school she had strolled through Presidential Fitness Testing reading a library copy of Keats's *Endymion*—but here she had to keep at it. She suspected that she would only be released to go mop a floor once she'd proven that she was making an effort. So she began to slap the machine and punch her fingers into the keys like they were eyes. The others began to hear a string of muttered curses from her lane.

"Crap*shit*! You sullen, blistering fuck, can you not do one fucking thing right? You stripy asshole. I hope you have a deeply damaging inner monologue and I hope it sounds just like this. You worthless fucksack. I hope you hear my voice when you're trying to fall asleep."

"Medea. This is not appropriate language for the workplace."

"Sorry. Sorry. *Buggery!*"

Colton smiled at his customers and imagined wearing their skins as a suit. They walked away feeling as if they had received excellent and yet profoundly unsettling customer service.

He still felt like if anyone made any sudden moves he'd probably scream. He could feel the key winding at his back and he wondered what huge grinning nightmare clown would pop out of his jack-in-the-box. He felt full of surprises.

From Medea's lane: "You curdled cursive shit. What the fuck were you recycled from, a Go-Bot?"

"*Medea.*"

"Sorry, I know I'm not supposed to insult the recycling program."

And over the sound system: *That's the Jingle Bell—that's the Jingle Bell—that's the Jingle Bell Rock!*

Colton shivered.

The day wore on. Brisket, borage, sumac, miniature maple bacon cupcakes, a Buddha hand lemon—Dylan waved it at a child, who started crying—Peruvian purple potatoes, purple cauliflower, purple onion, ras al hanout, rabbit loin, chicken-flavored donuts, emu egg. Beers called Vicious Bitch, Mud Flaps, Deer Tick ("just a hint of lime"), and Honeybuzzard. All of them cost more for a sixer than Colton would have paid for a handle of vodka. He felt smug about his cost-efficiency, until he realized that drinking bottom-shelf liquor wasn't actually on the same level as clipping coupons. Apparently there was a whole genre of people who bought bottles you didn't find on the ground outside of bus shelters on your way to work in the morning.

Medea was making a conscious effort to rein herself in, since there were children present. She believed that adults should never take away a child's innocence—that was a job for the children to do themselves. So she began replacing her cursing with whatever came to mind.

"Bumblebee," she hissed, ripping a receipt out of the printer and starting over. "Clusterfeather. Mustache Fist, the brotherpuncher." And then, in an especially loud and aggrieved voice (compensating in volume for the loss of her freedom), "*Jemima Puddleduck!*"

Two registers away, Sharptooth yipped. A small child

caught sight of Colton's face and began to shriek. He smiled murderously as he helped her mother load the groceries into her cart.

Sharptooth was working the express lane when she got a customer who was trying to check out an entire cart of groceries. She tried making a small "ahem" noise and pointing to the sign, but the woman didn't seem to notice or care. She said gently, "Excuse me, ma'am, this is the express lane. The regular checkouts are... all the other ones."

"Oh," the woman said. "I know, but I'm in a hurry."

"I can't check you out here."

"Why not?"

"...Because this is the express lane? And you have a lot more than ten items? There are people waiting behind you."

The manager came over.

The woman was into it now: "Are you giving me an attitude?"

The other customers had reconstituted themselves into an audience. They thought that they were angry, but they were going to savor this feeling for the rest of the day: the acrid glee of being in the right.

The manager told Sharptooth to check the woman out. She was stung by his scolding tone, and also confused. "But it's an express lane!"

"She's the customer. You're here to provide customer service. So serve the customer!" He shook his head. He'd thought all Americans knew that the customer was always right. Wasn't it printed on their money or something?

"That's right," the woman said. The audience behind her murmured darkly.

"But what about humility and self-responsibility? I have taken a fearless and searching inventory of her groceries and *she has too many items*."

"You are wasting time! Finish up with her and serve these other customers."

Sharptooth glowered, but she reluctantly began to scan the woman's cabbages. They bounced into the grocery bags like the heads of French aristocrats.

"So she gets away with it," Sharptooth groused.

"This is a grocery store! It is not *Law and Order: Produce Section*." The manager could feel a headache burrowing just above his left eye. "You are a cashier. You give parking validation. It isn't a judgment on a person's character."

"So you admit that she has character defects."

"You have customer-service defects! This is a much bigger problem since it is your job."

Over the sound system a grunged-up pop band slurred, *Fa la la la la, la la la la.*

The "Amends" cast were trying harder than the viewing public might realize. Dylan had given himself a stern, disappointed-coach lecture, and was now being relentlessly humble. He smiled and apologized and at the slightest opportunity he told the customers that he was being filmed as part of a televised alcohol rehabilitation program.

The manager, who did not feel that TV rehab was much better than parole, began to curse upper management under his breath. He took Dylan off the register and sent him to clean the bathrooms, which he accepted cheerfully as the reward due for his hard work.

As Dylan pushed the mop cart toward the men's room

he heard Medea's anguished howl: "Baldhockey! You workfare, slithy piece of tove, why won't you function? Take responsibility for your actions!"

He raised his eyebrows as he opened the men's room door. "Wow, this place smells like my *soul*," he muttered.

And from Medea: "*Robert the Bruce!*"

He heard something at her station break.

*   *   *

The exhausted talent climbed back onto the bus. "I feel like my mind is made of feet," Dylan commented to nobody in particular.

When they got back to Noah's Rainbow it was time to do their chores, which they grumbled and slogged through. Colton and J. Malachi were assigned to make dinner. As J. Malachi sliced carrots he found himself somewhat in awe of the knife. It glided through the vegetables; it kissed them and they fell apart. All of J. Malachi's knives at home were dull. He would rather saw his tomatoes apart than risk cutting off a finger during one of his drunken cooking adventures.

Jen had told them they should all make lists of the things they never allowed themselves before, the things they hadn't accomplished yet due to wasted time and energy, and all the other ways their lives could be better sober. There were lists pinned up in both bedrooms, with items like

I would know how my favorite movies end (J. Malachi),

I would know how my favorite movies start (Dylan, who never seemed to start watching *Harold and Kumar Go to White Castle*—he just looked up and there it was, playing, as if he was being haunted by a stoner poltergeist),

I would understand the contents of my refrigerator (Colton),

I would be able to get some keys to my fucking car, if I could figure out how you get replacement keys, which probably there's some way (Dylan, ruminative; he'd crossed out "fucking" because he was trying not to be offensive),

I could fill out the whole form at the doctor's office instead of skipping the question about how much do you drink (Dylan again, willing to lie to his coach and friends but too scrupulous to lie to strangers), and

When people ask me how things are going I wouldn't suspect them of trying to run an intervention on me (Colton, who was suspicious by nature, but in fact they all hated to be asked impolite questions like "How are you?").

J. Malachi mentally added *I could buy sharp knives* to his list. And then, on reflection, *and a laptop.*

He'd been working for years on a huge and hideous old desktop he'd "borrowed" from a friend's brother's basement, a thing so bygone and brutal that you could make it run MacWrite and MacPaint. The only game it understood was a pixelated snake's quest to eat pixelated apples. The only browser it supported—and in fairness, J. Malachi was grateful that it could connect to the internet at all—was Netscape Navigator.

He used this thing, whose keys made an audible *clunk*, this thing on which Mark Twain had typed "Journalism in Tennessee," this relic of the lost kingdom of Zork, because he'd maxed out his credit cards buying laptops to replace the ones he'd ruined with spilled drinks. After the third time he was told that his laptop couldn't be fixed because "we opened it up and it has... uh... *residue*," he gave up. He made the desktop computer his traditionalist affectation, the Washington journalist's version of agrarianism.

In reality, he hated it. He hated traveling because everybody else was working on their laptops while he sat and stared at the residue coating the inside of his skull. The realization that if he got sober he could have a laptop was a surprisingly powerful source of motivation. More powerful than being able to talk to his parents without miserable guilt, perhaps because J. Malachi had seen a laptop before and knew what they looked like.

*   *   *

As the talent slumped down for what they all considered a hard-earned dinner, they had another learning opportunity. Jen announced: "Today wasn't just about patience and learning to be ordinary. It was about the consequences when we don't practice the skills we're learning here. In the real world, where we all have to live most of the time, you'll get fired if you don't do your job right. It isn't cute and nobody thinks you're a hero for standing up for yourself or sticking it to the Man. You lose your health insurance—"

"What health insurance," Colton said.

"You lose self-sufficiency. You become dependent on others. So that's what's going to happen here. As you can see, we've got a pretty great dinner here: roast chicken, mashed potatoes. Let's all thank the chefs."

They applauded Colton and J. Malachi, apprehensively.

"The people who did well today get to keep their jobs. They get a 'paycheck,' which means a nice big plate of food. The people who put their own emotional needs ahead of the customers' will be fired. They'll be dependent on the others, and they'll only get to eat if somebody with food chooses to share."

"This is some 'Lord of the Flies' bullshit right here," Medea said.

"I realize that you have to find a way to invalidate the process, Medea, because you know you did poorly," Jen said evenly. Medea's face reddened.

"You're experiencing the same kind of emotional dependency and hunger now that you'll experience physically in a few hours. You can cope through making yourself indignant at me, or at Noah's Rainbow, or at the rules—those can all become your Higher Powers. Or you can turn to your *true* Higher Power and remember that we're all needy, but going without food for a night won't kill you. It doesn't even mean that you're worse than anybody else. It's an experience which will teach you a lesson—and I assure you that lesson costs much less here in reality television than it does out there, in reality *reality*."

She smiled. They could all smell the chicken—it seemed to smell much more strongly than it had five minutes ago.

"So, the people who will be getting a plate tonight are Dylan and Emebet. Please come up and take your paycheck!"

They shuffled reluctantly up to the food. Emebet darted unhappy little glances around like she was expecting someone to come and yank the plate away from her. She looked like she was committing a crime. Dylan looked like he was being punished for one.

They filled their plates. "This is sadism," Medea said. "It's very creative. All sadism is creative. *Justice* is always so thrilling, isn't it?"

"How do we share," Dylan said flatly. "There's four of them and two of us. And also only enough plates and utensils for us."

"We're fine," J. Malachi said, looking at Emebet. "Please don't feel that you need to share at all. You earned this food and we didn't. Take as much as you like!"

Medea was about to tell him that he was supposed to be humble with his heart, not his dick, when Dylan spoke. His voice was furious and miserable, and his face was set in a tight grin, which yanked up on one side as if it had gotten caught on something.

"Of course I get to eat," he said thickly. "Fucking obviously, I never have to take any consequences. I was born with a silver spoon up my ass."

He set his plate down angrily in front of the four miscreants. Mashed potatoes slopped over the side. His face was bright red from ear to ear.

"Rude," J. Malachi murmured. Several of the others hummed their agreement.

Dylan glared around at them all, unable to stop smirking. "I'm not hungry," he said, and stormed out.

"Left In Huff," J. Malachi said, and everybody laughed a little too hard, out of need. But Colton was watching the doorway and looking slightly nauseated.

Emebet nodded her head, then, and held herself very carefully, with her chin high. She had a precise, regal carriage, a dignity maintained with such obvious effort that it swung 180 degrees around and became painfully vulnerable.

"It's Friday," she said. "On Fridays I fast."

In fact earlier that day she had comforted herself with chicken fingers. But she gently laid her plate down in front of the other four. They felt that she could have created a Friday for herself even on a Monday or a Tuesday. They were slightly in awe of her—for J. Malachi, more than slightly—as she turned and left the room, switching her hips just a little; every Friday has a little Saturday on the tail end.

There was a long pause, and then J. Malachi's stomach rumbled. Sharptooth let out a giggle, and Medea snorted; and Colton gave Jen a level look and asked, "So, can we eat, or what?"

After dinner Colton came into the dorm where Dylan was lying in bed with the covers over his head. "I know you're awake," he said. "I brought you some leftovers."

Dylan sat up slowly. "Thanks," he said, watching Colton. He forked up the cold chicken and potatoes and chewed. "Tastes like... I don't know what this tastes like." His light voice was wary, and more tired than usual.

"Tastes like recovery," Colton suggested, smiling.

Dylan grinned a little too, but his mouth still had that fishhooked hitch upward. "No way, man, this is actually good! You guys must've dumped like a tub of butter all up in this bitch."

"Better not let Sharptooth hear you disrespecting the female dog, son. Also, 'all up in this bitch'? Did you wake up on the wrong side of 2008 this morning?"

Dylan was grinning for real now. "Watch it, motherfucker. I could go full Walmart on your face if you mess with me."

"Do you cuss your mother with that mouth?"

"If you want to know what I do with my mouth, you should be asking *your* mom."

Colton shook his head. "You know, sometimes I tremble for my country when I behold the flower of its youth."

"I don't think there's too much left of my flower of youth.

I can act real shy, though."

Colton was throwing around a koosh ball they'd stolen from Jen, trying to kick it back into his own hands; he didn't succeed, and had to crawl to fetch it from under the bed. Dylan chewed meditatively, and then asked, "So the idea for tonight was that we just pass mashed potatoes back and forth like some kind of butter-based money laundering scheme, I give you mine and then you give me it back, and this is supposed to teach us... humility?"

"I'm not sure what they expected," Colton said. "I think they definitely didn't expect both you and Em to just LIH with your food on the table."

"Emebet huffed? Ha. I feel better about myself now."

"She huffed hard. You can probably guess where our other roommate is right now."

"Aww. Hey," he said, dragging the tines of his fork across his plate, "are we cool?"

Colton clutched at his head. "Oh my God, stop poking at it! *Yes*, we're cool, I approve of you, I will go to your Little League games."

Dylan's grin looked like the grin of a teenage kid who'd been hit in the face several times, so Colton tried to pull himself together. *Face the fuck up to it*, he told himself.

"Look, I'm sorry I snapped at you," he said.

"No, no, I'm the one who—I was a jerk, I wasn't taking your thing seriously."

Colton shrugged. "Not everything is about my thing."

He would not have thought that having to apologize to the idiot rich for their rich idiocy would make him feel better about himself, and yet there they were.

J. Malachi came in then. He walked over to the bulletin board with Dylan's trophy cup, Colton's sloth, and their list of things they could have if they stayed sober. He added to the list *sharp knives, laptop* and, with a quick little grin, *Kiss girls and not worry about puking or crying or losing a tooth*. Then, after a shy pause, he crossed out *girls* and wrote *women*.

Dylan whooped for him. "Did you really?" he asked.

J. Malachi's grin widened. "That is for me to know. And for you to find out when this episode airs, I guess."

He headed into the bathroom. Dylan lay on the bed for a moment, pondering. Then he made his decision and jumped up. He went over to the list, crossed out *women*, and wrote *cougars*. He admired his handiwork for a moment, and then looked at the empty paper trophy cup pinned up next to it. He slid the little twist-tie champagne bottle out from behind the bulletin board and dangled it in front of the cup. He considered it, and himself, with the level of drama appropriate to his age; he moved his hand so that the champagne bottle hovered over the wastebasket. In the end he decided not to choose, and put the bottle back where it came from.

Colton had been watching him from his bed throughout this bout of shadow-boxing, but when he opened his mouth, it was only to say, "I don't think I can handle TV rehab with a wolf *and* a cougar. Gettin' a little too 'Wild Kingdom.' A little too 'Wild Kingdom' all up in this bitch."

*   *   *

From the "Amends" thread at Idiotbox.com:

dollparts: Disappointed but unsurprised to see that they're being coddled here. Their big punishments are literally working a cash register and then sharing their chicken wings.

On most TV shows that would be the happy ending!

At my rehab they wrote stuff like DRUNK or USELESS on our faces and made us work along the side of the road picking up trash, in those black-and-white striped prison uniforms. The idea was that if we worked hard enough the sweat would wash the words off. I remember one little kid thought I was the Hamburglar—he gave me his Happy Meal so I wouldn't have to steal anymore.

CheeseSniffer: I wouldn't want to be out on the side of the road, with everybody taking pictures of me on their phones. I'm guessing these people would really like that, though, since they signed up for the show.

dollparts: This was in the early '90s. I didn't know anybody who even had a cell phone until I went to rehab. He got so upset when they threw it away. Nowadays I think he's some kind of Nietzschean out in Silicon Valley. Some people can't handle normal life—they always have to be achieving something.

Chapter 11: A Meditation, Concerning Fun

The day after retail therapy started with group, to which Medea arrived in a costume intended to compensate for her various failures at customer service the day before: a zebra-print sheath minidress, scarlet leggings, and fingerless black elbow gloves. Colton whistled.

"You are a cautionary tale today," he said, and she acknowledged the praise with a slight nod of her head.

The others reacted as well: Emebet gave her a raised eyebrow which was unexpectedly maternal, and said, "You look expensive," which was not the word Medea herself would have chosen. Dylan said, "You look like you play a sexy sport, in a dystopian future where women fight with their feet." Jen attempted not to react at all, as Medea simmered in her direction.

Jen started them off with another word problem. "Let's say you're mopping a floor. You mop and mop and the floor just keeps getting streakier and dirtier. What's going on? Why is that happening?"

Dylan suggested, "Are you mopping with mud on

purpose? Are you, like, the janitor at a mud-wrestling pit?"

"You have sexy fighting on the brain," Medea said.

Jen shook her head. "This isn't a trick question. Just a normal life event which could happen to one of you later today, maybe happened to you yesterday. Why is the floor getting dirtier each time you push the mop across it?"

"Because the mop is dirty," Medea said, with unexpected practicality.

"That's exactly right, Medea," Jen said, and let her preen. "The mop is dirty. Now, when you get out of here you're going to need a lot of help. You're going to need people you can rely on to help you stay clean. But how do you figure out which people are good mops, who will help you keep your spirits bright and shiny, and which people are dirty mops who are only going to make things worse?"

"I feel like I had this lecture in middle school, except it was about my purity," Colton said.

"I don't think it's right to reject a mop just because it is dirty," Emebet said. "Maybe your floor needs to be made dirtier, so that you can be humbled in the eyes of others. The bad mop may be a gift."

J. Malachi perked up, and wondered if he could take this as a compliment.

Jen smiled, with a smile that was more of a frown. "The point is just to learn discernment. That means learning which people we can rely on to support our recovery. When we get out of here, we'll need a lot of help," and she smiled harder into their *What do you mean, "we"?* stares. "Some of you will use twelve-step programs, and you'll need to find a sponsor. Others will find other ways of getting the help you need.

Because none of us can do it alone."

She smacked this last sentence onto her point like a store-bought, pre-tied gift bow. "Remember that old comic strip, Goofus and Gallant? Some of you must remember it. Well, today we'll hear from a few speakers who will help us learn to tell the Goofuses from the Gallants."

"Gallant always seemed like a total enabler, I'll say that for him," Medea put in.

"Let's all welcome our speakers."

There were three of them, and they made an aggressively unmatched set. The first one appeared to be a human male, tall and spindly and chewed-looking, a sallow Giacometti with an old tennis ball for a head. He limped in like regret. Behind him strolled a short, plump white woman, a sort of hexagon, with short dyed red hair and tiny hands and feet. And last came a medium-sized black man with a small pot belly and unpersuasive facial hair. He carried a thin, bright yellow book in one hand. The talent shuffled around and pulled chairs up so that they could join the circle.

They introduced themselves, but the talent instantly forgot their names. Jen explained that they each had different approaches to discernment, which they would explain one at a time. "We believe in diversity here, and we don't want to confine you to just one way of looking at things," she said, and the Giacometti frowned and shook his tennis ball.

He went first. He was a recovering alcoholic with forty-two years sober. "The most important thing for you to know is that someone in genuine recovery does not make choices," he said. "You think that you're here to learn how to make good choices, but that's completely wrong. If you truly surrender your will to your Higher Power, there are no more choices to be made. Before each action you will consult your Higher Power, Who will tell you what to do."

They could all hear the capital letters.

"If you try to choose for yourself you *will* relapse. There is no other way. Promoting 'diversity' in recovery is promoting death. And not the death of your ego! The death of your soul. If you want to go to Hell by way of the gutter by all means try to 'make good choices.' If you want recovery, turn your will over to God." He lifted one thin lip and bared a fang at Jen.

The others looked slightly terrified—all except Emebet, who looked engaged and intrigued.

Then the plump girl made her pitch. "Well, I completely disagree," she said, with an offended air. "The important thing in recovery is figuring out who will support *you*, and who will do things the way you want them."

Suddenly she seemed to glow with inner happiness—a self-sufficient, battery-powered satisfaction. "I thought the way... uh, the way you did," gesturing toward the Giacometti, whose name she too had apparently forgotten, "for several years after I first got clean and sober. I thought it was a miracle that I was drug-free and I was willing to turn my whole life over to whatever had caused that miracle. But then I realized: The miracle was me. It was all me, all along. So I turned my life over to me."

There is no "I" in team, but there is a "me" in miracle, Dylan thought, and felt discomfited. The plump woman's happiness made him feel younger and somehow smaller than he had been before.

"You don't have to have somebody else's recovery. You can

have a *me*-covery."

And with this closing line they all had to try not to look at Medea. She, however, simply shuttered and raised her eyelids very slowly, almost with an audible click, like a Krazy Kat clock.

The third speaker had a high, eager voice. He lifted up his yellow book—he had small hands too, and pale yellowish palms—and explained that he was the author.

"This is my book. It's called *Foolproof Your Friendships*, and it is a five-point plan to getting the friends you need and deserve, while protecting yourself from betrayal and disappointment. The five points are: Sanity, Maturity, Adulthood, Respect, and last of all, Time-Tested Trust. S-M-A-R-T. Maturity and adulthood are different," he said urgently, as if answering an objection. "If you read my book you can find out all about how to secure these five qualities in your friends. We talk about using protection with our sexual partners, but nobody talks about protecting your *heart* from the friends who will let you down."

Colton was powerfully reminded, again, of abstinence-only sex ed. *Next we'll all pull petals off a paper rose,* he thought.

They all waited, expecting the man to elaborate, but he simply waved the book at them and grinned. They realized that they were expected to purchase it if they wanted to learn, for example, the difference between maturity and adulthood.

"Does anybody have any questions?" Jen asked, with a rock-climber's intense, determined grin.

Colton, just to be a dick, asked the book-hawker to explain his five points, and got the non-answer he expected. He also asked if the book was discounted for people in rehab.

"It's $19.95 for everyone," the author said flatly. "I don't think any amount of money is too much to pay for peace of mind. This book is your security system, it's your preventative medicine. I will autograph it if you purchase it today," he conceded.

Emebet raised her hand. She addressed her question to Giacometti: "I understand that we must constantly ask God and only God for guidance. But can you tell us anything about patterns you have noticed? Are there some kinds of people who God seems to like more, or does it seem random?"

He listened to her with his eyes cast down to the floor, and as she talked he nodded his big head slowly, rhythmically. It was soothing to watch, almost hypnotic.

Several of them jumped in their seats when he jerked his head up and barked out an answer: "This is how you tell angels from demons. A demon will appear pleasant at first. He's good-looking and fun and he makes you feel good about yourself. But the more time you spend with him the more you feel afraid. You begin to feel that there's something wrong. An angel is the other way around. You may hate him at first! He's unpleasant, he's abrasive, he's even frightening. Or maybe he's someone you find silly and sad. But the more you get to know him the more you feel that you're in the right place. You want to be with him."

Sounds like a rom-com, J. Malachi thought, *demon played by Hugh Grant*. And Sharptooth thought, *This must be how he justifies being a crazy weirdo*, even though she knew that was very othering language.

Dylan had a question. "This is something I thought of

while Ms., uh... while you were talking, but I guess I can put it out there for anybody who wants to answer. So... do you think you *should* like yourself? I mean, is it wrong if you don't?"

It's that one kid who asks an honest question on the little index cards they hand out, Colton thought. *"Can you get pregnant on your period?" I should've known it would be him.*

The two men deferred at first to the plump girl, who looked uncomfortable.

"Well... I don't believe in 'should's," she said. "When you 'should' on me, I feel should-y. Have you ever heard that expression?"

None of them had, and none of them seemed to feel that it had enhanced their life experience.

"But I do think that as you work on your recovery, self-liking will come naturally."

Dylan didn't look particularly reassured by this answer.

Giacometti looked as if he might weep great gray chewing-gum tears.

"Nobody cares who you like," he said sternly.

Dylan nodded, eager and miserable.

"God doesn't care if you *like* yourself—it's a sin, like all forms of self-involved pleasure, but not a very bad one. You're supposed to love yourself. Love yourself as you love your neighbor. That's a different thing from liking, and much less fun."

After the Q and A Jen announced that their guest speakers would be joining them for lunch, which was a taco bar created by Sharptooth and Emebet. This was exciting, since Sharptooth was a passable, if vegan, cook, and Emebet was a genuinely good one. The talent grabbed plates and lined up, and then had to be reminded to let the guests go first. Embarrassed, they fell back in disarray, and were further confused and delayed when Giacometti insisted on going last.

The plump girl crafted three bulging vegan tacos, with double corn shells and a fried-tofu filling and lots of vegetables. She put a huge scoop of chopped salad into one taco before Emebet saw her and warned her that it was extremely hot. She laughed, saying that she loved spicy food, and Emebet wondered if it was rude to say, *This isn't American spicy; this is our spicy.* She tried to explain that it had Ethiopian flavors, but that only made the red-haired girl regard the taco filling as if it were an exotic vacation spot and Emebet as if she were a telethon orphan. Her eyes were very big as she looked from the taco to the cook and nodded with intense, sympathetic misunderstanding.

The rest of them had gotten their food and were sitting, waiting for Giacometti to finish so that they could begin— they were trying to be excruciatingly polite to make up for their earlier faux pas with the line. They watched him as he paused in front of each and every plate and tray. He processed along the taco bar as if it were the Stations of the Cross, and the talent scolded themselves for noticing that their food was getting cold.

Finally he brought his plate to the table and lowered himself onto his chair like the last dodo settling onto its petrifying egg. The talent held their breath. The other two guests had in fact started to eat at least two minutes ago, which only added to the acute awkwardness of the situation, as they watched Giacometti bow his head and put his hands together in prayer.

He prayed and went on praying.

This isn't hide and go seek, Medea thought, *you don't have to count to one hundred Mississippi. God is still right where you left him.*

He looked up, wrapped his long bony fingers around a taco, and began to nibble. With visible relief the others grabbed their own tacos and began to stuff their faces. At first he didn't appear to notice them—he seemed to find each tiny bite endlessly fascinating—but then he said, in a sepulchral voice, "I'm sorry for delaying you. I didn't realize that you were waiting for me. I thought that you were giving your food a chance to cool."

They stared at him and made themselves smile.

"We understand that it can be hard to make a decision when there are so many great choices," Jen said, with a big kindergarten-teacher smile for the two cooks.

Giacometti frowned, though. "I don't make decisions," he said sharply. "God decides. This may take longer—to ask God and to receive an answer—but it is the only way to lead a genuinely human life. You must surrender your will to God in *all* things. There is no exception in the Bible for taco bars."

"God told you to get salsa and not guacamole," Medea said. "He took time from his busy schedule of not intervening in wars and genocide, in order to fix up your menu plans."

He looked at her, and chewed. When he had swallowed he said, "You appear to seek attention. You should seek God instead. He will give you all the attention you desire and much more."

A few of the others, in some cases despite themselves, snickered. Medea attempted an air of queenly indifference, which is difficult while eating tacos in a dress shorter than John 11:35.

At that moment the red-haired girl bit into her Ethiopian taco. She made a stifled, high-pitched noise, like a child trying to blow into a recorder, and then began to puff and wave her hands in front of her mouth. Her cheeks were still stuffed with food. She began to turn red and to sweat, and her eyes bulged. Sharptooth jumped up to get her a glass of water; some of the others, notably Medea, simply watched with interest.

Emebet said quietly, "The water will make it worse. You need to eat something which will... distract your mouth."

The red-haired (and now red-faced) girl tearfully shook her head. With a supreme effort she chewed and swallowed, and then, as the peppers slid down her throat, she entered a new phase of the pain. She began to pant. She gulped down the water Sharptooth had set in front of her, and glared at Emebet when the warning turned out to be accurate.

"I don't think," she gasped, "that we should respond to difficult situations with self-distraction. We need—self-acceptance—and—meditation!"

"It's important to ask for guidance even in life's seemingly small decisions," Giacometti said. He calmly chewed his one, moderately-filled and mildly-spiced taco.

As a special treat after lunch they had Fudgsicles and Creamsicles. The talent tried to eat demurely; they felt that their usual clowning wouldn't go over as well in front of the guests. As Colton unwrapped his Fudgsicle and began pensively to suck the tip, he contemplated the others. He found himself wondering which ones would make it and which would fall back into misery. *Just a little more than a week left*, he realized. And after they got out the horror movie would begin, as these people he'd gotten to know were picked off one by one.

Sharptooth. She'd already gotten clean so she could probably stay clean, plus she was crazy so perhaps that was her new form of self-medication. She seemed very convinced that she was right, anyway, and Colton was under the impression that that attitude might help her. She reminded him of Jen in some ways, and Jen was clean and sober.

He didn't understand J. Malachi at all, but sensed a certain lack in him: some missing piece which left him permanently wobbling. Colton grinned and wondered whether Emebet might be the phone book shoved under his short leg to keep him steady. His grin wilted a little as he realized that it probably didn't work that way.

He looked at the others, at Medea biting her Creamsicle in half and Dylan licking ice cream off his wrist and Emebet taking little, frustrated bites and massaging her sore jaw, and he didn't want to play the game anymore.

You didn't do yourself, he thought, and then he definitely didn't want to play anymore.

Instead he turned to Giacometti. Their success story, the guy who was supposed to teach them how to live. "You have Fudgsicle on your face," he said.

The man simply nodded and kept eating. The fudge tracked along his cheek in a big dramatic slash, but he said, "It will help me with my humility." Emebet looked at him with an intensity which both Colton and J. Malachi disliked.

After the popsicles the guest speakers were allowed to leave, and the cameras focused on the talent to capture their envy and frustration.

After an interlude for cleanup and confessionals, they had more group. Medea raised a point which piqued the general interest.

"What I don't get is the all-or-nothing here. I usually *love* extremism," she purred, "but this idea that if alcohol makes your life a little messy, then you can't have even one beer—I mean that just seems superstitious. 'Take a sip of Jack, break your mother's back.'"

Colton lifted an eyebrow, and wondered if he wanted to get in on her side on this one. But before he could figure out what he wanted to say, Dylan laughed and put in, "Oh my God, who has one beer? Does beer even come in 'one'? Yeah, that sounds super fun, let's all *drink a beer* and like, have a *conversation.*"

"Plenty of people have one beer," J. Malachi attempted.

"Boring people," Dylan said.

While the rest of them argued, Emebet got stuck on that phrase, "super fun." She felt like she didn't understand very well what it meant for something to be "fun." Dylan seemed to use it to mean "catastrophic and degrading"; Jen always meant "therapeutic, but not too painful." Emebet had asked J. Malachi about it once and he'd said that it was a modern concept, "similar to joy or carnival, only plastic," which didn't help much.

Everyone had said that the man she'd loved had been "fun." He was known for it. She thought she was attracted to this fun.

The apartment where they had lived together was on the second floor, by a narrow concrete stairwell with an unreliable light bulb. Frequently as she was coming down the stairs the light would shut off, so that the stairs were close and black, full of the sound of her breathing. And then there would be a series of shuddering flashes before the light came back on.

He had been like that too. When she came up and smiled at him he would turn to look at her with lightless eyes, and it would take a few shuddering false starts before the fun came on.

J. Malachi was different. He lit himself up when he saw her. She didn't think he was fun; but maybe it had been a mistake to go for fun in the first place. Would she miss it? She missed it already.

But you hated it when you had it, she thought wryly. Maybe fun was always something that looked better when it was over.

"Can you get what you want from one beer?" Jen asked them.

"I can't get what I want anyway," J. Malachi said, with a diva's weariness.

*   *   *

After dinner Jen explained the activity for the evening, in which they'd get a chance to use their new skills of discernment. They would make a list of several people to whom they owed amends and apologies, and then pick one— and only one—who would gain the most from their efforts. They'd be allowed to make a confessional-booth video just for that person.

Jen reminded them that sometimes you didn't get to apologize, because breaking back in to another person's life might disrupt it. You weren't allowed to dredge up old memories just to make yourself feel better. And you were supposed to pick a person who would support you in your recovery. She emphasized that they'd only get one chance to do this.

Medea snorted. "This seems like false urgency," she observed. "Why can't I just make one video now, and then when I get out of here, go to the other people on my list and say I'm sorry in person? Or send an email, or a text, whatever. It's not like you're going to shoot us once we finish our *video confessional*, this isn't our last words before the cigarette and the firing squad."

"I don't think you're supposed to do amends over text," Dylan said, but in fact they were all interested in this question. They wanted to see Jen wrong-footed.

She disappointed them by handling it with aplomb.

"I'm glad you asked that, Medea." (They were getting sick of hearing her say their names. In real life people say your first name mostly when you're being scolded, but for television Jen had to use their names as often as possible to help orient commercial-break viewers.) Her voice got extra bouncy as she explained that all of the people who received their videos would be informed that the talent had had a chance to pick just one person, and they were the chosen ones.

"I think your words will have a lot more impact when your recipient knows that you considered them, and the amends you owe them, more important than anybody else."

Medea said sulkily, "I thought we were here to learn that nobody's more important than anybody else," but she acknowledged that she'd been beaten.

Jen passed out pens and paper, and they sat hunched

over, feeling especially humiliated by the need to balance the pads of paper on their knees. Lack of privacy was one thing—they all accepted that privacy was an outdated and slightly distasteful form of life, like arranged marriage—but lack of a desk felt unnecessary. They felt that the show was gloating over their dependence.

At least we don't have to write with crayons, Dylan thought; he was trying to be grateful.

The task proved harder than they'd expected. There were either too many names or too few. Dylan took up both sides of the paper writing down everybody who'd ever been married to one of his biological parents, then his various fractional siblings, and then his sexual partners with names or identifying marks, and then raised his hand.

He asked Jen, "I feel like we should go with either the person we have the most resentments toward—so that we can let that stuff go—or else the person who's done the most for us. If those are the options, which one should you pick?"

"Which one should *I* pick?" she asked, just like a teacher. ("I don't know, *can* you?") Dylan scowled, and she said, "Who are they?"

"I mean, the one I resent the most is a cliche I guess, but my mom. And the person who's given me the most is definitely my coach."

Medea spoke without lifting her head from her paper. "Your mother gave you half of your DNA, many of your habits I'm guessing, and the gift of life, just for starters."

Dylan thought better of several different responses before settling on, "Yeah, that's great, everybody give a cheer for the home team."

Colton didn't look up from his paper either. "I thought *your* mother was the away team," he said lightly.

Dylan laughed. "No, I'm the away team," he said.

"I think you should talk to the person who needs to hear it most," Jen said. "And ask yourself what makes an apology selfish. Don't be like the guy who gets his wife a grill for her birthday because *he* loves hamburgers. If you're making an amends to serve your emotional needs rather than your spiritual needs, you're probably not ready to make that amends."

She could see that she wasn't getting through, so she tried again: "Think of it as opening a door, not closing one. If you're trying to 'get closure' that's more of an emotional, psychological need, and you shouldn't use other people's forgiveness as a form of self-medication."

Dylan rolled this around in his skull, and thought it might answer his question. To his surprise, it gave him the answer which made him feel less dread rather than more.

Colton found that it was strangely hard to come up with names. Like taking a drug test when you'd just peed an hour ago. He wrung a name onto the page and crossed it out. He wasn't sure when he'd gotten so isolated—nobody left to burden or be burdened by, nobody left to let down or to be hurt by. He felt like something out of a fairy tale, one of the nightmare ones: Just yesterday he'd had friends, he'd been surrounded by people and their demands, and then today he lifted his head and looked up and there was dust on all the doorknobs.

All of the people Emebet could think of had vanished, and left no forwarding address—except, in a few cases, their headstones. She didn't know where her ex was; she knew exactly where her parents and her brother were, though she wasn't sure which direction they were going. And she didn't think they'd get to watch reality TV on their journey.

Can you open the door to a tomb? she thought. *If a dead person forgives you, does it make a sound?* She giggled. Her brother had loved that kind of puzzle, koans that had degenerated into riddles. He'd asked her, "What is the sound of one hand clapping?", and when she couldn't figure it out, he gave her the answer by slapping her face.

Medea was trying to remember if *Exes of Several Sexes* was already an album title, or if she could steal it for one of her plays. She also couldn't remember the names of most of the exes. Her dating tended to take place in a dark miasma of drunken scheming.

What Sharptooth really wanted was to redo the confrontation with her mother, since she felt that she hadn't expressed herself well. She always felt petulant and childish around her parents. She felt that in every other area of her life she was well-adjusted; if anything, the world needed to shift around to adjust to *her*. As she gained time in recovery she felt less and less any desire to apologize or be sorry for things she did. She felt more complete, and less like she was on a constant game of hide-and-seek with herself which had stretched out long past the point at which it stopped being funny.

She had figured out, she felt, the trick to being right most of the time. This made it hard for her to make friends or find a job.

It also made it hard to figure out who she could talk to in her video. When nobody understands you better than yourself, you communicate only to win converts. Sharptooth tended to identify as "offended" a feeling most people would call "lonely."

Medea paused to think, which was never a good sign. She felt oddly bereft. She was used to wanting things, and then having to figure out why it was okay for her to have them. Now she was being asked what she wanted and she wasn't sure. She felt unsettled, and wondered idly if breaking something would help.

In the end none of the videos were shown to anyone but the intended recipients. Bentley lobbied hard for some of them, but she was overruled; it was felt, in the upper echelons of Fainting Goat, that America didn't need or want to see Colton apologize to his drug dealer. ("*Former* drug dealer," Bentley muttered, as if it would make a difference.)

Dylan's coach did get to see the apology to him, which is how he learned who had stolen his clarinet and where he could find it. "But I would, uh, run it through maybe a car wash or something if I were you," Dylan said.

He added, "Also, I truly appreciate what you've done for me much more than I ever said, and I'm literally more sorry than humanly possible about everything."

I should get that on a t-shirt, Bentley thought when she saw his video.

Medea... well, Medea started out slow. She arranged herself carefully in front of the camera, fixing her hair and trying to touch up her lipstick in the camera's fisheye.

"Solange, I'm not entirely sure that I need to apologize to you too much. After all, *I* didn't break up with *you*. But I'm trying to 'see my part' in my relationships," which was true;

Medea was interested in tracing the workings of her own willpower, even if it meant she had to apologize for it, "so I will list the things I did wrong."

She had to think.

"I'm sorry that I didn't tell you before I slept with Tiamat. I didn't think you'd want to hear about it, or approve. But you weren't being very supportive to me—this was when my play was getting reviewed in *Backwash* and *Skunk*, I was making progress, and you were busy with your 'job' or whatever. I mean I hit it and quit it, it didn't go beyond the physical and also the fact that she admired my plays. A lot. Plus she was having her handfasting ceremony the next day and I thought she shouldn't take a step like that without testing her commitment. We'd never slept together, and I thought, you know, how awful it would be for her to always be wondering what I would have been like."

Here Medea remembered something. "I found out later that she and her girlfriend had an open relationship, though," she said ruefully. "I'm sorry I made assumptions. I feel like everybody's into being monogamous these days, but I should've known that Tiamat isn't a trend-follower. I regret that I didn't clarify that before I wasted the time.

"Still, you have to admit that turning your mother against me was just rude. My relationship with your mother was totally independent of my relationship with you! Not everything is about you. And you should have let me talk to her first, to explain things.

"But," she conceded, "I know I could have been a better girlfriend, if we're going to make judgments."

She tried to find the exact right phrase for what she

wanted to say. "I'm sorry that I was only *equally* supportive of you; I know the more successful partner should always be the more supportive."

She let that hang on her lips for a moment, touched her lower lip gently with her tongue-tip to taste it on her lipstick. She nodded.

"Anyway, I'm not totally sure why you haven't even bothered to get in touch with me in like a year. This is my attempt to put the past behind us and move forward. I've *always* cared so much more about you than other people do! I'm just hoping that we can get to," and she paused as she searched for a phrase, "a place of mutual understanding. I just want you to understand me."

Having delivered herself of this missive, she belched, and then lifted a feminine little hand to cover her mouth.

The staff of Fainting Goat, appalled, unanimously refused to air this Advent calendar of crazy. Nobody ever let her have fun for long.

When Medea was a little girl she'd read *The Phantom Tollbooth*, but she'd never really liked it. It gave her bad dreams. She still remembered the passage about Subtraction Stew, the stew that made you hungrier the more you ate. Coming out of the video confessional she felt as if she'd had ten bowls of it. The whole time she'd been talking she had felt free and comforted—she'd felt easy and voracious. She'd felt as if she were drinking, doing shots, speedy and secure. But now that it was over she felt empty. She kept thinking she'd left something in the booth, but she had her lipstick, she had her bracelet and rings; she couldn't figure out what she had misplaced.

*   *   *

Emebet's video was much shorter but stranger. "I would like to make my amends to the most important person," she said precisely, "Jesus Christ. I am very sorry. I have been trying to ask you what to do and for your guidance but I think maybe you are telling me something by not answering. The same way that when I don't believe in you, this is still a way of talking to *you*. When I don't believe, it's you I don't believe in. I think I've figured this out.

"I want to know what happens if I give you myself as a gift. You turned the water into wine; you can turn anything into a saint."

She shivered, as if she knew what she was asking: "Please make me a saint. There isn't yet a patron saint of dishonest beggars."

Chapter 12: Meat-Shaped Stone

Everybody felt the end of the show coming. The atmosphere among the talent was humid, heavy and tightening like the air before an August thunderstorm.

Those who cared enough to try, tried to keep it light. At breakfast the day after the video confessionals they were all chewing with silent, Gothic intensity when Dylan contributed, "I crapped out a huge long sausage link this morning. All coiled up like a *picture* of shit. Like a big fat cobra waiting for a snake charmer."

He illustrated with a waving hand motion. The others ruminated.

"I felt so accomplished, like I'd done something exactly according to instructions."

"I think I'm getting more regular," J. Malachi said hopefully.

Sharptooth frowned. "I don't believe in setting arbitrary standards for the frequency of elimination," she said, "or its shape. But of course, as you begin to lead a more self-beneficial lifestyle you'll feel much more comfortable."

"Oh, yeah," Dylan agreed, "I felt like I'd crapped my way to freedom. I was sorry to flush it."

That morning they tried to meditate, or at least hold still for twenty minutes. Jen gave them a few pointers, which were not fully-understood.

"*Hey*," Medea hissed to Dylan as she tried to get comfortable on the floor, "I wasn't paying attention, what the fuck is a third eye?"

"I have no idea!" he whispered. "I always thought it was your, uh, your anal entrance. I mean not *yours*, but a person's."

"Really more of an exit than an entrance," Colton said.

J. Malachi grinned. "Only if you believe in natural law theory."

"Excuse me, are we having a general conversation?" Jen asked; and they surrendered to a meditative silence.

In group Jen told them they would be exploring "how your beliefs and self-views have changed through these amends experiences." She pulled a bedsheet off of a table, which was supposed to dramatically reveal craft supplies, but unfortunately the sheet got snagged and the crayons and finger paints spilled onto the floor. The talent, however, had learned helpful and cleanly habits. Several of them hastened forward to pick everything up without even being told. Along with the paints and crayons there were scissors, paste, butcher paper, and stacks of magazines.

The assignment was to "make a picture of your Higher Power as you understand your Higher Power." (Jen had to keep repeating the phrase because she didn't want to pick between "it" or "Him.")

"This definitely does feel like the opposite of drinking, in terms of ways to have fun," Medea noted. "Finger paints and paste, in rehab. So stereotypes *are* based on truth!"

"Do we get kicked out if we eat the paste?" Dylan asked. "Because I'm pretty sure it's, like, un-American to prevent paste-eating. It's primarily a food source rather than an art supply."

Meanwhile Colton was calmly creating a picture of his Higher Power. He used green and red finger paints, one on top of the other so that where they sludged together they became brown, and drew a gigantic eye in the center of his paper. He gave the eye a burning red pupil and a greeny-brown iris, and fringed it with thick black lashes.

"Done," he said. "Can I wash off?"

Sharptooth painted three sausages on sticks, with Pac-Mans attached to their necks: wolves howling at the moon. She painted a somewhat messy scroll underneath, with "My Pack" inscribed in heavily curlicued lettering.

J. Malachi painted an empty throne, which he claimed represented the concept of submission to rightful authority.

Medea openly mocked him. "'The *concept* of *submission* to rightful authority,'" she giggled, and you could hear the italics. You could hear, J. Malachi felt, the serifs. "It's like you're mooning us with your brain."

Dylan remarked, to no one in particular, "I should say my Higher Power is the Leafs. ...Yeah, hockey humor. I swear that's funny to, maybe, Canadians. Canadians who aren't Leafs fans."

He had in fact drawn a hockey team gathered on the away-team bench. Their faces were all black scribbles, like stormclouds, because he couldn't draw very well and didn't want to try too hard, but they wore big boxy uniforms and they carried hockey sticks, so the idea was fairly clear.

That didn't stop Medea from kibitzing, "What's wrong with their faces? Is this some kind of Japanese-Canadian horror movie? 'Before you die, you see... *the puck.*'"

"Well, what the fuck is yours? A cubic foot of shit, wearing a hat?"

Medea drew herself up and pretended to be deeply offended. "This is a representation of a famous Chinese work of art from the Qing dynasty. It currently resides in the National Palace Museum of Taiwan and it is called the Meat-Shaped Stone."

Dylan, realizing that he had fucked up in a way which might actually be racist, smacked his hand hard against his picture in frustration. "I'm *sorry*. I didn't mean—I genuinely didn't realize."

"Obviously not. Western education is so limited."

Colton asked, "So what is it? Is it actually a stone shaped like meat?"

"Yes it is. It looks exactly like a beautifully-marbled piece of *dongpo* pork, but it's made out of jasper. It represents the triumph of art over nature." She looked at her own effort ruefully. "This painting doesn't do it justice."

"I wouldn't eat that," Dylan agreed. "I would eat a lot of things. But not that."

"How is a delicious hunk of art your Higher Power?" Colton asked. "Although speaking of, I think I'll get DELICIOUS HUNK OF ART on my business cards."

"Who's Art, and does he share?" Dylan asked, and bounced away as Colton threw a crayon at him.

Emebet, who was having trouble with her picture, had wandered over to join them.

"It looks like meat, but you can't eat it," she mused. This struck a Biblical chord with her, and she searched for the words to put it into English: "'Do not work for bread which goes by the end of the day...'" She couldn't quite get to the end of that thought.

Medea nodded hard, with the kind of enthusiasm which made people inch away from her on public transportation.

"No, this is the thing!" she said. "It doesn't look like meat, not exactly. That's why it's my Higher Power! Because it looks *better*. Better than the real thing, the boring meat you just eat."

Sharptooth was puzzled. "So you're... hoping to lose weight? You will, I think, if you avoid alcohol and choose a healthier meal plan. You'll get in touch with your inner ecology."

Medea rolled her eyes. "Yes, I'm sure my eyes will brighten and my coat will get nice and glossy, but that isn't the point."

Jen had come over to babysit them. "Dylan," she said brightly, "that's a very powerful picture. Can you talk to us about why the players don't have faces?"

"In his house in Edmonton dead Gretzky lies dreaming," Dylan said. When this got him a round of blank stares, he shook his head and tried again. "No, uh, it's because I don't want it to be one specific person. I don't think you can kind of... outsource your recovery to the extent that you make another person your Higher Power. That isn't fair to them. But you can consider, I guess, your responsibilities to others. So this is more about my responsibilities to the team."

"There's no coach," Jen noted.

Colton added, "But there is a scoreboard. I feel like it should be the other way around."

"I don't know," Dylan said. "I didn't think about it that hard! But *isn't* there a score, in life? In recovery. Like, 'I have two years,' 'I have six months and three days.' The first guy is winning."

"Your team is winning here," Jen said.

"Yeah, but I feel like there's a lot of time left on the clock," Dylan said.

"All of your pictures show not only the Higher Power, which is great, but also your Higher Power's relationship to you as a person," Jen said. "Your picture implies a story about who you are. Let's ask ourselves what our self-stories are."

When no one spoke up, she prompted, "Dylan?"

"Well, part of a team," he said. "Hope I don't get traded!"

"Part of something larger than yourself," Jen said. "Sharptooth's story seems similar to Dylan's," she went on—and then added hastily, "although it has many unique qualities!"

She didn't need to worry. Sharptooth found it refreshing to be classified as just another team player seeking a pack.

"Jaymi, this is a nice picture of a throne. Are you the king?"

J. Malachi laughed. "No, I'm the jester. Here, I'll draw it in," and he sketched a cap and bells bobbing in the empty air before the throne, at about the level of the king's invisible shins.

"And Medea, what does your picture represent about your relationship to your Higher Power?"

"I would like to know this," Emebet said quietly.

Medea bared her teeth in a big flashbulb grin. "I'm the person who would rather eat a meat-shaped stone than a steak. They call art 'the beautiful lie,' *la bella menzogna*, and I believe that what we call reality isn't as deep as the glamorous lies we tell ourselves. That's why reality television is so compelling: because it's better than reality."

Jen frowned. "I think life is more real without intoxicants," she said.

"That is exactly my point," Medea said. "Drinking is a way to get to the reality-show version of yourself, where you've got a soundtrack and a character arc. Even if it's a shitty one. Being a villain is a lot more interesting than just being a person."

"I wouldn't be so sure," J. Malachi said slowly. "I mean you may have been a much more artistic alcoholic than me. But for a while now the nights when I'm drinking have basically been about overcooking things, regretting things, watching Animal Planet with the sound off, and maudlin peeing."

Medea paused for a moment, and almost rethought her position but not quite. She had a certain fear of commitment, it might be said, a preference for the one-last-time. "Hit it and quit it" was her approach to all things in life, and not just pretty women.

But as Medea summarily kicked J. Malachi's potential insight out of bed, Emebet was nodding. She went back over to her own blank page, rummaged around in the magazines for one she had set aside, and instead of cutting out a shape or a word she tore a whole page out. She stuck paste on the four corners and tacked it to her white butcher sheet.

"There," she said, and brought it over to join the others.

They were more than a little puzzled, since what she was showing them was an ad for Wonder Bread.

J. Malachi attempted, "I like how colorful the polka dots are...."

"It's a reminder. A reminder of Holy Communion," she said simply. "Christ's flesh and blood. I agree with Medea—why would anyone want just bread and meat? We want what is more than meat. This life, by itself, is so... not enough. People give you bread or change to drag yourself from day to day and they don't understand why you're not grateful. But we want what is more than bread, more than everything."

"Everything in the whole world could never be enough," Jen said, thinking that she was agreeing with a self-diagnosis.

"I'm always on the side of the ungrateful," Medea said. Getting the last word was her preferred form of self-soothing.

Chapter 13: You Don't Have to Go Home, But You Can't Stay Here

The last day was approaching and they were all getting squirrelly. Dylan found himself thinking about getting drunk—not thinking about it in depth, in gory detail, but testing it, gently putting his weight on the thought, as if it were a broken leg about to come out of its cast.

He tried to think about what he would do instead of drinking when he got back "on the outside," but all of his ideas seemed to require other people's assistance or company, and that felt selfish. He wondered if any of the others felt the same way. He even managed to scold himself into asking them over breakfast, but everyone just looked away and said that he needed to reach out for help when he felt shaky.

They did an activity where they made inspirational posters to supplement the rehab center's already abundant supply. Dylan trotted out DON'T DROP THE HOPE, which made Colton cackle and Medea snort. He also contributed DRY UP WITH YOUR FLY UP.

Medea's own poster didn't go over very well. She put

DON'T LITTER at the top in block letters, and then drew the wolf nursing Romulus and Remus underneath. Sharptooth, understandably, took it as a personal insult, and began to cry some of the least intentional tears of her life. Medea first tried to pass it off as a joke, and then argued that she was saying people shouldn't reproduce unless they were prepared to take responsibility for their progeny, and then she tried to point out that the wolf was actually the hero of the poster for taking in human children. None of this worked, and in the end she had to crumple up the poster and deliver a strained apology.

They had a candle ceremony to mark the last night of filming—the last night of their amends experience, Jen corrected herself. She showed them how to make the candles by dipping string into buckets of colored wax. They all lost patience, their arms started to ache, and their candles turned out bent or oddly curved or scraggly.

"But the colors are beautiful!" Jen exclaimed, still pushing.

At dinner, as the lights from the cameras blanked out the windows, they chewed meditatively on burnt meatloaf. "Tastes like something ending," Dylan offered.

"It tastes like too much time," Emebet said, with a sad sharpness. "It crumbles away under your fork."

"I don't think these carrot bits are even cooked," J. Malachi said.

He poked at the meatloaf disconsolately. He had been one of the cooks, but that didn't explain his exaggerated feelings of failure. He felt that all of his emotions were being presented to him by funhouse mirrors.

That will help you with your humility, he thought, and giggled as he remembered the scrawny saint with the fudge-smeared face.

Medea looked up from her meal, which she had disassembled into a burnt carapace and undercooked innards. "Did anyone," she asked, "actually make amends to anyone else here? I would like to know, did that ever happen? Did even one of us make up for a thing we've done?"

There was a depressive silence. Then Colton said, "I think I did. I think I made up for some things I did wrong, yeah."

"No you didn't," Emebet said. They turned to look at her. She wasn't blaming him. "Nobody can make up for what they did. That isn't how it works. You did something better than that: You got to a place where even the terrible things you did became a... a place for repentance, and for someone to forgive you. That is much better than just getting back to the life before. I mean life before this happened just led to the things that happened. This way, the worst things you did became grace."

Medea grinned. "Then he needs to do more bad things, so he can get more grace," she said. Emebet didn't dignify this with a response.

"I mean," Medea said, "either a thing is really bad and you shouldn't do it, or it isn't that bad and it doesn't matter. You can't have it both ways."

J. Malachi laughed. "That's just your limited Western rationalism," he said.

He did like Medea; as a traditionalist he was inclined to defend even something horrible, if it had survived for a while.

They scraped their plates into the trash and put them in the big stained sink to soak, then went outside carrying their candles. The night was a soft blue-gray, a gentle night after a day of rain. The black wet trees and the black wires of the cameras stood out sharply against white clouds that covered the whole sky in an even layer. The sky felt close; it was impossible to imagine that there was anything beyond it. The wires hung like dead vines, kudzuing over the cameras.

Jen had set up an inflatable kiddie pool in the courtyard. She handed out little plastic cups and showed them how to help one another melt the bottoms of their candles so that they would stick inside the cups and stand upright. They lit their candles—although the hushed solemnity of the scene was somewhat diminished by the presence of television lighting—and set the candle boats in the water.

Bentley and Ana were standing in the camera underbrush, watching. Bentley was drinking a watercress smoothie. She contorted her mouth around the plastic straw. Ana could feel nervous energy pouring off her.

The candles bobbled and they all tried to feel important feelings. Jen beamed. Sharptooth's candle boat collided with Medea's, and the two long skinny candles knocked their tips against one another as their cups tilted drastically.

"Look, they're fighting, how cute!" Medea exclaimed.

Then the candles began to melt one another and slumped together, joined at the tips.

Colton grinned. "I wouldn't call that fighting," he said. "I think they're mating."

"Ew," Medea said, precisely.

Emebet's candle boat journeyed out far away from the rest. Some unseen ripple or tide in the kiddie pool struck it and it rocked, tilted, and fell over, splashing and overturning in the water, and its little flame went out. The fall sent shivers across the surface of the pool and rocked all the other cup-boats, but none of the rest fell.

J. Malachi watched Emebet anxiously—he didn't want her to take it as some kind of sign from God—but she giggled. "Splash," she said, and made a toppling hand gesture.

Medea, morbid with symbolism, glared out at Emebet's doused candle and her own boat still shakily afloat. She wished suddenly that she'd worn something with sleeves.

They had a little awards ceremony as the candles slowly burned themselves out on the water. Emebet won for both Least Offensive Cooking and Classiest Vomit. Colton, to his surprise, won Least Disgusting Use of Shower (Men's). Sharptooth won the same event in the women's competition.

Jen had lobbied against the whole idea of a competition or awards ceremony, even a playful one—she argued, and Medea's and Dylan's jangled emotions might have offered her support, that people in very early recovery were obsessed with comparing themselves to others and also didn't understand irony or jokes. But all of the talent pushed hard for the awards, even the ones who were ashamed to admit how much they wanted to win prizes and knew they wouldn't.

In the end Medea won Best Dressed (Colton commented that it should be "Least Dressed," and Medea accepted the compliment with a gracious cackle) and Dylan won Most Musical Snoring. "Hey, I have a broken nose, I'm allowed to snore," he protested, before remembering that Colton did too.

Both of them felt discontented, almost disconsolate. They knew that in a setting like rehab, even TV rehab, everyone would get a prize; and so they assumed that their awards were meaningless.

Dylan felt additionally shitty because he realized that he was actually finding ways to turn a joke into an insult. He could see himself doing it but he couldn't stop. It was roughly similar to the way he felt after winning big games: He suffered from a kind of post-hockey *tristesse*, in which his accomplishments seemed stupid and pointless, but he couldn't say so because it would insult his teammates.

After the candle ceremony they had cupcakes ("This tastes like a birthday candle," J. Malachi noted—and added, "that's not a metaphor, I think maybe some wax got into the frosting") and Jen made a speech about clouds. They hung around in the common area for a while, not wanting to leave, and eventually, raggedly wandered back to their rooms to pack.

"Packing sober sucks," Medea announced. She wound several scarves into a ball and threw them into her battered, one-legged scarlet rolling suitcase. "You know there won't be any surprises on the other end."

Emebet, overhearing this comment, filched Medea's rose-scented body wash and tucked it into her own fraying backpack. *That can be a surprise for her*, she thought fondly.

"I'm over scarves," Medea said. "I think my thing is going to be jackets. Or no, I should get some artificial flowers for my hair. Fake hibiscus. That's not a bad title, actually. *Fake Hibiscus: A Comedy in Three Acts*. ...Or maybe I should do underwear on the outside, like Madonna."

"Like Superman," Sharptooth giggled.

"Madonna is a far greater superhero than him," Medea said. "Madonna *is* underwear on the outside, and that takes courage."

In the men's bedroom they were taking down their inspirational cork board. Dylan rolled a thumbtack between his thumb and forefinger as he contemplated the little paper Stanley Cup and the miniature champagne bottle. He threw the bottle away first, then the cup, and felt that he was making some kind of personal statement. Colton slipped the sloth into his wallet.

"Does anybody want this list?" J. Malachi asked, holding up their list of things they could have when they got sober. The other two shrugged and waved it off, so he folded it up and put it at the bottom of his suitcase, under his tweed jacket with the traditional leather elbows. He threw away the picture of Veronica Lake, but he did it with care, tucking her chivalrously into the trashcan.

They all took long showers, mostly to kill time (and, in the men's cases, to jerk off). But at last the long sleepless night had to be faced. Dylan tossed and turned in the dark, thumping his head in frustration against the pillow until Colton said pointedly, "*Good night*, Dylan."

"Good night, darling," he said; but he rolled over onto his back and stared quietly at the ceiling. His DON'T DROP THE HOPE poster stared back at him.

J. Malachi tried to count sheep, feeling that this was a practice which should be revived in the modern era, but he got bored after about seventy. *This is what I get for being a deracinated postmodern,* he thought. *I've lost touch with the agricultural roots of culture.*

After that he got "Hit Me Baby (One More Time)" stuck in his head for about three hours.

*   *   *

The last day didn't dawn so much as ooze into consciousness. The soft, rainy air of the night before had become thick, low-hanging, chilly fog, which drifted through the courtyard and slurred its way around corners. Everything outside the windows was awash in gray. The fog took the edge off; it gave everybody beer goggles.

Breakfast was undercooked pancakes, for which Sharptooth apologized. The runny, undecided circles were so obvious in their meaning that nobody even bothered to say, "Tastes like the weather." Everyone except Sharptooth poured thick gouts of Mrs. Butterworth onto their plates; Sharptooth, for her convictions, suffered without the relief of high-fructose corn syrup. Dylan mashed his pancakes and syrup into a kind of pudding.

"That's a good idea," Emebet said, and briskly chopped up her own meal with the edge of her fork. J. Malachi watched her with a damp besotted look.

Despite the insomnia of their last night, all of them looked a little fresher than they had when they arrived, and Emebet would probably win Most Improved. Her face was already a bit thinner, and the skin was much smoother and softer. She had a certain luster, like a bronze helmet in sunlight. Her dulled eyes had brightened and the tension in her mouth and shoulders had eased. Where several of the others seemed slack and tentative, she had an air of restrained purpose. She was waiting for the gate to open so she could leap forward. He was, perhaps, waiting to watch her do it. Waiting to cheer her on.

*   *   *

Bentley was sitting outside in the cold fog drinking a vanilla milkshake into which she'd poured four cups of coffee. She was morose and twitchy, a lost little hedgehog. Her t-shirt said, I'LL FIX IT IN POST. She told herself that "Amends" was out of her control now. *And so is everything else.* She tormented a lump of melting ice cream with her straw. She checked her phone but nobody had called in the past five minutes.

Emebet wandered out then. She'd wanted to go for one last walk in the fog. She was startled to find Bentley on the stone bench. In the otherworldly atmosphere of the courtyard they looked like monsters, strange and beautiful, almost sisters. A unicorn meeting a kirin, a narwhal encountering a mermaid. An archaeopteryx, suddenly coming across a phoenix.

Emebet looked at her for a moment, impressed against her will: *This is someone who works in television!* She studied Bentley, and wondered whether she would get to be like her if she stayed sober. Then she noticed something.

"Aren't you getting wet?" she asked, gesturing toward her behind.

Bentley, who in fact was just realizing that the dew had soaked through her jeans, grimaced her way to a smile. "Oh, no, it's nice out," she said.

"Yes. I thought it looked just like... what is it called? The paintings they make where everything goes around like this," Emebet said, waving her hands in a way she hoped conveyed "watercolors." "So I thought I would go and walk around one last time."

"One last time," Bentley echoed.

Emebet waved at her and, evidently considering the conversation closed, sauntered off to walk her delicate circuit of the courtyard. She quickly disappeared into the thickening mist. She was thinking that Bentley must be so focused on her craft that she didn't notice mere inconveniences of the flesh.

Bentley remained on the damp stone bench. Her bare arms were covered in goosebumps. She was used to thinking of Emebet as "the homeless woman," "the Ethiopian," "the Christian—we need a Christian, lots of drama and controversy there." Now for the first time she'd noticed Emebet's swaying walk and her considering, tender expression.

I'm not comfortable!, Bentley thought; but didn't move.

*   *   *

The six stars of "Amends" were standing in the parking lot waiting for the bus to take them back to the airport. They were still being filmed from afar, but they'd been given the go-ahead to take off their mikes. They felt self-conscious now without them. They scratched idly at the marks left by the tape and wondered what to say.

Sharptooth was scratching at her shoulder blades as well. Medea noticed and decided to teethe on her for a while. "What are you scratching for? You don't have eczema, don't plagiarize somebody else's medical condition."

"What? No, I respect your right to your disease. My wings are itching."

Everybody turned to look at her.

"Look," Medea said slowly, "I realize that I was high all through biology class, but I'm pretty sure that wolves don't have wings at any stage in their development. The common or garden wolf does not cocoon itself and then blossom into a glorious wolfafly."

Sharptooth wouldn't be badgered. "Many 'kin have unique body parts or mixed identities. I always thought I was just regular old wolfkin—"

"Werewolf," Medea muttered.

"—but this has been a profound experience for me, and sometimes deep spiritual experiences can reveal elements of our kintype which we hadn't noticed before. In this case, wings."

"That would scare me," Medea said. "If I could suddenly wake up with, like, a tail or horns, just because I'd had a *profound spiritual experience*, I think I'd stay at home all day watching 'Punky Brewster' and eating Twix."

"That's because you're afraid to get in touch with your true self," Sharptooth said. She added, as a compliment, "I wonder whether you might be 'kin yourself. Sometimes the things we have the strongest negative reactions to are parts of ourselves we refuse to welcome."

"I wonder if I should take up smoking," Medea said, in a blatant refusal to reply.

J. Malachi nodded. "It's traditional for people in recovery," he said.

There was a pause. They were uncomfortable with situations in which they weren't sure exactly what to do, so they made an effort to look busy; most of them tried to look as if they were examining the fog for signs of an approaching bus. Others fiddled with their luggage or checked their newly-returned phones.

Dylan said quietly, "I know it's weird, but I've honestly really enjoyed this place, after I stopped puking. I think if I could have a room or a house that was just me and a group of other, you know, people with drinking problems—even Medea—and no alcohol, and a bunch of toilets for me to clean when I get edgy... I think I could be happy with that."

"Does the room or house have a door?" Colton asked, dryly but fondly.

Dylan grinned. "Yeah, that's the problem. Everything has a door."

"Where is everyone going after this?" J. Malachi wondered.

"Home sweet hovel," Colton said, and Medea chimed in, "Me too."

"I'm staying with my coach through the end of the season, which... will be stressful," Dylan said. "I get to be the unsinkable Cheerio."

"My mom's," Sharptooth said, daring them to challenge her.

Emebet looked away, and fussed with her scarf. "I am living in Jaymi's apartment for a little while," she said. Several of the others made schoolyard noises.

"It's—I'm staying with a friend," J. Malachi said quickly. "She's looking after my apartment. While I'm not there. I'm gonna call some friends when I get back in town and set something up. She's babysitting my shrimp."

"I thought your shrimp died?" Medea asked.

"I'm getting new ones."

"They won't be the same, though. You shouldn't talk as if they're the same," Medea said. "You can't just *replace* pets. You can't just order shrimp from a catalog and expect them to be these perfect little animals, just like the shrimp you used to have."

J. Malachi looked at her in bewilderment. "Actually that's exactly what you can do," he said. "They don't have a ton of personality."

"I just think you're being very cavalier about your responsibilities. And putting a lot of expectations on these shrimp."

The bus pulled into the parking lot. Six small, uncertain people disappeared into the bus, and after a pause, the bus shuddered and disappeared into the fog. The show was over.

Chapter 14: The Gift of Failure

Bentley was twitchy and akimbo in her seat, in jeans and an unwashed t-shirt at this meeting where everybody else was carefully casual. Bentley had been more careful and less casual than she appeared; the t-shirt today read, IT'S NOT ME. IT'S YOU. She'd treated herself to lunch before the meeting: a classic addict's meal, a salad of tofu and winter greens followed by nine peanut butter fudge bars. She felt sticky, granular and sick. She wanted another fudge bar.

"I think it was a fine idea on your part," a very young and highly-polished man said.

This chromium fetus was trying to make her *feel better*; she was appalled.

"To show a different side of alcoholism and recovery. But the thing is—"

"They behaved too well," Whelkin Jeames laughed. He was a small man with a giant laugh, a big deep crinkly Santa Claus laugh coming from his thin pursed mouth. "No fucking, no fighting. They *courted*."

"There was fighting!" Bentley protested. It seemed

259

somehow important to say that her alcoholics hadn't been so well-behaved as all that.

Jeames nodded. "Right, they talked at each other. Fighting about German philosophy or what it's like to be a zoo animal or whatever it was. Fights nobody understood. Also, what happened to the production-assistant angle? We were supposed to follow that woman, Ana, as she coped with the stresses of producing a reality show. Very meta. *Especially* meta because it didn't actually ever happen."

Bentley tried to figure out a way to avoid saying, *I got bored.*

"That was a deliberate decision on my part," she said, choosing self-responsibility over strict honesty. "I didn't want to create an easy outlet for the audience's empathy. I wanted them to have to look at the world the way our talent looks at it."

"'Talent.' The thing is, people don't want to see the world the way a bunch of alcoholics see it. They want a sympathetic viewpoint. Anyway we thought about repackaging it as a reality-comedy, one of those shows where you're supposed to laugh. Maybe call it something like, 'I'm Not As Smart As I Think I Am.' Like a reality version of those sitcoms where you hate all the characters."

Bentley nodded intensely. "Yeah. Yeah, like 'The Daily Show.' That could work!"

Jeames looked at her for a long silent moment. "No. Now, I know you have a really nice education—"

"Which you worked hard for!" the fetus interjected.

"No I didn't," she said.

"The point is," Whelkin Jeames said, "there's nothing here

to clip. None of this makes any sense to anybody if you're flipping channels, or these days, if you're watching a five-minute YouTube trailer. It's hard to market and I'm not saying that's your fault. I'm just saying this is the lowest-rated reality show we've ever produced." (This was before the Urinal Girl episode aired, prompting a brief but sharp spike in the viewership.) "They're great people, I'm sure, or at least they're the kind of people you said they were, but," and with those three letters he yanked a steel security curtain down over his face. "We're done with this."

She practically bounced up out of her seat. "Okay!"

She held out her hand. Whelkin Jeames was still sitting. He stared at her protruding veins and red, bony knuckles until he realized she expected him to shake. He put his small, soft, moist and oddly formless hand in hers, as if he were giving her a newborn animal. She was afraid to squeeze it so she just moved her hand up and down aimlessly and then let him go. She almost lost her balance and had to stutter forward in her stilettos; then she was a little too close, so she stuttered back.

"Okay," she said, regrouping. She wasn't done. She was never definitely done. "I appreciate the opportunity, and I appreciate your honesty. And I know this will be—just one step on our road together. On our road...s," she tried again, "our different, personal, individual roads."

"Please do feel free to pitch us on your next idea," Jeames said.

The fetus gabbled some enthusiastic kiss-off, but Jeames had already left the room in spirit. Only his small body was hanging around waiting for her to leave.

*   *   *

Emebet stood at the window of J. Malachi's apartment and watched an early snowfall feathering the streets where she used to live. The weather had turned the day they left rehab, and each day of the past three weeks had been colder than the last. Three weeks sober on her own: It felt longer, even though in fact J. Malachi was the only one whom it impressed.

She'd cut her hair, and she still felt a little lightheaded from the absence of familiar weight.

J. Malachi had argued against this change. "I don't want to tell you what to do," he'd said, which wasn't a prepossessing beginning, "but I remember how I wanted to change my appearance when I first got on the show. I didn't want to be recognizable. And so I was planning to just stop shaving. This is one of the advantages of being a man: We can grow our own disguises. But in the end I'm glad I didn't do that. I had to face up to it with, you know, my face."

"Hm."

"Besides, guys love long hair! I mean me, but also other men, if that's something that interests you."

"That's true."

"Your hair is beautiful."

"Hm."

And the next time he'd seen her, it had been shorn. But he had been right that it hadn't helped.

She'd been living in the apartment, applying for jobs— first the jobs she actually wanted, answering phones at law offices and immigration services, and then the jobs J. Malachi thought she should get, doing social media for community newspapers, and finally all the other jobs.

She was restless and she found regulated life as exhausting

as the streets. She had all the same scares and nightmares as when she was homeless, the same fragmented sleep and jumpiness, but now people noticed and acted like she was being crazy. She had told J. Malachi a few days ago that she felt like she was living a life made out of his things, his friends, his ideas, his apartment, his advice.

"Like a wasp's-nest," he'd said, and nodded like he knew what she meant. "Gummed together out of old gray pieces of me."

"I don't know what that is," she said, in a low furious voice. He thought she sounded like Bette Davis, caged and undefeated.

"A wasp is a small stinging insect, it has a painful sting like a hornet or—or a sort of super bumblebee, and they build these—"

And she had screamed a little then.

That had been their first fight, and he had fought excruciatingly fair; he'd fought like the penitent capitalist in *This Little Piggy Joined the Workers*. (He'd fought like his parents.) He'd apologized and literally taken notes on how he could be a better partner, in the reporter's notebook he had bought for her. She had lectured him and then apologized for lecturing, and they had agreed to chew the walls of their home together, and that had helped. He'd asked her what had surprised her about their fight ("I always ask that! It's a great way to get sources to open up") and that had not helped as much.

It would be a long time before they learned to fight well. J. Malachi hated conflict and tended to fling apologies randomly in the hope of never having to talk about his mistakes again, whereas Emebet needed time to do what she called thinking and he called brooding. Still, they were trying.

She had just sent a cover letter and her limping, bandaged resume to a service which provided therapy for people who'd had bedbugs. She hoped it focused on cognitive behavioral techniques rather than exposure therapy.

Emebet opened the window. The air outside was soft; snowflakes blew in, and melted against her skin. They caught in her eyelashes. She wanted to be out on the street again, with a pint of bottom-shelf vodka and the certainty that she was unloved.

Instead her phone hummed. She left the window open and padded over to retrieve it: Jaymi had texted, *What r u doing?*

Snow, she texted back. She didn't want to tell him about the resume yet. She wasn't sure she had the energy for his encouragement.

Her phone buzzed. *Snow? Stop staring morosely at snow.* He texted a follow-up: *Or walking morosely in snow.* She shook her head, almost laughing despite herself, and opened up her dictionary app; then she did laugh.

She was surprised—this was one surprising thing, although she hadn't thought of it in time to tell him when he asked—by how much she liked it when he knew her. He caught her doing things like staring morosely at snow. He made all her moody self-indulgences, all her confessions and excuses and personal anathemas, into inside jokes.

Her phone buzzed again: *Uh sorry i dont mean to tell you what to do.*

She took a picture of the view from the window and sent

it back to him: *Picture to hang inside wasps nest.* He sent back *Lol we can have this picture instead of a window.*

She imagined taking photos of everything she wanted—a wall with photographs of liquor bottles, dollar bills and candies, jewelry, a thousand flowers, her family all around her—and she laughed, hard, with the snowflakes drying on her cheeks.

*　　*　　*

Dylan was forty minutes late to Dinner with a Sinner. Somebody had jumped in front of a subway train. Dylan was fidgety, then muttering out loud and holding too tightly to the metal pole, then guilty and sorry when the conductor made his announcement and the whole train started to murmur and decipher it. And then angry again. He held a whole argument in his head, not with Gair of course but with the other, unknown Christian who'd accompany him. In Dylan's mind this person was slightly older, maybe just out of college; he had a turned-down mouth and condescending facial hair.

You're very late. Have you been drinking?

No! Of course not—

There's no "of course" about it, this douchebag Christian said, and Dylan was especially angry with him because it was true. *We have this Breathalyzer here*—no, that was unrealistic, that probably wouldn't happen. He wouldn't be lucky enough to get a chance to prove that he was telling the truth.

We've been worried. This is very thoughtless of you. You could at least have called.

I forgot my phone. But anyway I couldn't've gotten a signal underground. It's not my fault!

So by the time he finally arrived at the unknown Christian's house, he was aggrieved and defensive.

"Hey," he said roughly when the man opened the door. (He was doughier and a bit older than Dylan had imagined, but he did, in fact, have a wispy little beard that seemed to flourish only in the cleft of his chin.) "I'm *sorry*, there was an accident on the subway."

The man had the gift of raising just one eyebrow. Dylan barely restrained the impulse to head-butt him right in the beard.

He tried to be companionable during dinner, but he kept mistiming his jokes and interjections. He found himself talking over Gair or the other man, who turned out to be named Lance—short for Lansing, Michigan, "where I was conceived." Dylan got frustrated with his own rudeness and retreated into silence, only to realize that he looked sulky and childish.

Lance excused himself, with another lift of the eyebrow directed at Gair. Dylan looked at the tablecloth. He thought it was probably self-centered to apologize. Maybe they hadn't even noticed that he was being an asshole. *Not everything is about you*, he told himself sternly.

Gair gave a quiet laugh. "You look *miserable*," he said.

Fuck. "I'm sorry—"

"I forgive you," Gair said easily. And then, "I'm sorry we're annoying you. I know you're not all about church stuff or—"

"*No*, seriously, please don't apologize. I'm the one who's being awful. I have no idea how you don't get sick of me."

"I do," Gair said. "All the time! But you know better than anyone that getting sick is no reason to stop the party."

A genuine grin snuck onto Dylan's face. "So you're saying that our whole friendship is based on the principle of 'boot and rally.'"

"Put it this way, I'm not saying that's *false*."

"I really am grateful. I'm a very grateful asshole."

Gair grinned. "That is actually the target audience of the Christian faith," he said. "Look, do you want to just be quiet and let us talk, maybe let us pray over you after dessert? Or do you want to talk about whatever it is that's making you crazy? Something's clearly driving you nuts."

"*I'm* driving me nuts."

Gair nodded—and then gave a sudden, startled yelp of laughter. "You know that's a sin, right?" he said, giggling.

Dylan cocked his head and looked at him quizzically.

Gair, immensely pleased with himself: "Only your wife is supposed to drive your nuts."

Lance walked back in right at the punchline. "I'm not sure we should be discussing what does not prosper us," he said. "If the salt lose its savor, how shall it be salted?"

"I can verify that Gair hasn't lost his—uh, I, shutting up now. I rebuke myself." Dylan made a "zipping the mouth" gesture. But he felt better.

*　　*　　*

In a booth at Bargaining, Ana was sipping a gin rickey while Bentley was judging it. Bentley was slumped with one arm lolling across the table and her head nodding bleakly. "I'm grateful for this experience," she said experimentally.

"Why?"

Bentley glared at her. She hadn't expected to have someone demand that she make up a reason. "Every moment is a gift," she attempted.

"No, but that would apply to anything. Why are you

grateful for *this* experience? I'd like to know." Ana sipped, delicately, like a researcher dabbing deodorant on a rabbit's eye.

"It'll keep me humble," Bentley said. "Everybody in TV is so inflated. Infatuated with themselves. When you meet somebody who's genuine and down-to-earth it must be so refreshing—you'd want to, maybe, help that person out."

This rang very false in her own ears. She generally preferred to help the fake and the fatuous; she preferred credit and counterfeit to cash. She liked taking people at their word, as she liked every form of wishful thinking.

But Ana was nodding, co-signing every syllable. "Humility is the best policy," she said.

Bentley, in her slough of humility, watched the ice cubes watering down Ana's drink.

"You do have a gift, though," Ana said. "I believe that we were all given life on this planet for a purpose. We each have a unique, never-before-seen gift, which we can bring to the world if only we don't squander it."

"Very 1970s."

"Maybe your gift is failure."

Bentley said, after a pause, "That's a shitty gift. That's the worst fucking X-Man."

"You know so many things! So much about *life*. You said yourself, addicts have insight. I don't know myself very well because I haven't failed as much as you have."

Bentley grabbed the menu. She glared at it and jabbed a hard-bitten fingernail at the cocktail list. "Look at this thing. Seabreeze with beet juice and salmon foam, there's an asterisk so they can tell you they mean the actual salmon fucking fish, and raw radish. You know, I feel like these days I'm haunted by radishes? Everywhere I go. *Veal-infused* cardamom bourbon. Veal! 'Waiter, there's a cow in my drink!' These are the fucking end of days."

"So everyone says," Ana said.

Bentley sighed. "Ah, addicts are all such apocalypse junkies. We love this idea of the end of the world, we kind of test-drive it in fact. I bet it was awesome to be an addict during the Cold War. You could pass out, secure in the knowledge that the Soviets would blow us all away before your hangover hit.... No morning after. And maybe in the new devastated world you'll do better, you'll change...."

The waiter brought her another iced tea and she sucked it down morbidly. *Better luck next time,* she thought: the addict's war cry.

"Gotta go to the john," she said. "Hold my grudges for me."

She pulled herself up painfully from the low seating. She locked herself in the little unisex bathroom and stared at the wall ahead of her. There were pornographic paintings of women masturbating, for some reason. She looked up at the ceiling and it was painted with a hundred eyes.

"These people are trying too hard," she muttered. She felt small and jangled and cheap; and then, like something falling over, she thought, *I'm going to drink today.*

Her heart was pounding. She told herself that she'd had that thought many times and hadn't done it. *You always act like it's over before you've even started,* she thought, *but in fact you don't have to do anything. This is just a thought, it's not a vision of the future.*

But Bentley was superstitious about bathrooms. If a thought struck her in a bathroom she gave it much more weight than if it occurred to her in a kitchen or on the subway. She'd spent too much time on her knees throwing up to avoid investing the toilet with mystical authority.

She walked back out to Ana with her smile tacked to her face like a flyer with none of the tags ripped off. HAVE YOU SEEN ME?

*   *   *

Jaymi had a hard time explaining to his parents that he wanted to marry Emebet, in that first year after "Amends." He was trying to ask for their permission—he wasn't able to ask her parents for her hand in marriage, so he was using his own as substitutes—but they were playing hard to get.

"Are you sure this marriage idea isn't just a phase?" his mother asked. "This... conservatism... I think a lot of young people these days go through a stage like that. It's a matter of delayed development."

"Do you have a lot in common with her?" his father said.

"Yes," he said.

There was a small raw silence when his parents realized that they didn't want to talk about the things Emebet had in common with their son.

"Anyway, I don't believe in having things in common," Jaymi said stubbornly. "She believes more or less the same things I do about marriage and she's very pretty. And we live in the same town. For millennia those were good enough reasons for the human race to get married. Why shouldn't it be good enough today?"

His mother shook her head. "I worry about you," she said.

"Well—at least it will be a multicultural marriage." (Emebet's own view on the cross-cultural enterprise of her marriage had been a long sigh, followed by, "At least I can be sure you're not my cousin.")

"You could argue that marriage is a form of peacemaking," Jaymi suggested. "Like, we're the pacifists in the war between the sexes?"

"You *could* argue that," his father conceded. "I wouldn't."

*   *   *

It was January 2, just over a year after "Amends," and Medea was wandering purposefully toward the liquor store telling herself she wouldn't stop there. *They probably aren't even open.*

After "Amends" finished filming she'd stayed sober for a startling ten months, for reasons she'd preferred not to articulate to herself. During that time she'd written a new play, *The Alcoholists*, about a political movement advocating personal irresponsibility, and gotten a grant to adapt *Nightwood* for the stage. She had extensive notes for *Fake Hibiscus*, which was turning out to be a Tennessee Williams pastiche. She'd lost twelve pounds and sometime in August she'd realized that her insomnia had been gone for over a month.

She'd always thought of herself as a person who slept badly. The challenge to her identity was, she suspected—to the extent that she was capable of sustained thought—the reason she was drinking again.

On the way to the liquor store she fed herself a lot of sticky-sweet platitudes. *I might just stop in and get matches, I should start smoking for New Year's.* That would be a great story: Her last time in a liquor store was just to look around and get a matchbook.

Of course, she thought, *if I do pick up something, it's good. It's part of the process. It's a way of proving to myself that I need to humble myself and do AA like everybody else.*

She liked this idea of forced humility. She had told herself several times now that in her joyless, lightless drinking she was embracing a countercultural experience of helplessness, she was enacting a spiritual surrender; she declined to notice that she was doing this entirely on her own terms.

She felt good about herself as she walked along the street, through the detritus of the New Year: plastic bottles of Dubrov and (for the discerning gutter drunk) Popov, Remy and even Wild Irish Rose, which struck her as a charmingly old-fashioned choice. She felt solidarity with this garbage. She felt that it, like her, was freighted with great and overlooked symbolic meaning. Others might pass trash by, but not her! She was a salvage artist.

Anyway, they're probably not open.

She smiled, happy and youthful: a gamine, a disingenue. Butter wouldn't melt in her mind.

The classy liquor store wasn't open, which didn't surprise her. She'd been there too much lately anyway. She needed to change it up. *And oh, it looks like there are some interesting Christmas displays still up on the street with Sav-Rite Liquors. I want to see those lights.*

As she reached the crosswalk she suddenly noticed something pacing her, just a few steps behind. She turned her head sharply to catch this deferential footpad and saw that it was a bird: a very big, ragged black bird, with the hunch of a vulture but a feathered head. It looked sort of like a seabird but much more like an alcoholic hallucination.

Medea caught her breath. She'd forgotten what it was like to recognize hallucinations and consider them normal. It made her feel empty and muffled. It made something in her feel closed-off. She remembered J. Malachi talking about a black box and a plane crash, and she didn't like this silent bird; it wasn't a friend.

She tried to shoo it away. She'd come to once in a vacant lot, with thorns in her fishnets and the contents of her wallet strewn around under bushes, and she could have sworn that there were two vultures courting on the low brick wall she'd crumpled against. She loved to tell this story—or at least, she'd loved to tell it before TV rehab. At Noah's Rainbow people had consoled her for the fear she must have felt, waking up in an unknown place, not knowing what might have happened to her, bruised and scratched and menaced by vultures. They hadn't thought it sounded awesomely hardcore.

This bird hopped a few steps away from her but continued to pace alongside her as she crossed the street. They were walking past the Christmas decorations now. She saw that the most lit-up house had a front lawn like a massacre: It had been filled with inflatable holiday balloons, Santa and elves and reindeer, but they had all deflated. The limp colorful carcasses littered the lawn.

A stone path wound between the dead balloons up to the blue front door of the house. The house sat on a tiny grass-covered hillock, and a short flight of concrete steps led down from the stone path to the sidewalk. Medea spotted something at the base of these steps which she thought at first was a fancy glass goblet filled with abandoned champagne.

She tripped toward it, with the black bird hopping beside her, but when she got closer she saw that it was a big plastic cup— and the liquid inside was definitely too yellow for champagne.

The bird made a hopping run forward and flapped up into the air. Soundlessly it flew up and away. Medea watched it go, and then looked again at the plastic cup of piss.

It's possible that my life is devolving into a sort of existential rebus, she thought. *Highlights for Bad Children. What's worse is that I think I know what this one says.*

She looked at the neon sign of the Sav-Rite and weighed her options. She had experienced the ecstasy of drunkenness and the pointlessness of being a drunk; and now she had experienced relapse. (This was the first time she'd thought the word "relapse" about her actions. She noticed that it had a certain kitsch appeal. It had a tawdry sincerity, which was the only kind of sincerity Medea could respect.) Long-term sobriety, by contrast, would be a new experience from which she could learn new things.

I bet being sober has a real dark side, she thought. *I bet it's got some hidden teeth.* This thought strengthened and comforted her.

She decided to have a large mocha at the coffee shop at the end of the block and then go home. And so her relapse ended.

*   *   *

Emebet was just slipping out of J. Malachi's apartment building when she heard someone yelling her name.

"Emebet! Hey, girl, hold that door!"

She turned and looked, and deliberately let the door swing shut under the wishful-thinking sign that read, EMERGENCY EXIT ONLY—ALARM WILL SOUND. She knew the man who was calling her.

He was an old man named Randolph, tough and gray, like a piece of gristle you'd chew and chew until you had no choice but to spit it out in your hand. He was drunk and he was dragging a girl behind him, a pretty young plump girl whose braids were unraveling at the ends. Emebet suspected that the girl herself would soon begin to unravel too.

"Emebet," he said with a disappointed tone, as he caught up to her. "Asked you to hold that door. You ain't do nothing for a person. I been like a father to her," he complained to the girl, "took care of her for years. And you see how she treat me."

"I'm sorry," Emebet said, but didn't mean. She was already running late for dinner with some of J. Malachi's friends, and she didn't like them enough to feel comfortable being late.

"I wanted to ask you something," he said. He coughed, and she could smell malt liquor on his breath, a sweet thick horrible smell that a dog could roll around in. Bad luck and bad ideas rolled off of him in waves.

"Fine. What do you want to ask me for?"

"I didn't say I wanted to ask you *for* nothing! I want to ask you a question. Can I ask a question around here? Is this a democratic, liberated nation?"

"This is DC," Emebet said. "You tell me."

"I wanted to ask you. Do you think I have a problem with alcohol?"

Emebet considered him. "If you're asking the question, you probably have some reason to ask," she said, and her voice was kinder. She didn't mind being of service, and she especially didn't mind the opportunity to give advice.

"What would be better in your life if you didn't drink?" she asked, and suggested, "You'd have more money."

"Yeah," he said mournfully. "Or I'd waste money on something different." This was a fair point. "I like to drink. You gotta weigh that in. You gotta weigh—does how much I like to drink outweigh how much I need to stop? That's the question."

"*That's* the question?"

"That's the question." But he couldn't quite remember where he'd been going with it.

"I like to drink," he said stubbornly. "My life would be worse if I wasn't drinking, because I wouldn't have no alcohol."

The girl was looking at him with a sort of sorrowful lust. Emebet didn't like her chances.

"I ain't drink yesterday," he offered. But then he remembered something: "Yesterday was shit."

"I have to be somewhere," Emebet said gently. "Walk with me."

The drunk old man, whom she had known as long as she'd lived on the streets, offered one arm to her and one arm to the chubby girl. He strolled down the street with them, stumbling and staggering a little so that they had to yaw and pitch with him, like God was playing with his desk toys and they were the knocking ball bearings.

Emebet talked to him about his self-esteem, his relationship with his children, his breath, his sweat, and all the other things which she said would get better if he got sober. He listened and nodded, and his mind sailed away somewhere else.

"I hear you," he kept saying. "But I do like drinking."

They walked like that all the way to the Belgian restaurant where J. Malachi's friends were planning a leisurely evening arguing over lamb brains about whether *Harry Potter* was conservative or libertarian. Emebet invited Randolph to come in and say hello. She felt that she owed him that; she didn't think she was allowed to care about the humiliation it would cause her. But Randolph shook his head. He had a tragic sense of life. He bowed to her as he left, sweeping his arm in front of him, and then he held on to his girl as they slewed off into the night.

Emebet spent most of dinner chatting with the oldest man there about her experiences in the civil war. She usually talked with him; he was a Cold Warrior of Polish descent, always up for revisiting the crimes of what she called the Derg and he just called Communism. He told her stories about his adventures running guns to the mujahideen ("That was back when they were on our side," he noted) and she talked about the time she found a grenade in her mother's shoe. "We were always finding things in the wrong places," she said.

Then he excused himself, and while Emebet was at a loose end, the girl on her other side leaned over to say hello.

She was a skinny white girl who did opposition research for the Senate Republicans, and she'd put away almost an entire bottle of Shiraz. She was wearing a coral business suit which had somehow become off-the-shoulder; her lips and tongue were dyed purple by the wine.

She was a giggly, skittering drunk, her eyes scuttling away from Emebet's like cockroaches under the kitchen light.

"I *love* your fiancé's stuff," she said. The word "love" was swollen with emotion, distended almost to three syllables.

She smelled like a grape-crusher's feet.

"Hm. Thank you."

"I wanted to ask you something." She looked around, hunching her shoulders as if she was trying to hide inside her own skin. She gave Emebet a conspiratorial grin. "I can't ask J. Malachi because I want him to respect me! But I wish you knew me, so I could ask you if I have a drinking problem."

Emebet said, for the second time that night, "If you have to ask the question, there's probably a reason."

The girl sighed for about a minute.

"I *know*," she said sadly. "But I'm such a better person when I'm drinking! I'm friendly, I'm optimistic, I put up with people's bullshit really well. It's just that when I wake up I'm hungover and I need to get Plan B and I steal stuff. I go way off-message. It's really the *hangover* that makes me mean. You know? It's not drinking. I'm a great drunk! I'm just... a really bad post-drunk."

"Do you have someone you trust, who you can talk to? In our church we have something called a soul father—"

"Oooohhhh," the opposition researcher said, and her voice got husky. "A *soul* father. Sssssexy."

"Have you tried taking a break from drinking?"

"Oh yeah. God, I was a total bitch. Everybody around me was like, 'Lizzie, this has been the worst week of our *lives*. Get back on the horse.'"

She nodded, gazing deeply into Emebet's eyes, enraptured by her own dilemma.

"I mean, you have to understand this about me," she said, ready to unveil her deepest secret, what set her apart from everyone else around her: "I *really* like drinking."

*   *   *

Clean for a Day
by Jaymi MacCool
Inside the Whale, February 2014

On the Golden Age television show "Queen for a Day," the housewife with the most harrowing sob story would win appliances and medical care by yanking on the audience's heartstrings. Viewers could indulge several different pleasures as they watched women abase themselves for hearing aids or silver-plated flatware: the pleasure of painless charity, the pleasure of preening one's own luck, and the old covert delectation of the back-fence gossip retailing other people's sorrows.

That's the parallel a friend of mine used when I got back from a stint in televised alcohol rehabilitation. I was a cast member on the first (and so far only) season of "Amends," so if you go online you can watch me vomit and make excuses for myself and cry. My friend called me a fame whore; I pointed out that whores usually get paid, whereas the rehabilitation itself was my only compensation from the show, and that's when he brought up "Queen for a Day."

It seems vain and perverse to become a "star," a "personality," by broadcasting one's most humiliating moments. Everybody's writing a memoir, everybody's going to Confession on Facebook (but nobody's willing to admit their sins in the mere privacy of the confessional), the humblebrag is our only new art form. We'd rather be recognized than respectable. What incredible self-esteem it must take to think that even our grimiest moments are must-see television!

That's one way to think about pride and humility: Pride

puts itself forward, while humility hides and, demurely, demurs.

But let's look at the question with even older eyes. Isn't the whole cult of privacy an early modern invention? Before privacy we lived in houses without bedrooms; we knew our neighbors almost as well as God did. Even concealed confession is an innovation. The early Christians, up through the age of Augustine, confessed once to everybody. Maybe reality TV is the return of the repressed desire for morality plays and charivaris—and for submission not only to God's judgment but to that of society.

Humility accepts submission to an outside standard. In private we can judge by private standards. We can say that other people just don't understand us. We can say that our apartment is "messy, but not dirty," and who will contradict us when our only regular visitor is the exterminator? We can gladhand our consciences and lie to our diaries. I grew an extra face when I was drinking, but nobody knew what he really looked like. (I puked on a guest once at a Heritage Foundation roundtable and everybody envied me because they thought I might have anthrax.)

Even when I went on "Amends," I was enough of a self-invested mess to think that I could smear some Vaseline on the camera lens. I thought I would prove that I was a smart, unique guy with some interesting personal problems, and everybody would agree that there was nothing more I could be doing, and then I'd go back to drinking myself to death in peace. But the problem is that once I was sober, I got to hear how I sounded to a sober person. Suddenly I saw myself through everybody else's eyes.

In the end "Amends" humbled me in two ways: both radical, both countercultural in today's self-justifying, Facebooking America. First, on "Amends" I learned to accept other people's judgments of me as more valid than my own. I had always praised society but I had never knuckled under; like everybody else, I considered myself the exceptional case. On "Amends" I learned to live like a statistic. This turns out to be what everybody else means when they say "common sense." This kind of salutary humiliation can only happen in public—it's the ascesis of celebrity. You're forced to see yourself as YouTube commenters see you. I think most of us would rather wear a hair shirt.

In our own moments of willful self-defeat we may think that the view of the comments-boxers is the *only* true view of ourselves. We may give in to the despair that provides its own comfort: If you can't change, you don't have to. And so I'm especially grateful for the other form of humility I learned on "Amends": I stopped thinking about the cameras. Eventually you get used to that itch along your skin that comes from being watched. You accept it; and at that point you stop trying to sell yourself. You let the cameras see you, in all your idiot glory, and from that point on it's *okay* that you're an idiot. You submit to being judged, and through that submission you learn to accept yourself. Having already let go of your own image of yourself, you are able to let go of others' images of you.

Learning to live without any images of oneself is extraordinarily difficult. Even now, I sometimes feel resentment when I'm unfairly criticized; this is proof that I still somehow believe that I'm a "good person," that fair judgment would always fall in my favor. I still hold on to this idea that people can offend against me by misjudging or misunderstanding me. Honesty and real humility would demand that I let go of the image and therefore let go of the offense against it. After all, I'm unjustly praised far more often than I'm unjustly criticized, and anyway nobody's opinions of me matter very much, including my own. Underneath all the scurf of opinion and fame there is just the next right thing, and then the next, and you do them and try not to think about them once they're done.

"Amends" taught me that I was a weakling when it came to willpower, a moral milquetoast; but because of "Amends," that usually doesn't matter to me anymore. It turns out that lots of great people are terrible people. One of those people did me the honor of consenting to become my bride. She is the beautiful exception to the rule that other people's opinions don't matter. She, and my parents, are the only Nielsen family I need.

So I've learned to love reality TV. But don't worry: I still hate "Big Brother."

*　　*　　*

He read it over. Frowning at "moments of willful self-defeat," he deleted "moments" and wrote "hours"; then deleted that too, and wrote, "years."

He was, for once, sufficiently satisfied.

"Em," he called softly, "can you come take a look at this?"

He ceded his chair to her and hovered. She tried to read the article with him lingering at her shoulder like bad conscience, but it was impossible. "I'd like some cocoa," she said.

"On it!"

He bounced away to the kitchenette, and she settled in to read.

When he came back with the cocoa she said, "'The Golden Age television show.' This is the third article you've asked me to read this month with Golden Age in it."

"I mean, I can't just say 'old'! It's disrespectful."

"Everything has Golden Age?" she said, teasing him. "What was yours?"

He considered this. "Probably in the womb, I think. It has to be something nobody remembers," he explained. "I guess I can say 'classic.'"

Emebet wanted to say that he didn't know what he was talking about. He was writing about how much he'd learned from being ridiculed in YouTube comments—how much that had helped him with his humility—but she had spent whole nights staring and scrolling, swilling the comments on forum threads and blog posts, dizzy and sick by dawn. Whenever she saw her face online (or sometimes just in the mirror) or saw her name in print, her heart pounded and her face burned. When she went outside she wondered, angrily or idly, whether people recognized her. Other Ethiopians stared at her; if they nodded or smiled then they were just clocking her as a fellow habesha, but if they didn't, she knew they were looking at Urinal Hair Girl. There were times when she chose not to go outside because of this, and those times were especially bad.

It had helped him; he had helped her. She looked up into his anxious, admiring eyes.

She shrugged. The decision to be gentle with him brought her some relief, although she thought it might also be cowardice. "I don't understand all of this, but I think maybe because I don't know all the words. Also, I'm not sure you can argue really that something you yourself did was an example of humility."

He lifted both eyebrows in dismay. "Oh. Huh. That's a good point. That kind of undermines the entire article, actually, which is bad because—well, weddings are expensive. Do you think I just shouldn't write it? Should I email Attanasio and apologize?"

"I think you should make this decision yourself. Take self-responsibility," she said, not without fondness.

"That's still not a word," he said, distracted. He sighed. "Maybe I'll just send it in and let him decide if it works or not."

"If I noticed this problem, readers will notice it," she pointed out.

To her surprise, J. Malachi brightened. "Oh, good point!" he said. She tilted her head at him inquiringly.

"It's like the ultimate act of humility, to submit yourself to the judgment of the reader," he said. "That's my whole point! It looks arrogant to defend myself, but I'm actually putting myself in their hands! ...Huh, I never thought of reader-response theory as a form of ascesis before. I'll leave it up to Attanasio," he decided. "And then up to the readers!"

She kissed him then, with the same mixture of wonder and irony with which she kissed the cross in church. She didn't always understand that, either.

*   *   *

It was three years after "Amends" was canceled, and Dylan was on TV again.

"Hi folks, and welcome back to the What the Puck Hockey Sportscast: Where the masks come off. Today we're speaking with Dylan Hall, *former* rookie of the year, *former* NHL first draft, formerly nicknamed 'The Next Big Thing.' Dylan, thanks for being on the show."

"Thank you for inviting me." He was trying to look engaging and maybe flirtatious, but it wasn't quite coming off. He looked like some of his pieces were missing.

The host, Bear Hobart, was a big bearded guy who prided himself on being blunt. He had a loud, insistent voice and pushy clothes, and he was paunchy and a bit faded around the edges. The people who watched his show left comments like, *LOL I love it, what a dick.*

"Look, I'm an up-front guy," Bear Hobart said. "I have to be honest with you—"

Here it comes, Dylan thought. He was pretty convinced that you didn't ever *have* to be honest with someone; maybe you should, and maybe you wanted to, but "I have to be honest with you" was a self-defeating sentence, since it was never true.

"In my opinion, which is the opinion of a lot of fans, you went from being the next big thing to yesterday's news without ever hitting the part in the middle where you give us great hockey! You're a might-have-been. You're propaganda. I mean you coach peewee hockey now. What's the deal with that?"

"I like coaching." His voice was low and rough. He looked hungover when in fact he was just uncomfortable.

"Yeah, you definitely come across like a role model. I'd want *my* kids to learn from you. What was your last championship—beer pong?"

Dylan laughed, which only made Bear more aggressive.

"Look," the host said, "I've followed your career very closely—"

And then the dimple popped out on Dylan's cheek like a bad memory. "Whoa, well, that makes one of us," he said.

Then, more seriously and a bit defensively, "Look, I have no idea why anybody would ever follow my 'career' for any purpose other than entertainment. Or moral education, I guess."

The rest of the interview was just Dylan laughingly agreeing with all of Bear Hobart's criticisms of him while Hobart became increasingly baffled and irate. "I think the main issue is that I lack discipline," Dylan said easily. "Discipline, perseverance. I don't train well."

"And also, you're an alcoholic."

The word, the name of it, caught him badly off-guard. It took a brief, punished hesitation before he could figure out how to answer; but when he spoke his voice was young and light.

"Well, nobody's perfect." He gave a spurt of creased, bleary laughter.

Chapter 15: How to Be Sorry

A list of the jobs held by Colton Rodman in the ten years after "Amends":

-Sign-twirler

-Ball pit lifeguard

-Professional wingman

-Rickshaw pedaler

-Second Naked Scarecrow, HellBound X-Treme Haunted Hayride! of Kansas City

-Picketer

-Scab

-Picketer

-Scab

-Coffin salesman

-Experimental subject for Applebee's

-Slumlord (alleged; Colton, in his defense statement, argued, "How am I a slumlord if I live in the damn building? That is a slum *serf* is what that is.")

-Taco Bell team member (wore salsa packet costume at
   edge of parking lot)

-Model prostate-exam patient for medical students

-Career consultant

-Snoopy

-Line placeholder for Apple products

-Underwear model

-Peppermint Patty (stand-in)

-Assistant developer of erotic fanfiction for HarperCollins

Despite this resume Colton stayed sober. He lived with his
sister and her son, Deserve. He worked a rich vein of irony,
which allowed him to acknowledge that even screaming his
head off in beige underwear in a freezing cold corn field was
better sober. (Alcohol lowers resistance to cold, and also, the
portajohns were almost a mile away.)

He yelled at Rian for smoking pot: "You're going to retard
that child's development."

"I'll retard your *face*, motherfucker. If I smoke a little on
the weekends it's not gonna kill him."

"Oh, well, if it's not gonna kill him go right ahead! Let's
keep our standards high."

"I don't even know why you're complaining! You seen
how I get when I don't smoke. You think *volcanic tiger-fucking
rage* is good for child development?"

"You're overpaying, by the way. I saw what was in that
baggie and I can tell you, that dealer does not take pride in
his work."

In the past he would've walked away, nursing the watered-
down victory of the last word. Now he was trying to love

people, so he lost a lot more arguments.

Colton liked the people from "Amends"—he felt he had more in common with them than with the hard-luck local types at the AA meeting he intermittently haunted, the meeting he called "Redneck Rehab." But he didn't stay in touch, and neither did they. Dylan drunk-dialed him at first, until even a bag of rice couldn't save his phone and he lost Colton's number. The depressing truth of the "geographical" is that you can't move away from your problems, but you can move away from your friends. Wherever you go, there they aren't.

And anyway Colton's life was so busy that it was hard to find the time to chat. There was always some school event for Deserve—Colton had the parent's delight in learning how dinosaurs had changed since he was a kid, the joy of being corrected about the brontosaurus—and he worked two nights a week as the token heathen at a Christian debt-counseling service. He'd begun working there about a month after the show wrapped. He didn't like to talk about it, but he was the most popular volunteer there, largely because he had no qualms about lying to banks.

He learned to cook, and Rian taught him to do nails and hair. They both picked up some spare cash in the underground economy as unlicensed cosmetologists. There was always the job hunt, since he never dragged himself out of marginal employment, so that took up a lot of his time. He felt that every week he pried up some rock inside his soul and discovered another squirming little resentment; and this, too, was steady work, for which he was always eventually grateful.

Deserve was a happy kid: Colton and Rian never tired of

exclaiming about it, praising him for it, being surprised by it. He "lost" his coat so many times that Rian yelled at him and shook him, and he tearfully admitted that he'd given the previous two coats away to other kids.

"Those kids got more money than we do," Rian said, shaking her head, trying not to grin. She swiped at her eyes with her elaborate nails. She posted about it on Facebook and tried to make it sound like a complaint.

Both of them looked at the boy and wondered if this was the "before" picture. Would they look back on this time and say, "But he was such a happy kid"? They couldn't trust it.

Familial dysfunction, like every form of abuse of power, has no firm outer boundary. It swells and shrinks, and when it meets its generations-awaited end, the people who killed it don't even know, because they're still afraid. Abuse of power ends—when it does end—invisibly, and much later than outsiders would expect.

Out of all of them only Sharptooth and Colton never drank again. Colton was also, and perhaps relatedly, largely forgotten. He never got arrested, he never became a meme. He was a news ticker whose tick had tocked. One is never sufficiently grateful for ordinary life; there's no time to notice it when it's happening.

*   *   *

From the "Amends" thread at Idiotbox.com:

brunchingehenna: Reviving this thread to post this snippet from Yahoo! News. This is for @princedog!

"WOLFGIRL" TAKES A BITE OUT OF CRIME

Shayna Miller, better known as "Sharptooth" from the short-lived reality series "Amends," used a unique crime-fighting tactic to save a woman from mugging.

Shareece Harold, a mother of four who works nights at a CVS in downtown Atlanta, was walking to the bus stop after work when three men approached her and began to push her, demanding her purse. Miller, who considers herself to be "spiritually a wolf," saw the encounter and ran up to the men, howling and waving her arms.

"Wolves are prosocial animals," Miller explained. "I feel a responsibility to combat stereotypes of wolves and those who identify as wolves. We're not all running behind troikas eating babies."

"I thought she was crazy," Harold admitted. "She was yelling, 'I'm gonna bite you! I'm gonna claw you!' And howling like an actual wolf would howl. It was fairly frightening, to tell you the truth, but it worked."

The men ran off, presumably in fear, and Miller—without further howling—escorted Harold to a police station.

princedog: *_____* How is she so great? Seriously.

sharpercanine: I registered here in order to apologize for the language I used in the news article you have posted. I regret arguing that not all wolves engage in antisocial behavior. I don't believe in the "politics of respectability"; I support wolves and those who identify as wolves, regardless of any aggressive acts they may commit or allegedly commit. All wolves are valid.

*   *   *

As Gair approached the door of his apartment, five years after "Amends," he felt the old familiar dread come out to greet him. Gair, Dylan, Dylan's drinking, Gair's dread: a lot of roommates for a one-bedroom. Plus God, presumably. He sighed and tried not to think about it. His left side ached from where he'd slammed up against the boards during practice. *How much longer do you think you can do this?* Well, how long will it take?

He opened the door and whatever was happening to him clearly wasn't over yet.

"Ugh, turn this off," Dylan said, waving a sticky hand at Gair's television. "Seriously, did Sandra Bullock make this movie to convince people she *didn't* have a drug problem?"

"You're the one who turned it on," Gair said. "I just got home. You saw me."

"She's a really unconvincing addict," Dylan said.

"Okay."

"...You're mad at me. Look," and Dylan pulled himself upright, as Gair braced himself for yet another of these conversations—sentences Dylan started with "Look" never went anywhere good. "I really am sorry. I'm fucking up. I just—I need a little time, you know? I want to get some stuff in order, I... if I want to get my shit together I have to focus on it, you know, and now isn't a good time. I can't be, like, lying in a bed puking all day and seeing creepy shit. I have to work on getting a job. Get my teeth fixed, get a job, work steadily for a while so I can get some time off, then I can do a nice little medical detox and start making something out of my life."

I just opened the door. I literally just walked in here!

Gair hated the sound of his own sighing.

"Great!" he said. "And then the marble will roll down the pipe and over the xylophone to set off the mousetrap which was holding up the bowling ball, which will swing through my window and hit me in my idiot head."

Dylan said, by way of apology, "I bet everybody in your life tells you to kick me out."

"No, my sister is very tolerant of our relationship."

This was true, although if she knew Gair and Dylan weren't sleeping together she would be significantly more concerned.

Gair noticed something, and said, "Thank you for doing all the dishes, that was thoughtful. ...Wait, what were you making up for with that?"

"So, I sort of peed on your couch again. I Febreezed it."

"Well, you can't take it with you." Gair was practicing detachment from his material interests. Dylan, it appeared, was also practicing detachment from Gair's material interests.

"Your sister is great," Dylan said, slurring. "The rest of your family is horrible."

Gair's mother sent him cards on his birthday with verses from Leviticus and the phone numbers of therapists who hugged their clients into heterosexuality. His father's face spasmed every time he mentioned dubious subjects like hip checks or locker rooms, or Canada.

Gair told Dylan what he generally told himself: "They're better now, since I paid off their mortgage. Anyway, I love them."

"Of course you do, otherwise you'd hate them. ...Man, everybody you love just sucks. You need better family, you need better friends. You need better everything!"

Was that really true? Gair didn't think so, when he thought about it. He loved Jesus, and most of the time he loved the Father, and as far as he could tell neither of them had ever let him down. He didn't want to bring that up with Dylan again, so he took a moment to see if he could come up with any other areas where his life was genuinely sufficient.

He thought of one, and brightened. "I think my hair is pretty great," he offered.

"That's a good point," Dylan said. "You have been crowned with a mighty crown." He belched.

Dylan was the first person Gair had ever told about his sexuality. Dylan had grabbed him and, as he froze in terror, hugged him for about a minute. It remained the most unnerving comfort Gair had ever received.

And after that Dylan had gone around for weeks talking about how brave the gay athletes he'd found on Wikipedia were, and hitting people who used the word "fag." It was like having a very stupid knight-errant at his side. And when Gair said that he didn't want to be set up with cute figure skaters or Dylan's gay ex-stepbrother, Dylan had actually listened. (Sort of. "Oh, so Jesus is like your boyfriend," he had mused. "Okay. That makes sense. I mean not normal sense, but it makes Christian-sense, if you know what I mean.")

Dylan was the only person in his life who thought he was doing an okay job of being a person: not an abomination, not an embarrassment, not a closet case, not a self-hating religious fanatic. Dylan looked up to him—well, he spent a lot of time incapable of standing so he looked up to everybody, but he looked up to Gair more.

Gair wished he knew what to do. He had tried tough love with Dylan; now he was trying the other kind. It seemed to have basically the same result.

Dylan fumbled around with the remote control and managed to turn off the TV. He had poured whatever he was drinking into a two-liter Coke bottle, although drinking directly from the bottle removed any plausible deniability he was hoping to preserve.

There was a mostly-empty box of Girl Scout cookies on the floor in front of him. He leaned over, grabbed at a cookie like a bear trying to catch a salmon, and almost fell.

"Whoa," he said, rearing back in his seat, holding the snickerdoodle aloft. "Hey, guy," he said softly, to the cookie. "Om nom nom nom."

He munched, as Gair watched him in numbed, exhausted bewilderment.

With a mouthful of crumbs, Dylan asked, "Is this okay, is it okay that I'm eating you?"

He held up the last chunk of the cookie to his ear, listened to it, and said, "Thanks, bro. I appreciate it," before popping it into his mouth.

He looked at Gair again and his eyes were bad-idea bright.

"I could start paying you rent," he offered.

And then Gair realized that Dylan had skated past even the "talking to food" stage of drunkenness, as his friend said, "I mean, not paying with money. But with other stuff."

Dylan pulled himself up and stumbled over to Gair, who stepped back to avoid him.

"I like you a lot," Dylan said. "We could have fun. Just, like, guy fun, bros bein' bros... bros without clothes." He scrutinized Gair's face. "I want to give back," he said. "Attitude of gratitude, man."

"First of all," Gair said, "it's not a pity fuck if you're doing it to pay rent."

He heard what he had just said and his face turned bright

red. He never knew what to do about Dylan when he was drinking.

"Uh, I mean," he said, and coughed. "I don't want to hurt your feelings here. But this is not attractive to me, what you're doing."

Dylan pouted.

"I mean, you're not even gay! ...Are you?" He felt that it was polite to ask, just in case, although he had no idea what he wanted the answer to be.

Dylan waved a sloshy hand. A grin smeared itself across his face. "Gay, shmay," he slurred. "Shhhhhhhmmmmm*ayyyyy*. Sashay, chante! I could totally be gay."

"Oh, speaking of unconvincing," Gair said. "Go to bed! Try not to piss yourself. Try not to break anything important! Your own body parts don't count."

Dylan looked at him, swayed toward him, then got the message from Gair's intensely disappointed body language and slumped back down on the couch. He pulled a blanket over himself. Gair sighed and retreated into the bedroom.

In the morning he was surprised to find that Dylan was awake and shuffling around the kitchenette, miserably making breakfast. "Thank you," he made himself say, trying to figure out how to start.

"No problem," Dylan said; he stopped suddenly, hung on to the edge of the countertop and took deep, wide-eyed breaths, then belched and kept assembling bacon and eggs. "Ooohhh," he moaned, "I feel all gurgly. I feel, personally, like a gurgle."

"We need to talk about last night," Gair said.

"I'm so sorry," Dylan said immediately. "I was horrible.

You know I hate myself when I'm like that. Please tell me if there's anything I can do to make it up to you, or what I owe you."

"Do you remember anything about what you said after I came in?"

"Oh, shit. That sounds really, really bad. Your voice sounds bad. Uh... no. I don't."

"I *really* hope you're telling the truth," Gair said.

"I—me too. Uh, is it okay if I throw up in your sink before we do this, though?"

Gair, unimpressed: "What happens if I say 'no'?"

Dylan looked around the kitchen, then down at himself. "I could use my shirt," he offered.

"Oh God. Sorry. Yes, go throw up in the sink."

"Thanks!"

I am a tree, Gair thought, closing his eyes. *I am a tall, majestic palm, swaying gently in the tropical breeze.* Then the noises Dylan was making drove any calming imagery out of his mind.

As Dylan coughed and spat, Gair outlined the events of the previous night in a clipped, police-report paragraph.

"Wow," Dylan said, and he seemed genuinely surprised by the depths of his own awfulness. "That's—I'm so sorry."

He nodded, staring at the countertop.

"That's terrible, I wouldn't have thought even I could do something like that. I really am sorry."

Gair let out a thin breath. "Okay."

He wished he knew where this conversation was supposed to go.

There was a long pause while Dylan cooked the bacon,

took the strips out of the pan with his fingers, and cooked the eggs in the bacon fat. He took the plates over to the table, carrying them on his arm like a waiter so he could wiggle his burnt fingertips. They both bowed their heads and Dylan reached his hands across the table. Gair didn't want to—and anyway, weren't Dylan's fingers supposedly just burnt?—but he took Dylan's hands anyway, and sat there in silence for a moment hoping that whatever he was doing counted as praying.

When he let go of Dylan's hands and lifted his head, Dylan was watching him. "So, this is kind of a shitty question but apparently I'm a shitty person, so... was I at least a little bit of a turn-on? Like, have I still got it? Wow, I'm turning into my *mom*, sorry about the phrasing, but was I kind of sexy in a train-wrecky way?"

"*No*, you were not 'sexy,' *ugh*," Gair snapped. "You were *pathetic*. You haven't been 'sexy' to me in years! When I fantasize about you nowadays it's always from back when we were still in juniors, which is kind of gross and sad, by the way, and makes me feel like a dirty old man."

"You're still totally young to me," which was Dylan trying to be helpful.

"Besides which, you were blackout drunk and I'm not a rapist."

Shit, I just admitted that I fantasize about him, Gair realized. *Although I guess he knew that, which is why we're having this conversation. I would really super like to eventually have an experience that isn't humiliating.*

Dylan waved his hand to dismiss the rapist thing.

"You really don't think I'm hot anymore?" He sighed. "I

guess I'm not the Next Big Thing these days."

"This is not the conversation we need to be having."

"No, right, you're right. Look—I should just go. Right? I should just take off, and then things would be good for you."

"Oh my God, *stop trying to solve your problems!*" Gair's voice rose in an abandoned wail.

"Wait, what? Why is it bad to try to solve my problems? I thought that was what you wanted me to do!"

Gair took a slow breath. "You are constantly looking for some solution, the thing you can do that will make you better and kinder and—and burn fifty pounds using this one weird trick. You're looking for the *answer*, like once you find it, getting your life in order will be easy. Stop looking for an answer and just do the things. Even when you don't know how."

"How?"

"It doesn't matter how! I can't *believe*," and this was something Gair had never allowed himself to say out loud before, "that you get to sit there and destroy your life however you want to, and I have to keep trying to do the right thing! You get to live like *that*, and I have to live like this."

Gair immediately regretted saying this; and regretted it more when Dylan looked at him, with an expression Gair couldn't read at all, and said quietly, "If I could trade with you I wouldn't."

Dylan shook his head. "I'm sorry. I do try, I know you can't tell. I don't know why it doesn't stick. I just—I always mean it, you know?"

Gair knew; and had no idea what to do with it.

"You need to persevere," he said gently.

"But that's the thing that doesn't stick around," Dylan said, "the thing I persevere with."

He felt betrayed, stupid, embarrassed, exhausted, obnoxious, regretful, smelly, self-defeating, worthless, stubborn, deeply frightened, apparently no longer sexy, and confused; he summarized this to himself as, *Ugh, I am so hungover right now.*

Maybe today Jesus will return, Gair thought, in much the same way that Dylan thought, *Maybe I'll be hit by a truck.* Gair felt a lot of very familiar regret, but he knew that there was no point paying attention to it; it would be replaced by newer and sharper regrets soon enough.

*   *   *

Welcome to Atlantis: Howl Back Girl
The Atlanta Alternative, August 22, 2017

In "Welcome to Atlantis," we give you a taste of Atlanta's wildest and weirdest denizens. And what's wilder than a wolf? Well, maybe a wolf who looks more like Little Red: reality-show mascot Shayna Miller, a.k.a. "Sharptooth." We interviewed Miller at her mother's home in Sherwood Forest.

TAA: Tell us a little about yourself.
SM: My name is Sharptooth, and I identify as a winged wolf, Canis lupus. I'm a vegan, in recovery, polyamorous, currently unpartnered, a social change agent, Jewish, temporarily able-bodied except for the species dysmorphia, and I have three animal companions.

TAA: Also wolves?
SM: No, cats.

TAA: You call yourself an "otherkin."

SM: Yes, that means that I've done a lot of introspection, a lot of self-work, and I believe that spiritually I am a wolf. My soul and mind don't match my body. Most people's don't!

TAA: What do you do for a living?

SM: I'm a life coach, and I curate the Fur Afield news pages and also moderate there. I'm the author of a forthcoming self-published memoir, *Terminally Unique.* I'm certified in conflict resolution. And I'm the drummer for Disobedience School, an otherkin agit-pop, trip-dub group. Actually we don't use the term "group"—it's very exclusive. It creates artificial boundaries between the people who are in the group and the people who aren't, between the artist and the audience. So we say that we're music facilitators.*

[* *Babar, the frontman for Disobedience School, emailed us to say that Miller is not affiliated with the group any longer. I emailed Miller for her response, and she replied, "I identify as the drummer for Disobedience School." She did not elaborate.*]

TAA: You've been on a few reality TV shows. I think "Amends" was the first? But then you did "Reality Bites," "The Sultans of Sting," "Possum Perfect," "Tila Tequila's More to Love," "Pet Hotel: Luxury Suites," "American Ferret"...

SM: And you can see my mom in the background in several scenes from the Lhasa Apso episode of "Dog Show Divas."

TAA: Would you say that you're a fame whore?

SM: No, I think that's very othering language. I think of myself as a fame worker. I'm an advocate.

TAA: You spearheaded the protests at the Humane Society last March, which accused them of using "speciesist" language and marketing. Don't you think that's aiming your anger in the wrong direction? I mean, these are people who are trying to help animals.

SM: Condescension is never helpful. We believe that oppression begins in thoughtspace. Words have meaning! And so changing the language we use is actually the most important step we could take. It's ridiculous to call compassionate behavior "humane." Humans don't have a monopoly on kindness.

TAA: We don't have a monopoly on violence, either. Do you believe in prosecuting animals who kill other animals? Are dolphins rapists?

SM: First of all, that's profiling and stereotyping. Not all dolphins engage in unwanted sexual activity. Second, there's a lot of debate about this subject within the animal-rights and 'kin communities. Personally I'm a noninterventionist when it comes to interspecies violence, but I know that many people believe that stance to be a form of complicity. The two big camps here are liberationist and noninterventionist. You'll also sometimes hear the problem framed as a choice between managed conflict resolution and anarchecology.

TAA: Is "managed conflict resolution" among animals... basically a zoo?

SM: I would compare it more to the United Nations.

*   *   *

Six years after "Amends," Bentley was parked behind a blond fake-wooden table and a stack of books. Five rows of empty chairs confronted her. "Okay, now put your chin on your elbow and kind of slump over," the photographer from the local alternative weekly said. "Like you're really feeling down."

Bentley, in a t-shirt which said YOU DESERVE IT, obeyed. "Great!"

She looked at the cover of her book, *The Gift of Failure: How to Reach the Top by Bottoming Out*. She kept having to tell people that it wasn't really about "getting to the top" at all—it was about a whole change in your mentality! It was a much bigger thing.... Usually they started talking before she finished that sentence. The book was about the theory of recovery, which was the part she liked best.

She wondered if she'd still be staring at those empty chairs in fifteen minutes, when the actual reading was supposed to start. When she was a little kid she used to play pretend book signing. She made the covers for the books—*The Fun Puppy*, and then when she got older *Splinters from the Unicorn's Horn*, and then *I Hate Your Handbag and I Hate Your Heart*—and then she'd sign them, with a theatrical flourish. They were blank inside, of course.

The idea of having her own, real-life, somebody-else's-tab book signing would have blown her away back then. It was the ultimate in success, total validation. "Why is everything always the thing *before* the real thing?" she muttered.

She twisted her hand in her necklace chain. Her one-year chip pinballed between her breasts and then sprang out of the top of her shirt collar.

"Congratulations," she told herself. "I thought this moment would be taller."

An old lady with white soft-serve hair came and sat down in the front row, and folded her hands over one knee. She smiled sweetly and expectantly at Bentley, and then checked her watch. Bentley glanced at her phone, which was on the table in front of her, and realized she had to get her game face on. When she looked back up at the woman a smile was throbbing on her face like a swollen vein.

*   *   *

Colton was on a first date at a Long John Silver's, so already things were not headed his way. Rian had nagged him about dating, and he'd thought it might be good to do normal things now and then, so this was his attempt. The man was a Christmas tree farmer, which led to some customer-service bonding; the tree farmer made a "my balls in your mouth" joke when Colton stole his hush puppy, which Colton chose to ignore.

He could hear his sister's voice in his head: *Get back on that horse and ride 'em, cowboy! You got to get to know guys who aren't "sponsoring" you like you're a starving child. There's plenty of fish in the sea—or whatever, I don't judge.*

Colton was already feeling that he had cast his net a little too wide when the tree farmer recognized him.

"Oh my God, weren't you on that show with the Urinal Hair Girl? What was that called?"

"...'Amends.'"

"Oh my God. We used to get high and watch that thing all the time. Too bad it got canceled. We tried it with

'Intervention' but that was just depressing—you guys were so funny! Oh man, I remember you! And your sister. She was fucked *up!* 'Who gonna ride the ruffle bus? We *all* gonna ride the ruffle bus!' Oh man!"

The tree farmer danced a little bit in his plastic seat, miming a sort of hula as he chanted, "Who gon' ride the ruffle bus? *Who* gon' ride the ruffle bus?", in what he imagined to be Rian Rodman's accent. He was laughing all over his face.

"She was a trip," he said.

Colton gnawed meditatively on his Corn Cobbette. He accepted his own powerlessness over this situation. He couldn't fix this; he couldn't undo it or make up for it, and this man could never pay what he really owed. But you have to do *something*, don't you?

Colton stood up and casually flipped the tree farmer's tray onto the floor.

"Ladies and gentlemen, this man has sex with cocker spaniels," he said, loudly and calmly, and walked out.

Behind him commotion broke out.

"That's disgusting!"

"Those are beautiful, trusting animals!"

"Wait, I don't—"

"If it was a Doberman I could see it. Those are some nasty dogs. Those dogs will do porn for *free*. But a spaniel?"

He let the door swing shut.

*   *   *

FORMER HOCKEY STAR ARRESTED IN DUI HOMICIDE

(Associated Press) April 2, 2018 -- Dylan Hall, former National Hockey League Rookie of the Year and first draft pick, was arrested for vehicular homicide and driving under the influence in Michigan. The victim, 16-year-old Althea Wray, was on her way home from basketball practice at the time of her death.

Hall was arrested late March 31 after Wayne County sheriff's police received a call from a man who reported that an unknown man had walked uninvited into his home and demanded to use the telephone to call the police. The man appeared intoxicated and said that he had just hit someone with his car. When police arrived on the scene they found Hall, whose blood-alcohol level was 0.20, well above the legal limit of 0.08.

Hall appeared in the reality television show "Amends," which followed several alcoholics through the early stages of addiction treatment. In the course of the show Hall, then a teenager, revealed that he had destroyed his car keys in an attempt to avoid driving while intoxicated. For the past three months he has been working as a janitor at a skating rink in Dearborn. Hall's friend and former teammate, Detroit Red Wings forward Gair Cupek, said that Hall planned to plead guilty, "of course."

*   *   *

Dylan served four years in a minimum-security prison. "Somebody has to," as Gair put it.

After the initial shock—after everything acute became chronic, terror maturing into exhaustion—prison was in a certain way livable. He was used to navigating arbitrary and changing constellations of rules and authority figures: Between divorce and hockey he'd seen his share of unreliable referees. He adapted. He accepted the purgatorial surrealism of prison life, the stench and the noise and the way everybody made fun of the video that was supposed to teach them how to not get raped. He learned to avoid the cafeteria dispensers that said FRESH MILK but were filled with clumps of orange sludge peppered with cockroach shit. (FRESH OJ dispensed clumps of peppered powdered milk.) He got a pet.

"Hey," he said, when Gair visited him. "Help me name my spider."

"Your *spider*? Wait, *your* spider?"

"Yeah, he sleeps on my pillow. He's a cute little guy. Or she. I haven't checked."

"Uh... Fluffy? I hope it's not fluffy. Peter Parker? Uncle Ben?"

"Nah, all the guys name their spiders that shit. I want something original."

Seeing Gair's face, he shrugged and looked away.

"It gets fucking bleak in here," he said. "Don't judge my pet."

He swiftly figured out that the money Gair put in his commissary account for toothpaste could become barter; so he bought pruno from his sponsor. A guard caught him drinking from the bag of fermented canned fruit, laughed in his face and told him the night shift pissed in that bag.

It felt oddly comforting to be able to laugh at the extended punchline he felt his life had become.

"Oh man," he said, shaking his head, as the guard giggled. "Don't rain on my parade, man! Don't rain on my parade."

And then at times he would remember Althea Wray and things would fall apart.

"What did you *think* would happen?" his ex-stepbrother had asked him, afterward, in the awful period between the arrest and the trial.

"I was really trying to stop," he said.

"Look, I'm sure you hit the brake, but that isn't going to—"

"No, I mean stop drinking," he said, looking down and away.

It was inadequate, obviously; and like everything he said, it had a complex relationship with the truth. About four months before the accident Gair had finally taken the advice of literally everyone in his life, including Dylan, and told him he had to leave if he wouldn't get sober. He'd left. It had seemed obvious to him that this was the next right thing. He'd gotten a job, which made Gair feel hopeful, and then horrible because maybe this all could have happened years ago; and then he'd gotten a car, because he needed to get to his job.

And in the weeks before the accident he had been going to AA meetings again: hungover, miserably sucking coffee he'd bought on the way over (he felt like it would be unfair to take their coffee given the state he was in), silent.

After two weeks of this one man had taken him aside after the meeting and said, not unkindly, "You know, you don't absorb this stuff through the skin. If you don't want to get better, why are you here?"

When Dylan whined something about not knowing what to do, the man had said, "We'll be here when you're ready to do what it takes."

Can't I just do the first step twelve times? Mathematically that should be the same thing, Dylan had thought. The first step was the only one he was good at.

Althea Wray's father wanted to meet him. He submitted to this meeting; he felt like he shouldn't, like he was helping

Brian Wray somehow punish himself for losing his daughter, but he also felt like he couldn't refuse. They met in the visiting room. Dylan had tried to get at least a little drunk beforehand but had only succeeded in giving himself a headache, for which he tried to be grateful.

Brian Wray was a short man—his daughter had been willowy, but she got that from her mother—with fraying hair cut a bit longer than you'd expect from him. He had a careful, intellectual manner, and when he spoke his voice seemed to wander off to a quiet place deep inside himself. He was like a library closed to the public.

He explained that he wasn't sure why he was there, but he felt a need to see Dylan and let him know that he was forgiven. That was the way he put it, in the passive voice: "that you're forgiven." He said that he was a Methodist—Dylan at first thought that this was his job description, before remembering that it was a church—but lately he'd been going to a nondenominational church.

"I'm not sure why I told you that," he said.

Can't help you there, guy, Dylan thought; and immediately felt guilty. He felt that there was no way they could understand one another, and trying would only hurt them both—which he deserved and Brian Wray didn't.

"I suppose it's because my faith is part of how I approach this question," Brian said. He had this public-radio way of phrasing his thoughts. "I feel that we all do things which aren't... 'All have sinned and fall short of the glory of God.' What I mean to say is that I keep thinking, 'Well, I killed Jesus, after all.' Do you see?"

"*No*," Dylan said, startled. "No, I think that's totally wrong,

I know Christians try to make themselves think this stuff but it's so obviously wrong! You're not—you haven't. You haven't killed anybody! It's not the same. Just let yourself see it, let yourself see that you're one of the good guys."

"'One of the good guys,'" Brian repeated, in his wandering voice. "Yes, that's the thing I don't understand."

Dylan braced himself.

Brian Wray asked, "Maybe you can help me with this—do you think I should feel angry?"

There was a pause, and the man struggled to express his meaning. His expression was entirely inward; he was looking toward Dylan but not at him.

"Everyone says I should feel angry. At you. They're actually quite upset with me, I think, because—I don't. I just don't. My wife is very angry with me for coming here. She's Presbyterian," he added, as if in explanation.

"Do you think that's, I don't know, inhuman? Wrong? It's not about forgiveness," Brian said quickly. "They're good people. They don't have a problem with forgiveness if it's something you feel called to do, if it makes you feel better. But I think it bothers them on a deep level that I don't *feel* hatred toward you, in my heart."

Yeah, Dylan thought, *I don't understand that either. You probably should.*

But he wanted very badly not to make this encounter all about himself. Dylan searched for a response which would have no reference at all to his own needs or emotions, and so, in one of those hidden acts of self-denial by which we are all surrounded, he said, "You can only have the emotions you have. You don't control it, you know?"

Brian shook his head a little—he wasn't sure, and in fact Dylan wasn't sure that was true either, so he tried again: "In rehab they taught us that forgiveness is like rat poison. If you give enough of it to the rats they... die? Uh, I don't think I'm remembering this part right. Maybe the rats are resentments."

That made Brian nod a lot, in jerking uneven motions. "That's good," he said, and nodded some more.

"I just worry that they're right, that it says something about who I am as a person," Brian said. "Like there's something dead inside me that should be alive. Should be fighting back. I guess—I think what they don't like is that it isn't fair. It feels like it isn't fair to—to Althea," and here he looked down and composed himself, and his head shook slowly from side to side. A thin, embarrassed smile stretched his lips. His voice thickened a little as he said, "Like I'm not doing justice to her memory."

Dylan thought, *I need to be present in this moment.* He was able to pick out a couple of words from Brian's speech and say, "They tell us—here—not to focus on things that are fair or unfair. There are a lot of people here—not me, but like, practically everybody else—who have such awful stories of the things that have happened to them. And it's *not* fair. But that's dwelling on the past."

"Are you a Christian?"

"Uh—kind of, I guess."

"You should come to our church. My new church, my— recent church. When you get out. Yes," and Brian was back to that intense, painful nodding. "You should come fellowship with us. Or maybe at my old church if you'd feel more comfortable there. I think it would be good for all of us."

"That's really kind of you."

"I don't think that I *do* forgive you," Brian said, unexpectedly. "I don't know what that means. I don't think it's my place to forgive, to decide. But I want you to know that you're forgiven, by whoever... does these things."

Dylan, in a strained voice, said, "There's—I would do anything I can to make amends, but all of it—I feel terrible, I'm happy to be here and serving my time, I'm going to meetings and I'm trying to—the point is that none of it fills up the hole. I don't think it does."

Brian Wray nodded. "Like a penny into the ocean."

"Yeah. Yeah. So I don't know either. Doesn't forgiveness require the other person to—being sorry for what you've done, which I am, but also making up for it? But I can't. I mean I do feel sorry. I think I feel all the stuff I should feel. But I can't, there's nothing that can make up for it."

Dylan was trying very hard to breathe evenly. He had spread his hands out on the table, palms upward. He'd heard in a meeting that this posture represented openness.

"So I sort of don't see the point of forgiving me, to be honest. You should do what makes you feel better, whatever helps."

"You destroyed the most beautiful thing in my life," Brian Wray said, and there was so much wonder in his voice. "I didn't believe it was possible that—that things could happen like that. That a person could do that."

Dylan felt immense relief when their meeting was over. He could handle being in prison as long as he could pretend that all the people within the walls—the guards, the inmates, the visitors who used their one authorized kiss to transfer balloons of heroin to their boyfriend's mouth—were complicit. He hated the thought of an innocent in that place.

It wasn't until the year he was released that he began to see things differently. That year he watched a wife-beater shepherd his retarded cellmate from the cell to the yard, carry his tray in the cafeteria, clean up his piss and shit, and take his blame for assaults and generalized yelling. The wife-beater spent two weeks in Ad Seg because he'd jumped into a fight in defense of his cellmate.

Dylan had done solitary several times, never more than a week, in the bad company of his own thoughts. He couldn't imagine accepting even two minutes of that abandonment and disintegration voluntarily.

His own mother went in for a different kind of awful husband, the kind who missed his kid's birthday because he was tanning. That kind would never hit a woman, because breaking a mirror means seven years' bad luck. Dylan knew why most of the other inmates despised the wife-beater and he felt guilty, in a way, for having enough distance from the situation to begin to respect him. But he was starting to see that if you think in terms of guilty and innocent, innocence is something you can only lose. This was something Brian Wray had said to him: "No parent wants his child to die innocent."

Dylan said all of this to Gair, in one of those jolting visiting-room conversations where they tried to jam everything they could bear to say into the shortest possible time, and Gair said, "Well, obviously. I mean a wife-beater is a shirt, not a person. You're not defined by the worst thing you ever did. The first time they show Paul in the Bible he is literally cheering on a crowd as they straight murder a man. Only God is innocent."

"You think?" Dylan said. "I mean you could say that God has the ultimate martyr complex. 'There, I killed my *son* at you, are you happy now?'"

"You don't believe that," Gair said, not as sharply as he might have.

"Please don't put any more money on my books," Dylan said, and his voice was clotted.

Gair looked at him for a long moment and said gently, "Do you want to tell me why?"

Dylan explained, red-faced, moving his hands restlessly over the scarred surface of the table between them. An unsteady grin tilted all over his face. He was ashamed of how calmly Gair took the news: He'd hoped he was still capable of surprising Gair.

"I try to think a lot about transformation," Dylan said. "Anything can change here, you know? Anything can become something else. Like, I saw a guy get killed with a toothbrush, you can file it down and shove it into somebody's gut and just pull."

He made an eloquent hand motion, and Gair swallowed hard.

"Or the other day, a dude splinted his leg with a mop. And mopped with it! There's a guy here who makes eyeshadow out of Vaseline and pencils. So that's kind of hopeful."

Gair sat there trying to look on the bright side of a shanking, while Dylan searched his face. He couldn't help asking, "Are people killed here a lot? You've never said anything about it. Are you safe?"

Dylan looked away. "I mean, it's not that frequent, I wasn't trying to make a point about that specifically. I mean how safe is Detroit, you know? I'm okay."

Gair's cheeks burned, and he felt sorry for asking. To shift the conversation he tried, "How's Jonah? All eight legs still kicking?"

Dylan grinned tiredly. "Maybe! Probably one of his grandkids, by this point. Have you—did my mother get back to you?"

Gair shook his head. "Sorry...."

Dylan had been reduced to communicating with his mother through Gair, like siblings around an especially tense Thanksgiving table, because she wouldn't come see him.

"She says prison is like time-out for adults," he'd explained to Gair. "If your kid's in time-out you can't always be coming to check up on him and play with him, or he won't learn his lesson."

"It's just as well," Gair said, trying to be gentle. "I'm pretty sure your parents are banned by the Eighth Amendment. And maybe the Geneva Conventions."

The dimple sunk into Dylan's cheek, slowly, like the mark a spade leaves when it socks into the earth.

About five months after Dylan was released from prison, Gair got the flu. Dylan was living with him, rent-free—"You can pay off your restitution faster this way," which wasn't an argument Dylan felt he could counter—and so he wandered into the bedroom to check on him.

"Hey. How's the suffering coming?"

Gair made unintelligible pity-me noises and burrowed deeper into his blankets.

"Aww," Dylan said. "Can I get you anything? Soup, toast?"

Gair lifted his head from the pillow and said, as precisely

as Rapunzel's mother: "Schweppes diet ginger ale in a can. Please. They have it at the Exxon."

And then, as an afterthought: "Keys are in the whale."

He was too feverish to remember that Dylan's license was still suspended. The nearest convenience store was three miles away; the late January wind howled against the window. Dylan paused for a second, then shrugged.

"Okay."

He bundled himself into sweater, coat, scarf, gloves, boots, hat. He passed the sign taped up in the dark front hallway, above the side table with the souvenir Yale Whale from Ingalls Rink: DYLAN IS NOT ALLOWED: ALCOHOL. Underneath, in Gair's loopy handwriting, EVERYTHING ELSE IS FAIR GAME. He grinned unevenly and tagged it with his fingertips, for luck.

When he opened the front door the wind and cold punched him everywhere at once. He gasped and panted against the frigid night. By the end of the block his eyes were watering. He walked through their fancy suburb, talking to himself—encasing himself in words, an astronaut taking a spacewalk in the protective suit of his self-image. By the time he reached the highway he was shivering enough that he'd stopped talking; there were about two miles to go. He walked faster.

Electrical wires creaked overhead. In the freezing night he felt too cold to look up at the stars. Very few cars passed by; when the rare headlights cut across his body he felt obscurely ashamed, as if he were performing community service, roadside cleanup in a jumpsuit. He could taste blood on his cracking lips, and he thought his nose might be trickling blood as well. He beat his arms against his coat to see if that helped, but it didn't.

In the freezing, bloodied silence, he became aware of the night as something alive and beautiful. It was huge, black, and pulsing as if he were near its heart. It was so big that he got lost in it. He had known the Michigan winter night for a long time; it was like family to him, and yet now it was loving and haunting and strange as well.

The relentless wind swept through his mind and left a cold, stinging happiness where his small warming thoughts had been. He accepted the miles in the dark with only this huge living animal night for company.

And then he felt that he was a part of the night. He was being breathed by it; he moved through the world as a part of its body. He, too, had a place here and a purpose.

A car slewed toward him at high speed, pushed onto the shoulder by a gust of wind, and he stumbled away so quickly that he fell to his hands and knees. He scrambled up as his heart pounded. The car sped away, fishtailing a little. He tried to breathe.

Holy shit, that thing almost hit me. That could have killed me.

And then: *Well, if I die tonight, I could live with that.*

To his surprise, this wasn't a despairing thought but a peaceful one. He was glad that the car hadn't hit him.

"Need to get that fucking ginger ale," he muttered. The living night eased up on him, and seemed to laugh along with his scuffing, coughing laugh.

"Fucking arctic polar deserted highway." He grinned and sniffled. He could feel his identity beginning to solidify again.

"Who do I have to blow to get a drink around here?"

After a long time the lights of the gas station appeared. He stayed in there for five minutes, shivering uncontrollably (and wondering why the owner was staring at him—he'd forgotten that he had blood on his face), and then made himself go back outside and go home. Gair was asleep when he got back. He smiled, took the ginger ale out into the hall so the sound of the tab wouldn't wake him, and opened it so it would be nice and flat when Gair woke up.

Afterward Gair said, "You found God. Good for you!"

Dylan wasn't sure. He didn't know if he could put a name on it; but he had felt that he was a part of something larger than he could understand, something which could consume his catastrophic life and turn it into living, flowing purpose. Something which could kill him if it chose, and so if it kept him alive, that must mean that he worked better for it alive than dead. He had very little religion—much less than he wanted to have—but this little bit helped.

*   *   *

The last time the cast members of "Amends" were all together was two years after Dylan's release, twelve years after the show. Emebet was speaking at a small Ethiopian Bible cafe in D.C.

The cafe was jammed in between the Scientific Rational Barber Shop and Wonder Chicken, a little storefront decorated in red, green, and gold. Big white letters read **IN GODS HA**—and then, huddled up in much smaller letters, the **NDS** which formed the rest of the cafe's name. The sign-painter had lacked forethought.

Inside, all the talent of "Amends" (plus Bentley) were greeting one another. The heels of Bentley's high heels were peeling and her black t-shirt read, WHAT'S MY MOTIVATION? Dylan was still having a tough time looking people in the eye. He'd had his epiphany but epiphanies can be slow-release drugs.

Emebet was standing with several other Ethiopians, both men and women. She was laughing, big vivacious laughter which shook her curls; her hands were working excitedly in the air and she was tossing knowing glances at the women. Sometimes she'd glance over at J. Malachi, checking up on him, and then she'd quiet down. She was louder and brighter with other Ethiopians but she returned to her husband with relief.

Now she was complaining about one of the women she'd counseled at the crisis pregnancy center where she volunteered once a week.

"Every month it's the same," she said, as the other women murmured and commiserated. "She agrees with me about her problems, she knows that this relationship is not good for her. We come up with a plan to make progress. And then next month nothing has changed!

"What I have suggested again and again is simple, it is obvious, it is clear, it would fix her life. I can't understand why she doesn't just do it," said the alcoholic.

All of them were sober, right at that moment: Medea's eighteen months, Bentley's seven and a half years, Sharptooth's fourteen-plus which Medea wanted to count in dog years to make it sound sillier. Dylan's four years. It was strange how six months had felt like an enormous accomplishment, but four years felt like nothing. All of them were a little too aware of the intense sincerity of the recurring question, "How *are* you?" A little too aware of the present tense.

Bentley was the only one from the production side: the only one who ended up with the drunks when it was time to pick teams. Medea asked where Ana was, "can't remember her name, the cute awful one with the... she dressed herself like a pill bottle or something? Do you know the one I mean?"

"I remember that," Sharptooth said. "That was very triggering for me, her clothing choices."

Seriously? Bentley thought; but she was trying to be a person, so what she said was, "I'm sorry about that."

She felt unexpectedly ashamed that she didn't know what Ana was up to. She was always having these weird echoing shames, which weren't about the experience itself but a different experience it reminded her of—in this case, the experience of losing track of all her old running buddies. All the old dead-enders.

Dylan found Colton, and steeled himself for a familiar janitorial duty. "Hey. I just wanted to apologize for—all the times I called you when I was fucked up. I know that must've been hard for you, when you were working on your own recovery."

"Actually it made things easier for me. Talking to you," and Colton only realized how bad this would sound once he'd already started the sentence, "made me realize how much I wanted to stay sober."

"Wow, really? I helped you? Ha, go me."

Medea was doing research, which was her proxy for taking an interest in other people's lives. She cornered J. Malachi and asked him, "Are you really a Christian?"

He laughed.

"I've missed you," he said. "I'm a Christian in the sense that I go to particular buildings at particular times and say particular words. I subject my body to discipline: I stand up when everybody else stands and prostrate myself when everybody else does. I do the things."

"Do you talk to Jesus—do you seriously talk to Jesus the way you talk to the rest of us?"

He shrugged. "Sure, why not? I talk to my *Higher Power*, is that sincere enough for you? Jesus Christ, my co-pilot."

"You're sure you're not just talking to your wife?" (Medea made "wife" sound like an insinuation.)

"Pretty sure. I don't think Emebet would appreciate my communicating with her without her knowledge. I liked your play, by the way, *Our Initial Goal Is Voluntary Compliance.* You should do more political stuff."

"Thank you," Medea said—and despite her personal growth, she couldn't resist saying, "I thought it could be like *1984*, but inspired by rehab instead of the BBC."

J. Malachi laughed. "Yeah, I got that, you weren't exactly subtle about it."

"I don't believe in subtle," she said. But there was a new, undefended warmth in her voice: a prickle of laughter, like wine pricking along the veins.

After a little pause, awkward and tilting—they weren't sure how much they still had in common—she asked, "So, do you speak her language yet?"

"I'm learning," he said. "I understand maybe fifteen percent of what she and her friends say. I think it's good, though. If she's angry at me, we can still go out together—she'll complain about me to her friends and I won't even know what she's saying. She relaxes, I get to spend time with her, plus I get husband points for letting her friends laugh at me. Everybody wins!"

"Don't you get bored?"

"Boredom, serenity. To-may-to, to-mah-to. I think it's good for me. Oh and look, I can eskista!" he said, and demonstrated: He pigeoned his toes out and bent his knees, then did a sort of hopping jig with pumping arms akimbo. He looked like David Byrne, in the sense that David Byrne looks like a distressed chicken.

"Does that *help?*" Medea asked, and he had to concede that it didn't really.

Emebet, watching them, hoped he wouldn't tell the story about the posters. Jaymi had come home with several Spanish Counter-Reformation prints ("Anytime the museum wall caption starts, 'In response to the spread of Protestantism,' I know I'm gonna love that painting") but she'd nixed them. She thought of icons as the opposite of religious art. "The saints are exaggerations," she said.

Jaymi loved this opinion of hers, and waved it around at parties; she worried that it made her sound demanding. He liked to be thought of as the kind of husband who takes orders but she didn't like to be thought of as the kind of wife who gives them.

"Welcome, friends," a tall, rangy man said. About half of the crowd was white, the rest Ethiopian or Hispanic. The man was dressed in a bright, geometrically-patterned shirt and fraying blue jeans. It was July, and there were small standing fans in every corner of the store, trying to roll back the heat but settling for detente.

"Our speaker tonight is very famous. She is known on the Internet as 'Urinal Hair Girl,' and you have seen her on many 'memes.' But tonight we will look beyond the memes. We will hear this Urinal Hair Girl speak about her life, her faith in Jesus the Lord, and her salvation, how God rescued her from the prison of addiction. God has brought her from below the urinal to a place of refuge in the house of the Lord! Please, show your appreciation."

J. Malachi had heard this kind of thing said about his wife many times. They laughed about it, how Emebet's shame got treated like a badge of honor just because it had made her *very famous*. She was, in a certain sense, an American success story.

J. Malachi told himself that it should be just as humiliating to be introduced as the President of the United States, or a Congressman; it should be more so. At least you couldn't order drone strikes on wedding parties if you were passed out under a urinal. *Although I don't know*, he thought, *I bet LBJ could.*

Emebet stood up, and made her way to the microphone with a poise and delicacy which meant she was feeling more than usually ashamed. Jaymi clapped harder for her, and she turned—as regally as Gloria Swanson—and favored him with a small, game and toothy smile.

What Emebet told them wasn't new: We are not saved by our own efforts but by the power of God, we are not healed by our own suffering but by the wounds of Christ.

The cast of "Amends" had long ago decided what they thought of this approach and they responded according to their settled habits. Dylan nodded intensely and tried to yank himself up into hope by the bootstraps. Medea and Sharptooth theorized and mistranslated. ("She's right, we all need to find our place in an interdependent ecology.")

Colton judged the others for having opinions about what Emebet was saying, when they should just be grateful and happy to see her doing so well. Judgment of others' judgmentalism was Colton's only new sin, the one character defect which was a side effect of the medicine rather than a symptom of the disease.

Bentley took notes and chewed things.

Emebet found her way quickly to the end of her speech. "What I wondered, as I was learning English, was why you have this phrase: 'I'm sorry.' Why do we have to say it, and what does it even mean? Most of the time when there is pain you don't *have* to talk about it. There is usually no moral rule that you must say 'I have caused you pain,' or, 'I am in pain,' and often to talk about these things makes them worse."

J. Malachi patted his knee and murmured, "Hear, hear." Bentley frowned.

"But in this case we must talk, and what we must say is: 'I'm sorry.' Why? At first it seems irrelevant. I did something bad; why does it matter how I feel?"

Dylan nodded.

"It may seem like we are humbling ourselves by saying we are 'sorry,' we are pathetic. 'I'm sorry,' we say, and the other one says, 'You certainly are!'"

Medea giggled.

"But look at the structure of it. I *am* sorry. I have become sorrow for my misdeeds. I have become penitence. This is a promise to the other person, like wedding vows—and also, like wedding vows, you may see it as a threat!"

Lots of laughs and some embarrassed glances at J. Malachi, who was grinning and nodding along.

"You are promising that you will come away changed from your encounter with the person you have hurt. Changed into something new. We think of 'making amends' as returning everyone to how it was before, but that doesn't happen."

Her voice became vibrant and raw, veined with passion. "You can never go back to the past. You can't heal their wounds or your own. Even God will not do this for you," and this was a bit controversial with her audience, but she believed she had proof: "Jesus himself was not healed—he came back from the dead with the wounds still in his hands and his body. He came back changed, but not healed. Saying 'I'm sorry' is saying that you will be different from now on. Your identity stretches to accommodate the thing you did to them. And in this way a relationship is formed between the person you have hurt and yourself.

"When you say, 'I do,' you *cannot* be sincere, because you cannot know what you're doing. You may want some idea called 'being married' but you have no idea what being married will actually require of you. And so your sincerity and your strength of character don't really matter. If you are a morally weak person you can still marry. You don't have to wait until you are ready, because you're never ready. And so it is with 'I'm sorry.' You can be insincere, you can be—what is the word I forget?"

"Callow," her young husband said softly.

"Callow, yes," she said, with great tenderness. "You can mean it very little, or you can be totally unable to imagine what it would mean. But it creates a relationship which you will learn to do as you go along. As long as you stay in the relationship, you will learn how to be sorry. And like marriage, this is one of the things we mean when we say 'love.'"

Applause washed toward her, liquid and sparkling. People in the audience held up their phones to take her picture, cameras held like candles. She had enough vanity left to wish for privacy. *In heaven*, she thought, tired and uncomforted, *the lights will be even brighter.*

Maybe there it will not be so bad to be seen for what we are.

Made in the USA
Middletown, DE
25 August 2015